JAYAPURA

WALLACE F. BROWN

Solebury Press

SoleburyPress@comcast.net

Jayapura

Published by Solebury Press

ISBN 978-0615622859

Sometimes a man can meet his destiny
on the road he took to avoid it.

- Eric Singer

Prologue

The captain of the North Korean freighter watched the barometer with growing concern. The wind was already gusting to thirty knots, driving a hard rain against the bridge. His ship rode restlessly in the choppy waters of the Yellow Sea and he ordered the helmsman to bring the bow closer to the wind. The fishing vessel was three hours overdue and there was still no sign of her. He could see nothing through the deteriorating weather but he knew that soon the seas would begin to roll and their mission would be in peril. He would have abandoned the mission two hours earlier, had it not been for the security officer who stood behind him, watching his every move. He was a mindless, political hack who knew nothing of the sea and cared nothing for his men or his ship, but the captain knew a bad report could cost him his command and, perhaps, his freedom. To transfer cargo in this weather, in these seas, was insanity but the choice was not his. He also knew full well, that if the cargo were damaged or lost, it would be better for him to follow it into the sea. And so he stood and watched, and waited.

There was a stillness among the crewmen. They were an experienced crew and they did not voice their fear, but he could see it in their faces. They did not like being dead in the water with a storm coming in. The wind, moaning through the steel winch cables was like the

1

howl of a Kraken, waiting for them in the dark. As if things were not bad enough, they were blind. Their ancient radar equipment had failed only an hour out of port and the technician did not have the parts to fix it. The captain rechecked the ship's position. He knew that the storm closing in on them was not their biggest problem. His real concern lay to the south where a typhoon was steadily working its way across the Pacific. He had calculated there would be ample time to reach port before it hit, but that had been three hours ago. The radio operator stepped onto the bridge and handed him a printout. The typhoon was moving west-northwest and was now tracking directly for Manila. It would be a close thing. If the typhoon held its forward speed they would avoid the worst of it. When it crossed Luzon it would lose some of its strength, at least for a while. Once it entered the warm waters of the South China Sea, there would be hell to pay for any ship in its path.

Suddenly, a cry came up from the aft watch. Lights off the port quarter. The captain turned to the first mate and told him to prepare to take on cargo. The captain watched warily from the bridge as the fishing vessel came alongside. There was nothing he could do but try to keep his bow into the wind and hold his ship steady against the storm.

Everything else depended on the skills of another captain, and the vagaries of the sea. He did not envy the task. The smaller vessel came alongside and the hawsers were cast. His men rotated the davits out over the rail and the sound of the winches filled the ship as the lifting hooks were lowered. On the smaller vessel a hatch cover was lifted and, inch-by-

2

inch, a pallet rose out of its hold. It held a rectangular shape, about the size of a refrigerator lying on its side, and was covered with a green canvas tarp. As soon as the pallet cleared the deck of the fishing vessel it was manhandled aft. The crewmen struggled to secure the twin hooks, which were slamming against the hull of the freighter as it rocked unevenly beside them in the turbid water - an ominous drumming in the dark night that gripped the hearts of the seamen like an icy claw. The rain and wind tore at them and it was all they could do to keep their footing. Suddenly the ship lurched and one of the hooks slammed into the group of waiting men, sending two of them sprawling across the deck, and casting them into the sea. The deck crew scrambled to save them as the pallet slipped precariously along the wet deck. The captain of the fishing vessel shouted orders above the din. The men looked up at him angrily, but they did not disobey. They threw a flotation ring over the side and returned to their work. One of the crewmen had been helped back on board. The other was surrendered to his fortune. The men knew the danger they were facing. They knew delaying to save one man's life in these seas could cost them their ship. They cursed the weather and returned to their task. There was no time to think about it.

Finally, the hooks were secured and the men guided the pallet as it inched its way upward toward the deck of the freighter. As soon as it had cleared their heads, they ran to release the hawsers, anxious to get free of the hulking vessel that loomed over them like a leviathan. Without warning, an enormous wave hit the small vessel broadside. Had they been on the open sea they would have rode over it like a cork, but they were only a few feet from the hull of the freighter and the wave lifted them and slammed them into the side of the larger ship like a toy. The wooden hull strakes cracked and the air was filled with the ominous sound of groaning metal, and the cries of terrified men. Seawater began to spray through the cracked hull of the fishing vessel and below decks, the engine crew struggled to wedge timbers against the damaged strakes. Above them, the pallet slammed into the hull of the freighter and the cargo shifted as the restraints started to give way. The men on the freighter had no time to worry about the fate of the fishing boat, as they struggled to keep from losing their cargo to the sea. It took every ounce of their strength, but they finally managed to swing the pallet on board and lash it to the deck.

Below them, the smaller vessel rolled violently sideways and the sea washed over the gunwales and began pouring into the open hatch. The small vessel tried to right itself but she was pinched against the hull of the freighter and too much water had run into her hold, disrupting her center of gravity. She was listing badly. Another wave hit and she was slammed again into the hull of the larger vessel, this time crushing the deckhouse and spilling the captain onto the deck below. With no one at the wheel, the small vessel began to lurch and buck. The deck hands succeeded in releasing the aft ropes, but before they could move forward, another wave washed over the deck and threw them into the sea. The stern swung itself away from the freighter and lifted violently, sending its bow into the side of the freighters hull. The freighter shuddered, as if staggered by a blow.

The fate of the fishing boat was now sealed. The forward lines snapped and she rolled slowly over onto her side. The men on the freighter stared in horror at the inverted hull of the fishing vessel, staining their ears against the moaning of the wind for the cries of the crew. They heard a few screams, and then nothing. A searchlight snapped on and swept over the debris floating below them, but there was not a man to be seen. Slowly, the stricken vessel slipped into the deep. The captain ordered a boat to be lowered but the political officer countermanded the order. He insisted the captain get underway immediately. The captain delayed as long as he could, claiming he feared the wreck could still be lodged under his hull. They threw an inflatable life boat over the side and remained in place for another ten minutes, searching the dark waters with their powerful light, but they could do no more. At last, the captain gave orders to get underway. He stepped out onto the deck and looked down at his cargo. A dark shape, that appeared to grow out of the steel deck like a malignant tumor. What was this thing that moved through the world in the darkness and killed the men and ships that bore it? Something evil. Something that would bring no good to the world. He ordered it stowed below, so he would not have to see it again. The mate asked if the incident should be entered into the ship's log, but the captain just shook his head and stared out into the darkness and the gathering storm. He whispered a quiet prayer for the crew and their captain, and then he called below and told them to give him everything the engines could take.

The tall man entered the building at ten to four in the afternoon. It was a marble and glass box of forty stories that would have seemed unremarkable in any Western city. Here, on the streets of Bangkok, it was an unwelcomed reminder of a fading culture. A monument to the relentless sameness of the new century. He crossed the lobby with long confident strides and smiled at the receptionist, a lovely Thai woman with the face of a porcelain doll and hands as delicate as a child's.

"Good afternoon, I'm Chuck Allan. I have an appointment with Mr. Juntasa."

She smiled back at him briefly and then glanced at her computer screen. "Would that be Mr. Annan Juntasa or Mr. Chalong Juntasa?"

"Annan Juntasa, please."

She picked up the telephone and waited for the connection. "Mr. Juntasa's 4 o'clock appointment has arrived."

"Thank you, Mr. Allan; Mr. Juntasa's office is on the twenty-fourth floor. The elevators are directly behind me on the other side of the mural wall. Would you sign in please?"

She smiled at him as he scrawled his signature and then she passed the magnetic stripe of his visitors badge through a reader and handed it to him. As he walked away he pretended to clip it onto his suit coat, but instead, kept it in the palm of his hand. He paused and waited by the bank of elevators. A group of Japanese businessmen had been behind him at the registration desk and he waited for them to sign in and head for the elevators. He stood behind them and followed them into the car. As he entered, he stumbled and fell against one of the businessmen. As he did so, he unclipped the man's visitors badge and at the same time dropped his own badge at the man's feet. He apologized profusely, picked up the badge from the floor and handed it to the man, who smiled and bowed but said nothing. He clipped the businessman's badge on his own coat pocket. There would be no record of Mr. Kitagima leaving the building that evening. It would be written off as a computer glitch. When he exited the elevator he was greeted by another attractive Thai woman. She was a bit older than the receptionist but had the same sweet smile and she bowed slightly and asked him to follow her. As he walked down the corridor he checked for security cameras but found none. The woman led him into the room and introduced him. Mr. Juntasa stood, offering his hand.

"Hello, Mr. Allen. It's a pleasure to meet you."

"Call me Chuck, please. In any case, the pleasure's all mine. Thanks for agreeing to see me."

"Would you like some tea, or something else to drink?"

"No thanks, I'm fine."

"Do you live here in Thailand, or are you just passing through?"

"I live in Hong Kong at the moment. I cover most of South East Asia from there."

"That's a lot of territory. It must keep you busy."

"Yeah, I spend a lot of time in airplanes."

"Tell me about it. Anyway, I understand you have a new ball valve design to show me. I have to tell you we're fairly happy with Kitz valves we've been using, but I'm always willing to listen."

Chuck opened his brief case and removed a stack of folded drawings. He nodded toward the drawing table. "May I?"

"Of course."

He opened the drawings and spread them out on the table. For the next half hour he went through the designs in detail, pointing out features and reciting benefits that he had committed to memory back at his hotel room. As Mr. Juntasa examined the drawings, Chuck looked around the office. The computer and mouse pad were on the left side of the desk. There was a document safe against the rear wall at the far left corner of the office. A filing cabinet stood on the opposite wall, next to the drawing table. He checked the ceiling for surveillance cameras or motion detectors. The office was not alarmed but the document safe would be an issue. It was nearing closing time and he could see Mr. Juntasa was anxious to wrap it up and go home.

"Can you leave these drawings with me for a while, Mr. Allen? I'd like to discuss them with my engineering team when we have an opportunity."

"Of course. Why don't you keep them for a week or so and then I'll contact you to set up another appointment."

They exchanged business cards and shook hands.

"Can you find your way to the elevators?"

"Sure, no problem. Thanks again for your time."

Chuck walked down the hall and entered the men's room. He knew it would be crowded with departing employees in a few minutes and he needed to work quickly. The lock on the janitor's closet was a common pin tumbler and he was able to pick it in less than thirty seconds. He entered the closet and relocked the door. His watch said four fifty-five. He stood quietly and waited, listening to the sounds of toilets flushing and the ratchet of the towel dispensers as employees cleaned up in preparation for their commute home. He had observed the building for three nights from an adjacent roof top. The janitorial crew started work at five. Each team handled a five story section of the building starting at the highest number and working down. The crew responsible for his floor would start at the twenty fifth. It took approximately one hour per floor so he would have an hour to get it done. Plenty of time, unless something went wrong. Something always went wrong. By five-fifteen the room had gone quiet and he slowly opened the door. He checked the stalls to make sure they were empty and then he removed a pair of overalls and a cap from his briefcase. He put the overalls on over his suit and pulled the cap down low over his eyes. It was a little uncomfortable but it would have to do. Finally he put on a pair of surgical gloves and pulled them tightly over his fingers.

Placing his ear against the door, he listened for sounds of movement but it seemed quiet. He cautiously opened the door and poked his head out. The office lights were all off except one. It looked like someone was working late and that would be a minor inconvenience. The occupied office was along the back wall with no direct line of sight to the corridor he was in, but there was no telling when its occupant might decide to leave. He walked quickly down the hall to Mr.

Juntasa's office and let himself in. As soon as he entered the room, he crouched and moved quickly behind the desk. It was locked, but desk locks are child's play and he had it open in less than ten seconds. He placed a small pen-light between his teeth and began a methodical search of the files. There were three file drawers in the desk and it was time-consuming work. In the end he came up empty. He pulled out the top drawer but there were no files in it. There was a stack of papers on top of the desk and he riffled through them, finding nothing. Next he moved to the credenza and examined each folder and went through the stacks of folded drawings. Again, he came up empty. Next he went through the filing cabinet, drawer by drawer. It wasn't there. That was the last of the easy options. Five thirty-four.

He turned to the document safe. He removed a small spray bottle from his pocket and squeezed a light mist of liquid onto the keypad. The Iodine/benzoflavone mixture would raise prints from a smooth surface but they were difficult to read. He didn't need to read them. He only needed to see which keys had been pushed. In a few seconds, faint blue ridges began to appear on four of the keys. Assuming a four digit code, he now knew the correct numbers, but not the sequence. If each number were used once, there would be twenty-four possible combinations. If not, it was going to be a little trickier. He examined the ridges again. Three of them were more or less horizontal but the ridges on the number five were slightly tilted to the left. That would be the first key. The motion of the hand toward the keypad while pressing the first number would cause the finger to be slightly skewed upward toward the right for a left handed man. Five was the first number. If he were lucky, that would leave six possibilities. On his fourth try the red light turned green and he pulled the door open. There was a stack of folders inside. He didn't want to remove them all but he guessed the straggler would be leaving soon and he didn't want to use the penlight if he didn't have to. He stopped for a moment and listened. The building was still quiet.

He checked his watch. Five fifty-two. Still plenty of time.

He removed the files and went through them one by one. His file was half-way down the stack. He examined the contents. Normally he would have photographed each of the pages and returned the file as if no one had touched it, but he couldn't risk a lamp with someone still on the floor. Instead he removed a manila envelope from his briefcase. It was already addressed and stamped. He put the contents of the file in the envelope and sealed it. He then removed some papers from a different file, placed them in the empty folder and returned everything to the safe in the same order he had removed them.

He stood and looked around the office, making sure everything was as he found it. Five fifty-six. As he started to open the door he saw the light go off in the other office and he crouched down behind the desk and waited. In a couple of minutes he heard the chime of an elevator arriving and he waited for the sound of the closing doors. Finally he stood up and exited the office. There was a mail slot next to the elevators and he deposited the envelope. It was a bit risky but better than being caught in possession of stolen documents. Besides, he enjoyed the irony of having a company

11

personally mail him the documents he was being paid to steal. The elevator bell rang again as he passed the doors and he dashed to the fire stairs and onto the landing. The door closed with a click, just as the cleaning crew stepped out of the elevator. Two minutes past six.

There were people using the stairs above and below him, so he moved cautiously on the balls of his feet and kept to the wall. On the ninth floor someone opened the door just below him and he had to go back and wait in the hallway. There were cleaners working on the floor but no one saw him. At last he made it to street level. The door was alarmed but it was only a contact pad. It was designed to keep people out, not to keep them in. He detached one of the wires. Before opening the door he removed his overalls and hat and then walked out into the sweltering Bangkok night. He dropped the overalls and hat and gloves in a dumpster and walked calmly out to the street. Ten after six. He was slipping.

2

Jack stood before the half open louvers and felt the late morning sun against his body. Bands of searing light illuminated the patchwork of scars that decorated his lean, muscular frame like some forgotten constellation. Indelible reminders of a war fought for honor, and of other, darker battles fought for survival. Each one a story he did not wish retold. Below him on Khao San Road, the shopkeepers were beginning to stir, sweeping the sidewalks and stocking the tables lining the street. A motorcycle raced by, spewing a trail of acrid fumes that drifted up toward him, leaving the taste of metal in his mouth. The whine of the two-cycle engine gradually subsided until it was indistinguishable from the buzzing of the flies. The room became still again, except for the groan of an ancient ceiling fan pushing against the hot, wet air, like a galley slave strapped to an oar. The hotel was little more than a flophouse but they accepted cash and didn't ask questions. He needed the anonymity. He had been here two nights, waiting for the envelope to arrive. It was addressed to the fictitious name he had used to register. He glanced at his watch. There was still plenty of time. The water in the shower was tinted with rust and cold enough to discourage lingering. Rooms such as these were not rented for their comforts. He dressed and then walked out into the hall, not bothering to lock the door. The stairway smelled of stale smoke and urine. There were a couple of kids slumped in the corner, sucking ya baa through a rolled up bill, their eyes glazed over and unseeing. They didn't even look up. He walked down the stairs quickly as his mind made use of the last quiet moments of the new day. Solitary thoughts that ended abruptly as he opened the door into the lobby and felt the chaos wash over him.

Mr. Zhang was behind the front desk, dressed in his serious suit as usual. It was double breasted and a bit worn, but he kept it neatly pressed. He wore thick-rimmed glasses and had his hair slicked back like an extra from a 30's film noir. The whole lobby had that look about it, right down to the potted palms, strategically placed to hide the peeling paint. Mr. Zhang still used an abacus and it was never far from his hands. There was always money to be counted. You could tell by the look on his face if it was coming in or, tragically, slipping away. He was arguing with a guest who had long since realized he wasn't going to get anywhere, but needed to further express his indignation. Mr. Zhang was happy for the excuse to change the subject.

"Good morning, Mr. Thomas. Wait a moment please I have a package. I bring it for you."

Mr Zhang disappeared into the back, leaving the guest arguing with himself. He finally gave up and walked away. In a few minutes Mr. Zhang reappeared with the manila envelope and handed it to him.

"You need taxi today, Mr. Thomas?"

"Morning, Yuan. Yeah, Is JoJo around?"

"You wait. I find for you."

He always tried to get JoJo. JoJo was a scholar of the streets of Bangkok and a retired gangster. He had lost the use of his right arm after a small disagreement in a dance bar in

14

Klong Toey. His friends called him the one-armed bandit and he steered the cab mostly with his knees. He needed to keep his good hand free to express his displeasure with everyone else on the road. JoJo was wired into the hard life of the city and his instincts were seldom wrong. Riding with him was not for the faint of heart but he could get you out of a jam pretty damn quick. He liked people with the stomach for a little excitement and he knew Jack was a player. There wouldn't be any drama on this trip, at least no more than the kamikaze Bangkok drivers would provide.

There was a noodle stand next to the front entrance. The hotel advertised a restaurant on the premises but nobody complained. There was no one to complain to. No one who would listen anyway. It was food, mostly safe to eat, and it was in the lobby. The toothless old woman behind the counter short-changed him, but he pretended not to notice. He had reached an uneasy compromise with the jackhammer in his head and there was no way he was going to upset the balance. The coffee was wretched but the noodles were edible. He swore they boiled them in seawater. Mr. Zhang reappeared again.

"Fortune with you today, Mr. Thomas. JoJo here very soon. Outside, five minute. You wait for him. OK?"

He dropped the plastic containers in a trashcan next to the door and stepped out onto the sidewalk. This part of the city had an atmosphere all its own. It was a cloying mixture of flower petals, exhaust fumes and overripe fruit. The motor scooters were flying by like a swarm of mosquitoes. Tuk Tuks, mostly empty in the morning, vied for road space with the Japanese cars and taxis. The street was lined with stalls and shop fronts, decorated with garlands of flowers and exotic plants. They called this area the 'backpacker's paradise.' The prices were good and the street was already filling with shoppers. He didn't even notice the heat anymore. It was always the same, except during the monsoon when it was just as hot, but so wet you could drown just from breathing too hard.

A slightly rusted green and yellow Nissan pulled up to the curb. JoJo jumped out and opened the door for his customer. He was a businessman and JoJo did not seem pleased by the tip. If there was one. He stared daggers at the foreigner's back as he entered the hotel and muttered 'kee nok' under his breath. It was the Thai word for bird shit. JoJo turned and grinned at Jack flashing a gold front tooth.

"Where to, boss?"

Jack climbed into the back of the cab. "The Ambassador."

"We need to run over anybody, boss?"

"Not today, JoJo."

He looked a little disappointed. Jack sat back and watched some young women walking by, wearing ankle length dresses and holding brightly colored parasols to shield them from the sun. JoJo lurched out into the traffic without looking, causing a rear end collision, an overturned fruit cart and a lot of interesting hand gestures. He didn't throw the flag. Jack always paid at least double what the flat rate would be, plus a tip. The extra was for information. JoJo always had information. Most of it was of no great interest, but it was always a good thing to know what was blowing around in the wind. JoJo was looking at him in the rear view mirror.

16

"Mani wants to talk to you."

"Oh, yeah? What about?"

"I don't know. Maybe a deal?"

"I don't think so, JoJo. I haven't been playing in his neighborhood in a long time."

"He says somebody else looking for you, too. He is farang-dam."

"A black man?"

"Yeah, and not so friendly, I think. Mani says he is jai khaeng. Won't do business with him."

Jack laughed. "Unless the price is right. What did Mani tell him?"

"He asked why he is looking for you. But the guy was talking bullshit. Mani says he didn't tell him nothing."

"Tell him thanks. Tell him I'll bring flowers next time I see him."

"I do that, he thinks you want to kill him. Flowers are for to bury somebody."

"Just tell him I left town."

"You leaving, boss?"

"I have a feeling."

Traffic was a little less chaotic than usual and they got downtown in pretty good time. JoJo filled him in on the latest turf war in the Chinatown. Jack wasn't all that interested but he listened as he watched the city go by. Bangkok was one of the most visually stunning cities he had ever seen. Modern hotels and corporate towers were sandwiched in between ancient temples and gritty street markets where exotic fragrances hung in the air like clouds waiting to envelope you. In some neighborhoods, elephants roamed the streets like stray cats, along with the pickpockets and hustlers and the ever-present prostitutes. They call it the City of Life, but for him it was life out on the edge. Out where the fall was quick and almost always fatal. The meeting wasn't for another forty-five minutes and he was dying for some eggs and a decent cup of coffee. The Ambassador was a little past its prime but it was a decent enough hotel. It was in a great location. There was a Skytrain to the Nana district, which meant the businessmen could enjoy an evening of debauchery without getting stuck in traffic. It was located in the heart of the commercial center, which was why the agency kept rooms there under contract. The businessmen had already headed out for their morning slash and burn sessions. That left the bright-eyed tourists getting ready for a new day of photo-op heaven. A hundred more snapshots, all destined to end up attached to emails and sent to people who really didn't give a shit. The sex tourists were still passed out in their single rooms, gathering the energy to fuel their addiction for one more night or perhaps wrestling with whatever was left of their consciences. The hostess wore a red, flowered silk dress. She greeted him with a smile and a bow with hands pressed together under her chin, as if in prayer. Everybody smiled here all the time. Even when they were kicking the shit out of somebody. Sometimes he missed New York.

He was sitting in the lobby reading an orphaned *Financial Times* when he saw Charlie step out of the elevator and sniff the air, surveying the lobby like a bear emerging from his den on the first day of spring. He was wearing a green, flowered shirt that looked slept in, over a pair of knee-length shorts and sandals. His legs were so thick and hairy he looked like a tree escaping from the rain forest.

Charlie Wingate. Ex Green Beret, ex CIA and expatriate Charlie was the agency's man in Bangkok, which meant he spent most of his time screwing and drinking while his local contractors sniffed around for opportunities. He had a beer gut big enough to house a family of four, a greying crew cut and cold, pale blue eyes. He was about six-foot two and didn't look all that tough, but looks could be deceiving. Jack had personally seen Charlie throw two very large men out the window of a whorehouse in Vientiane. He had mellowed just a bit with age but he still had a grip like a bear trap. He also still had the walk. People just got out of his way.

The agency was Iroquois Security Services. Among other things, it was a small free-lance army for hire, complete with the best weapons and technology money could buy, legally or illegally. If you had the money, they could provide an agreed upon number of unmarked aircraft filled with hard men, anywhere in the world, within 72 hours. Charlie's section handled intelligence gathering. It often involved the kind of work that could not be sanctioned by official government agencies. It really didn't matter what government was involved, as long as it was not an enemy of the West. A lot of it was pretty mundane tracking and surveillance. Jack was one of Charlie's boys. A contractor. It was just another name for someone being bribed into doing risky things he really didn't want to do. The pay was good, but there was no cover. They would help you out to a point but would not risk exposing the agency under any circumstances. Nobody was going to send in the cavalry. There would be flowers sent to the funeral home if there actually were any remains. Charlie was the exception, which was the only reason Jack was still in the game. It wasn't that he trusted Charlie completely, but they had some history together and it wasn't all bad. Charlie spotted Jack and ambled over to him.

"Good morning, Jack. How's the world treatin' ya?" His voice filled the lobby and elicited a few curious stares.

"This is the world? Anyway, my guess is you're about to tell me." He handed Charlie the envelope.

"That's what I like about you, Jack. You're a fatalist. Good philosophy for this business. Any problems getting the file?"

"No dead bodies."

"That's my boy."

"So what is it this time?"

Charlie gave him a sideways look. "What no small talk?"

"Sure, so how are the wife and the kid and the dog and the lawn?"

"Come on, lighten up, Jack, you're going to like this one. How about a nice little paid vacation in Singapore?"

"I don't do Singapore, Charlie. That was our deal."

"What are you talking about? You spend half you life down there."

"Yeah, well that's my free time. I don't do business there."

"Come on, Jack, this is a walk in the park. You won't even get your hands dirty."

"Yeah, well, Harry didn't get his hands dirty either. He just got his fucking head chopped off."

"Harry was playing me, Jack. He got what he deserved. Besides, they didn't chop his head off, they hung him."

"That's very comforting. Besides, those mean little bastards down there will cane you for spitting on the street. I'm allergic."

"What if I told you this would be your last time?"

"I wouldn't believe you."

"I mean it, Jack. I'm going to retire and go back to the States as soon as this one's over with. The new guy will have to find his own hounds."

"You? Retire? What happened? Did your dick fall off?"

"Look, I really need this one and you're perfect for it. I'd be willing to pay you double your normal rate. It will take you a week, ten days tops and I'll put you up at the Hyatt for Christ sakes."

"I wouldn't do it for triple my price."

"Come on. You know I can't make that fly."

"What the hell do you care, Charlie? If you're really getting out, your budget doesn't mean shit anymore."

Charlie sat back in his chair and waved to the concierge. He came over at a trot. "Get me a scotch, neat, and whatever my friend here wants. Make sure the bottle has a label on it."

Jack waved him off. Charlie was giving him the long stare and he wondered what would come next, the veiled threats or more of the old buddy routine. He didn't have to wait long.

"How long have we known each other, Jack?"

"Way too long."

"It was Hong Kong right? 1994 or around there. Back before the Brits pulled out."

"1995. Kowloon."

"Right, right. Some kind of trouble with the Chinese trade delegation?"

"Yeah, right. You got me out of a scrape. I was grateful. You were my best friend. Do anything for you. Have done ever since."

"Yeah, but you've been well paid well for it. Besides, you were made for this crap and you know it. If you don't do something illegal every now and then you get bored. Tell me I'm lying."

Jack knew it was true. He was an ex Army Ranger himself, and it had changed him. It was the other reason he hadn't tried harder to get out. The truth was he couldn't handle a normal nine to five. That was what got him into the business in the first place. Nothing like a little industrial espionage to liven things up a bit. It was a piece of cake really, but it did get the adrenaline pumping at times. The thing was, there was almost no risk. If you got caught with a few documents that shouldn't be in your briefcase you could almost always lie your way out of it. For the most part, corporations didn't bother with prosecution because they didn't want it to go public. Bad for the stock valuation. A couple of times he had actually been given a severance package in exchange for keeping his mouth shut. One of the companies he had burned offered him a job as a security consultant. It was all nuts. All you really needed were the balls to pull it off. In the end, who gives a shit whether some mega-corporation steals the recipe for some competitor's mouthwash? It wasn't like he was stealing State secrets. It was strictly free-lance, though, and the work was spotty at best.

But that was all before he got caught on the Chinese side of the border with some very embarrassing CAD files. They almost shot him on the spot but for some reason thought better of it. At the very least, he was about to grow old in some Chinese hellhole when his new best friend Charlie appeared. It seemed some of Jack's exploits had caught the eye of the boys who played in the big leagues. Word got around. The Chinese were becoming troublesome and several Western intelligence agencies were badly in need of operators who knew the neighborhood and weren't afraid to make late night visits to unauthorized places. What followed was a crash course in tradecraft, Iroquois style, and a brand spanking new Canadian passport with a background story to match. They even had people who would answer the phone somewhere back in Toronto and claim Jack as their long lost best pal who was off somewhere in Asia on important trade matters. It was great, except that the only severance package you would get in this game was the one that removed your head from your body. He was going to take the assignment. It was better than sitting around in the heat, wondering why you didn't have a life. The truth was, he didn't know what else he could do. This was just about playing hard to get and Charlie knew it.

"Look, Jack, double your normal rate and a business class ticket to wherever you want to go. That's the deal. Last time, I swear. Unless of course you want a letter of recommendation to the new prick in town."

Jack sat back and studied Charlie's face. It was impenetrable as usual, but he got the feeling he wasn't lying about getting out. It would be a different life without him. Charlie was predictable and he had a talent for knowing

23

what was doable and what was just somebody's wet dream.

"So what are you going to do back in the States?"

"Fucked if I know. Go fishing or something. Maybe I'll open a little bait and tackle shop somewhere. Anyplace where I can get a decent cheeseburger. The world is not what it used to be, Jack. It's getting too complicated for me."

"If I do this I want a back door, Charlie, and I don't mean crawling through some fucking sewer somewhere. I want an extraction and I want it set up before I leave Bangkok."

"No problem. I can arrange that."

"And I'm not lifting anything that belongs to the government of Singapore."

"Nothing like that is involved."

Jack just studied his face for a few seconds, and then sat back in his chair. "OK, so what's the gig?"

"Atta boy, Jack. Let's go get some fresh air."

They walked along a paved path below a row of Eucalyptus Trees behind the hotel. Charlie handed Jack a manila folder.

"Meet Mr. Thomas Yu. American citizen and resident wonk at Psydyne Optics. It's one of those Silicon Valley brain factories that turn out a bunch of 'Buck Rodgers' crap for the defense industry. It appears that Mr. Yu is a bit of an entrepreneur. Some of his superiors suspect he has gone off the reservation. A lot of Chinese engineers and scientists have been recruited by Beijing to loot defense technology from the US. Mr. Yu is known to have communicated with some individuals of questionable intent, as we like to say. We want you to catch him with his pants down."

Jack studied the photograph. "OK, so what's my costume?"

"I was getting to that. It's why we wanted you for this gig. As of right now, you are the CFO of a tidy little start-up called R-Scan. It does radio frequency scanning and identification technology."

"Like I know anything about that."

"Don't worry. You can stop by the shop tomorrow and we'll have one of our tech geeks teach you everything you need to know. Besides, that's why we promoted you to CFO. If anybody wants to chat about the technology you can just give him the old 'I'm just the bean-counter routine'. Get a business card to give to your 'engineering manager' and then have an important meeting to get to. You know the drill."

"What's he supposed to be pedalling?"

"His current project is a high power laser tracking and identification system Psydyne is developing for the Air Force. It is highly proprietary and nothing about it is allowed to leave company property or be discussed with anyone outside of the project team. Somebody saw him making unauthorized copies of the design drawings but they didn't let on they knew. He hid the disk in his desk. Jim Richards knows Psydyne's CEO and they hired us to track the disk and put the hammer down on Mr. Yu. They had their own security people break into Mr. Yu's desk and swap out the disk with some Donald Duck cartoons. We want you to pick up this guy's trail in Singapore and catch him with his hand on his dick."

"Who's the buyer?"

"Don't know. Probably an intermediary. It doesn't really matter."

"When do I leave?"

"The trade show starts next Monday. Mr. Yu's flight arrives on Sunday morning. You should get eyes-on at the airport when he arrives. He'll be staying at the Hyatt also so it shouldn't be too hard to keep tabs on him."

"Somehow I knew you weren't putting me up there out of the kindness of your heart."

3

It was a short flight to Singapore. Jack hit the washroom before checking in and went through his luggage twice. That was how Harry got the long drop; 20 grams of heroin in his shaving kit. They would hang you for fifteen. It wasn't that he thought the agency was trying to burn him. It was just better to trust no one. In the business he was in, paranoia was a survival skill. Being thorough was what kept you alive and he knew too many guys who had gotten nailed just for being careless. It wouldn't be the first time drugs were hidden in a carry-on bag until some bright-eyed tourist, unwittingly facing the death penalty, carried it safely through the checkpoint. Or not.

Changi airport is one of the most modern and best organized in Asia. There were always more police standing around than anywhere else he had ever travelled. And those were just the ones in uniform. Singapore was a democracy, but you wouldn't want to stand up on a street corner and criticize the government. It was also the cleanest city in Asia but you could get arrested for chewing gum or spitting on the street. He had walked down Orchard road and more than once been offered the services of little boys or little girls by sleazy looking men who probably were undercover police. If you were bent, or looking for a walk on the wild side, it was not the place to be. It was like a smaller version of Hong Kong, but with a generous application of disinfectant.

Charlie was right. He was perfect for this gig. Dressed in a business suit and conservative tie, Jack was an executive. He was rugged looking. Broad shouldered and on the tall side with a little gray in his light brown hair and a warm smile. Most importantly, he had the look. Approachable, but with piercing blue eyes that told you to get down to business. His years in the business world had taught him the language of power. It was easy to tell the movers and shakers from the toadies. They were the guys who looked like they were on vacation, while everyone around them was having a heart attack. The Electronics Industry trade show was being held at the World Trade Center, located across Keppel Harbour from the island of Sentosa. Sentosa was a resort now, but you could still visit the Japanese interment camp where the British and Australian forces were starved and worked to death during the Japanese occupation. It was one of those places in the world that would never feel good again. He had visited it once and he never wanted to go back.

Every trade show he had ever attended was the same. Corporations paid a fortune to project their image at these things and for most it was a losing proposition.

It was a good venue to launch a new product if you had one. Most of the time they were flogging some new and improved version of the same old iron. They were there because they couldn't afford to not be. The big dogs had the most booth space and the most padded carpet. Some of the displays came complete with bar and lounge for the live prospects. If you looked like a buyer they treated you like a king. It was kind of entertaining watching a bunch of guys in suits fall all over themselves trying to become best friends with some slob with a budget.

Jack had watched Mr. Yu long enough to recognize him in a crowd. He was small in stature and his movements were quick, almost furtive. At one point he had dropped someone's business card and he nearly knocked a display over in his eagerness to pick it up. That was a big part of the game. Watch a target for a while and, unless he's a pro, you will learn his body language. Learn how he moves when there isn't anything going down and when the action starts he will flash like a neon sign. Jack had seen guys run into the men's room and puke just before a deal. He followed Mr. Yu up and down the aisles while the legions of eager, fresh-faced salesmen tried to reel him in like a tuna. Jack wasn't worried about Mr. Yu spotting him. The guy was oblivious. Experience told him that the prospective buyers also had an eye on Mr. Yu and would be looking for anyone showing too much interest. After an hour of walking around behind him, Jack backed off and kept an eye on him from a distance. Nothing was going to happen on the trade show floor. Too many eyes. It was, however, likely going to happen sooner than later. The disk would be feeling like a hot potato in Mr. Yu's pocket and the sooner he unloaded it the better he would feel. It might happen in the evening but a guy like Mr. Yu would be feeling very pleased with himself indeed, and would be wanting to go out to play. The best time was during lunch or during an excursion sponsored by one of the alpha-dog corporations.

Mr. Yu left the show floor at 2:00 o'clock and got in line for the ferryboat going to Sentosa.

Jack took the Skyride cable car and loitered around the ferry dock until the boat came in. He was taking photographs of the Singapore skyline with a Nikon digital camera equipped with a 70 – 300 mm zoom lens, when Mr. Yu walked past with the rest of the passengers. Jack casually wandered off down the footpath about 50 feet and as many heads behind his quarry. He was taking pictures of the birds and furiously consulting his field guide. He solicited opinions from some of the passers by. He wasn't just watching Mr. Yu. He was looking to see who else might be interested. In particular he was looking to see if he had been spotted.

Jack had been wondering along at a safe distance behind Mr. Yu for about twenty minutes when he noticed a change. The body language was completely different. He looked like a teenager about to shoplift a pair of jeans. *This is going to be easy*, he thought. Mr. Yu sat down on a bench and in a few minutes was joined by another Chinese man. He was a larger man and his demeanor seemed more formal. Jack guessed he was military. They made a big show of having a heartfelt reunion but their faces were hard and tense. Jack got some excellent full-face shots of both men. Charlie would have the pictures as soon as Jack could get back to his hotel and, if his friends at the CIA were still cooperating, there was a possibility he would have an ID on the contact before dinner. It was just a precaution in case the contact slipped him.

The next part was a little tricky. If the disk were passed in a paper bag or obscured in a file of some kind the pictures would be ambiguous. When it finally happened, Jack couldn't believe his eyes and neither could the buyer. Mr. Yu took the disk out of his pocket and just handed it to the guy. Jack laughed and just kept snapping pictures. The buyer looked like he had just been handed a ticking bomb. He had a stunned look on his face for a second and then he quickly dropped the disk into his briefcase. They talked for a while and then the buyer got up and walked away, leaving a manila envelope on the bench. Mr. Yu very casually picked it up and put it in his bag. He sat back on the bench with a big grin on his face. Jack had a terrible urge to go over and tell the guy what an ass he was, but he would find out for himself soon enough.

The buyer did not seem concerned at all about being followed. Jack kept a safe distance but had to double-time it when his quarry entered the MRT station. It was a job that should have been done by rotating teams of watchers but this wasn't the CIA. If anyone was covering the target's tail they would have picked Jack up pretty easily, but that was the life of a contractor. All he could do was keep looking at his watch like he was late for a meeting. He was sweating like a lawn sprinkler but just managed to jump on the last car of the train the target had boarded. It was the north-south line, which probably meant he was headed for the hotels up on Orchard Road near where Jack was staying. The whole thing was going way too easy but he was into it now and there was no time for second-guessing. Jack just needed to see what hotel the target was going to. The Psydyne geeks had hidden a short-range location transmitter in the disk case. He needed to be within about thirty feet to pick up the signal, but that was plenty. He could walk down the hallway of a hotel and find the room it was in. He got off the

31

train, keeping a safe distance from the target, and followed him until he entered the Grand Central hotel. Time to get back to the Hyatt and see if he could find Angel.

Angel was probably the most exotic looking woman he had ever known. Jack wasn't fooled easily but it had taken him two hours and a very expensive dinner to find out she was a call girl. A very pricey one at that. She was born in Jakarta. Her mother was from Malaysia but her father was French. She was taller than most of the girls, with the best pair of legs he had ever seen and a face that you couldn't stop staring at. Her hair was liquid ebony and stopped just short of the small of her back. When she walked though the lobby you could hear necks snapping like popcorn. She had no regard whatever for men, except possibly for Jack, and not always for him. What they felt for each other was a little like love, except that there was no commitment and no surrender. They were more like co-conspirators in a game that they both played by their own rules. It was a game played on the razor's edge of legality, and sometimes it was more fun than two human beings ought to have together. She was a woman who had become comfortable with her power over men and she wielded it like a stiletto. When she was in the mood she could go to a bar and orchestrate a puppet show to whatever outcome she fancied, leaving broken men gasping for air.

Her favorite haunt was the bar at the Scotts Lounge in the Grand Hyatt. It was one of the reasons it was Jack's favorite hotel in Singapore. He wandered down to the lounge at five and took a seat at the bar. He was on his second bourbon when he felt a light touch on the back of his neck. He didn't have to turn around.

"It would serve you right if I ignored you completely," she said, in a low, silky voice."

He leaned back against her and gave her a kiss on the cheek. She was wearing a short, low cut, black dress that left little to the imagination, and stockings with a seam up the back. Even the women were staring at her. The pendant she wore around her neck, a token from one of her conquests, had a diamond that should have been locked away in a safe.

"What fun would that be, Angel?"

"So many men, my darling. So much money. Really I don't know why I bother with you at all."

"Because I'm the only man in Singapore who doesn't turn into a stuttering schoolboy when you pout."

"Not the only one. You stay away too long, Jacky. I get bored."

"That's OK Angel. I'm not the jealous type."

"So are you going to buy me the best dinner I've ever had or should I go looking for a schoolboy to seduce?"

"Anywhere you want to go."

"I want to go to Paris."

"Too cold this time of year. How about someplace in Singapore."

She pretended to be annoyed. "You are becoming a terrible bore, Jacky, but alright if you insist."

"I do insist. Besides I have a proposition for you."

"I accept. I'll need to fly to Rome to pick out my dress. You can choose the Cathedral."

"Not a proposal. A proposition."

"You mean a job? I couldn't possibly. I just had my nails done."

"All you have to do is seduce someone for me."

"Is he cute?"

"I wouldn't know. He's Chinese. Anyway, you don't have to sleep with him. I just need him to be distracted for a little while. An hour at most."

"Sleep is not what I do."

"I also need you to steal his key card for me and get it back into his pocket before you dump him."

"That's not work. I could do that for you for nothing. But I won't. You need to be punished for staying away for so long."

"I'll pay you a grand for it."

"Do I have to do it tonight?"

"No, tomorrow afternoon."

"In that case I want to go to the IndoChine. But only if they are serving the lemongrass crème brulee. You have to call them and ask."

"Bartender, could I have a telephone please?"

She put her arms around his neck. "That's OK, you bad boy. They always have the crème brulee."

The IndoChine, restaurant on the Singapore River near the harbor was one of Jack's favorite places, but he only went there with Angel. Something about sitting across from her out on the patio under the awning, with a light breeze coming off the water, got him to a state of being he couldn't find any other way. The menu was probably the best in the city and among the best in all of Asia. It was a slow, delicious seduction of the senses and they took their time with it. Afterwards, the waiter brought them a pot of Vietnamese coffee and they sipped it slowly, enjoying the moment of stillness and the anticipation of what was to follow.

"Why are you here this time, Jacky?"

"I came to see you."

"That's a very good answer, but it's a lie."

"It's only half a lie. Besides if I came down here too often you might get spoiled."

"I'm already spoiled. Let me count the ways."

"Have you collected any new admirers?"

"I had a banker who was amusing for a while. I think his wife found out, though. The last time I saw him he looked like he had indigestion."

"Too bad."

"Not really. He had horribly skinny legs and a big potbelly. I made him get under the covers or I wouldn't come out of the bathroom. He gave me a beautiful pair of diamond earrings but I think he expected me to be free after that. Can you imagine?"

"You are a very bad girl, Angel."

"So why don't you marry me and turn me into an honest woman?"

"First of all, you would get bored within six months. Secondly, you will never be an honest woman."

"Well, you're right about the second part, but I don't think I would get bored with you, Jacky. I have it all figured out. We could move to Monte Carlo and become professional jewel thieves. I would seduce the men into telling me where they were hidden and you would steal them for me. We could make love in their bed while they're downstairs having dinner."

Jack laughed. "I think you have way too much time on your hands. How do you come up with this stuff?"

"You have to have dreams, Jacky. Don't you have dreams?"

"That's not a dream, that's a fantasy. There's a difference."

"Not for me. But really, don't you ever want to do something else with your life?"

"Every day."

"So why don't you?"

"Because I'm like you, Angel. I don't know if there is anywhere to go from here."

She was silent for a while and Jack watched her, sipping her coffee and looking out over the water. He wanted to freeze the moment in time. In a while, she turned and looked at him with those eyes, filled with an unearthly fire, and he knew what was coming before she spoke.

"Let's go over to Sentosa. I want to make love with you on the beach."

4

Jack paid a visit to the Grand Central a little after midnight and a quick stop back at his room to check his e-mail. He had downloaded the pictures earlier in the day, but so far Charlie had not come up with a match. For now the target was still 'Mr. Who?' It was time for some legwork. He took the elevator to the second floor and began walking the hallways. The scanner was hidden in a transistor radio. He would hear a tone through the earpiece like a magnetic hum if he came with range of the transmitter. It was a high-rise hotel and he fervently hoped his guy was afraid of heights. He finally found the room on the sixth floor. He was tempted to just break in and get it over with, but there was no way to be sure the guy wasn't in there sleeping one off. It would take a little time to defeat the lock and he couldn't risk being seen.

The next part was the worst because it involved a lot of waiting. He was at the Grand Central early in the morning. He had to make sure Mr. Who hadn't checked out. Now that he had the disk, there was a risk he would just fold his tent and head on home. Hopefully he wasn't done shopping. Jack saw him step out of the elevator around 9AM and head right for the cabstand without his bags. It was going to be a long day. He told Angel to be ready by two. She whined about having to hang around at the Grand Central but in the end he just gave her another five hundred to assuage her pride. There was a café across from the hotel that provided a good view of the entrance. He had an early lunch and killed some time flirting with the cute little Chinese waitress who was just as bored as he was. The rest of the time he spent walking around outside the hotel, pretending to be talking on his cell phone, and sitting in the shade reading a newspaper.

It was a long wait but his luck held. Mr. Who got back to the Hotel at twenty after three. Angel was already in the lounge, shooing away barflies. She was an artist. When she didn't want to be distracted she put on a cubic zirconium ring that looked like it weighed four pounds. If a guy came up to her at the bar she just stuck it in his face as if to say, if you can beat this we can talk. If she found one who wasn't intimidated she gave him her number. Jack figured Mr. Who for a happy hour kind of guy but he told Angel to wear her bikini under her dress just in case. At 4:10, Mr. Who emerged from the elevator in his swim trunks. He crossed the lobby and headed out to the pool. It was show time. Jack gave Angel the sign and then found a place where he could watch her work. It was inspiring. She went to the ladies room and emerged in a bathing suit that you could pack in a matchbox, and what looked like a lacy black negligee.

Angel had already lifted somebody's key card. She probably got it from a coyote at the bar while he was trying to make body contact. After Mr. Who got settled in his lounge chair she took her oversized pocketbook, her drink and several magazines and strolled out to the pool. A couple of guys at the bar almost fell off their stools watching her walk by. When she got to where Mr. Who was sitting, Jack pushed the send button on his cell. Angel looked flustered as she tried to hold on to everything and find her cell phone in her purse. Finally she dropped the magazines and almost spilled her drink in Mr. Who's lap. He was falling all over himself trying to help. He looked like he had just caught Santa Claus coming down the chimney. Finally Angel put her drink down on the table next to his lounge chair, sat down next to him and flicked open her phone.

"Hello"

"Pretty nice suit. This is Singapore you know. You could get locked up for wearing something like that."

"Oh, hello, darling. Where are you?"

"You better go easy on the little bastard, he looks like he's about to have a stroke."

"But I already have reservations. What am I going to tell Tom and Jane?"

"How about we do the hot tub when this is over?"

"OK, but I was really looking forward to dinner."

"We can do that after. Did you locate the key card yet?"

"I already have it, darling. I'm sure it will fit just fine."

"You're unbelievable. I'll be over by the restrooms."

"OK, but don't take too long. I want you to be in by ten. Bye."

She was so smooth he hadn't even seen her make the switch. He watched as she thanked Mr. Who profusely for helping her and then asked if he would mind watching her bag while she used the ladies room. Jack watched her come through the door. She handed him the card and gave him a kiss.

"Hurry up, OK. I think this guy is going to grin himself to death."

"Just wait in the ladies room. This won't take long."

Jack walked over to the elevator with a deliberate, unhurried stride. He checked his watch. He was carrying a large shopping bag stuffed with tissue paper. There was only one other person in the car; an elderly man. They didn't speak and he exited the car on the fourth floor. On the sixth floor Jack walked to the room and quickly entered. There was a briefcase on the bed but it was locked. He flicked on the scanner. The disk was definitely there. He didn't want to waste time picking the lock, so he just dumped the whole briefcase into the shopping bag. He checked the corridor and found it empty. The fire stairs were next to the elevator. He walked down one flight, and took the elevator on the fifth floor. The whole operation took just under five minutes. Angel was waiting by the restrooms when he came back down. He gave her the key card.

"Call me in fifteen, OK? I want to get my nails done."

"Let him down easy, will you. I want him to stay at the pool for a while and not go running back to his room to jump out the window."

"Don't worry, Jackie. He's going to swear I'm in love with him before you get out of your cab." She blew on her finger and pressed it to Jack's lips.

Jack was in the game now and there was no wasted motion. He exited the cab in front of an office tower that had a Fed Ex box outside. He had picked the lock on the brief case during the ride. The shipping envelope was already made out. He dropped the disk inside and deposited

40

the envelope in the box. Mission accomplished. Back at the room he examined the other items in the briefcase. There were a dozen sheets of legal pad pages with what looked like the notes of a meeting, hand written in Chinese. He took a portable scanner out of his suitcase and brought the papers over to the table. Adjusting the light to reduce the glare, he began to methodically scan everything. He also found a Pentad dSLR digital camera and a black box, which was some kind of electronic equipment that he couldn't immediately identify. There was no cable to download the camera's memory and his cable wasn't compatible. He pulled the memory card and slipped it into his pocket. This was all a present for Charlie. He really didn't give a shit what it all was or whether it was worth anything. Not his gig. He examined the black box. It was about six inches by nine inches and there was an eyepiece on the top of the device next to a row of LEDs. An armored cable, about two feet long and terminated by a 24-pin Amphenol connector, extended from one end of the box. There was a slide switch on the other end. Jack put his eye to the cup. He didn't expect to see anything with the cable disconnected, but when he flicked the switch open a green dot appeared. It held steady for a few seconds and then did a counter-clockwise rotation, illuminating his eye. The LEDs flashed twice and then the device shut down. It appeared to be a retinal scanner, probably just another piece of pirated technology on its way into China. Next he connected to the server and dumped his entire memory. He sanitized the hard drive and then tore the documents into the smallest pieces he could manage and flushed them down the toilet. He didn't know what to do with the black box. His first thought was to dump it so there would be no evidence to connect him to the theft of the briefcase. In the end, he decided to hang on to it until he could discuss it with Charlie. The briefcase went back into the shopping bag and he closed and locked the door.

Orchard Road is like an Asian version of Rodeo Drive. Safe, sanitized and engineered to separate you from your money. He stood at a traffic signal and listened to the electronic sounds of chirping birds that changed in pitch when the light turned red. He did some shopping, keeping an eye out to see if he had picked up a tail. In years past he would have left the brief case under a bench and it would eventually disappear. Now, unattended briefcases drew the wrong kind of attention. Instead, he took a walk down an alley that connected a group of shops and tossed the whole shopping bag in a dumpster. It had been thoroughly cleaned of prints and there was no identification inside. Now he could relax.

Angel didn't want to meet until nine, so he decided to kill some time at the Long Bar at Raffles. It had been around since 1887 and was one of the best hotels in Asia. It was also the birthplace of the Singapore Sling. One part gin, one part cherry brandy, one part Benedictine, and a little pineapple. Top it off with some club soda and salute the bloody Queen. Some of his favorite writers had hung out there, including Joseph Conrad, Somerset Maugham and Rudyard Kipling when Singapore was still an outpost of the empire. "All the people like us are we. Everyone else is they." It was one of those places tourists went just to feel like they had arrived. He picked a table under a wicker ceiling fan near the courtyard, and watched the sparrows fly in to pick at the monkey nut shells the patrons dropped on the floor. He wondered what he was going to do next. If Charlie were really getting out, the landscape would be changing in a hurry. There was no way he was going to break in another handler. Charlie could be an asshole at times but he looked after his people. Maybe it was time to go back to the world. It would be nice to have Angel with him but he knew she would give him a heart attack sooner or later. Still, he wasn't sure he could go without seeing her once in a while at least.

There was an odd assortment of characters at the bar. Mostly tourists, but a few that Jack recognized by their body language and the expressions on their faces. He didn't know any of them personally, but he understood who they were. Singapore was a lot tamer than it had once been, but it still served as the major crossroads in Asia. The entrepot trade was not just in goods. The commerce included information that could get a man killed. It was neutral ground because the heavy police presence and liberal death penalty discouraged any kind of wet work. Enemies could sit across from each other at a table and have a drink without needing to watch the exits. It was like taking sanctuary in a medieval cathedral. The Long Bar had witnessed the last pleasant hour in the life of many a man, whose corpse had turned up later in some dark corner of Shanghai or Macao. The place seemed frozen in time. A man walked by and did a double take when he saw Jack. He wasn't tall but he was thick across the shoulders and powerfully built. He had tattoos on both forearms and his head was shaved, probably to hide the fact that there wasn't much left to run a comb through. Jack recognized him but it was too late to avoid a conversation. His name was Phil Bishop and they had met on an operation in Mozambique. It hadn't gone well. He walked over to the table and he didn't look happy.

"Well, if it isn't Jack Lawrence. I wondered if you were still alive."

"Up till now."

"You still with Iroquois?"

"I do some contract work for them. Nothing heavy."

"You know, a lot of good men got wasted back at that air strip, Jack. Some of them were my friends."

"Yeah, it went bad, Phil. Real bad."

"It wasn't supposed to happen that way. You were supposed to have transport for everybody."

"I did what I could Phil. I asked for three planes. They sent one."

"Yeah, well you got your guys out, didn't you?"

"That was my job."

"I spent six months in a hole in the ground because of you."

"So what do you want me to do, say I'm sorry? You knew the deal going in. We all did. None of us were risking it for God and country. Some times good men die."

"The deal was we were all going to get flown out of there."

"Look, Phil. If you want to go somewhere and have it out with me, just say so. I don't really feel like it, but I'll dance with you if I have to. Otherwise, you're ruining a good afternoon."

"No. I just wanted to tell you to your face what a waste of a life you are."

Jack stood up and faced him. "OK, you told me. Now get the fuck away from me."

It had been a long day and he wanted to rest up a little before he met Angel. The confrontation with Phil took a bit of the glow off of everything, but all in all, the gig had gone pretty well and he was feeling relaxed. He headed back to his hotel. Jack always used a side or rear entrance when he was on a job. Sometimes he had to wait until somebody exited, but he found an open door and took the fire stairs up one floor before using the elevator. He opened the door to his room and it took a second for his brain to process what his eyes were seeing. The entire room had been trashed, and in the middle of it was Angel. She was wearing a white summer dress and lying on the bed with her head to the side as if she were taking a nap. There was a pool of dark red blood that ran to the edge of the bead-spread and was slowly dripping onto the carpet. Her throat had been slit. Jack's knees went weak and he nearly vomited. He started to enter the room but then his training kicked in and he turned and stepped back into the corridor, closing the door behind him. There was no time. He walked quickly around the corner to the service elevator. It seemed like it took an hour for the door to open. He jammed his wallet into the door track to keep it from closing and then walked back into the main hallway and hit the fire alarm with his elbow. They would bury him for a setting off a false alarm but that was the least of his problems. He went back to the service elevator and pushed the ground floor button. The alarm was so loud it was hard to think but he forced himself to go calm inside. If he panicked, it was over. As the elevator began to move he did a quick inventory. He had his wallet but his passport and computer were back in the room. They were of no use to him now anyway. He had to get to a phone. Somebody was burning him down and, if it was the agency, he was as good as dead. He couldn't believe Angel was gone. Jack was trying hard to push the sight out of his mind. He couldn't allow himself the luxury of grieving for her. There would be a time for that later, if he survived.

The elevator doors opened into a bare, concrete hallway. He followed it to the kitchen, walking as casually as he could manage. The kitchen staff was still working but they had the doors propped open just in case they had to leave in a hurry. They didn't even look up. He exited to the alley and headed toward Little India. He would be on foot now. The police would not have circulated a description yet. That was what the fire alarm was for. They were probably waiting in the lobby and would want to take him in the room with the evidence. The fire alarm would slow them down, at least for the time being, but he needed to get out of sight. He walked with the crowds and tried to keep his head down. There were surveillance cameras everywhere. It was a long walk but it gave him a chance to start sorting it all out. There were only two possibilities that he could think of. He couldn't think of any reason the agency would want him dead. He wasn't really even on their radar. He was just one of Charlie's boys. On the other hand, they played by their own rules. Still, it didn't figure. The other possibility was that Mr. Who was connected to one of the Chinese gang families. Whoever did it had some help. Angel wasn't stupid. She wouldn't have just gone to his room without a reason. Someone had probably recognized her and made her give him up. He didn't want to think about it.

He found a small shopping mall and locate a pay phone. It must have rung twenty times before Charlie answered. The voice on the other end of the line said, "Speak."

"Is the back door open?"

"The door is open, are you injured?"

"Negative."

"What is your ETA?"

"About twenty minutes."

He heard a click on the other end of the line. Charlie had known who it was. It was Jack's call in number, nobody else had it. He stopped at a drug store and picked up some surgical tape and a package of condoms. By the time he got back out onto the street it was dark and he felt a little less paranoid. He kept his head down and ducked into some storefronts along the way to see if he were being followed. The address on Perak road was a typical two-story shophouse. He rang the bell and a heavy-set Indian woman opened the gate for him. She looked to be in her sixties and was wearing a red sari with a flowered uttariya covering her greying hair. Jack could tell she wasn't pleased by his visit. He waited in the open atrium briefly and then was greeted by a young man, also Indian. He was very dark skinned and had a neat moustache and thick, black, oily hair. The house reeked of curry.

"Can you tell me please, who sent you?"

"That would be Charlie Wingate."

"Thank you, come with me please."

He followed the man up a flight of stairs and down a hallway past an open airshaft to a room at the back of the house.

"The package is here, sir. We will depart in two hours. Do you need anything at all?"

"I could use a glass of water."

"Certainly sir."

The package was a cardboard box sealed with packing tape. There were no markings on the outside. He took out his pocketknife and cut through the tape. Inside he found a Glock 19, 9 mm automatic with two full, fifteen round mags. The Glock was optional. Sometimes you were better off without it. He knew this was probably one of those times but he tucked it in the back of his belt anyway. There was an encrypted Inmarsat satellite phone and a Canadian passport in the name of Jack Wilson. It had recent travel stamps from Hong Kong and Tokyo and one for Singapore for the date he had cleared immigration. An envelope in the box contained two thousand Singapore dollars. There was a knock at the door. He quickly closed the box. The man entered with a glass of water and a plate with some perakiya.

"In case you are hungry, sir. Let me know if you require anything else."

Jack listened to the man's footsteps recede down the hall and then he switched on the satellite phone and dialled the number he had been given. Charlie answered right away.

"Jesus, Jack. You really know how to start a shit storm. What the hell is going on down there?"

"They killed Angel, Charlie. They left her dead in my hotel room."

"I'm sorry, Jack. I really am, but you are in a world of shit and you need to get the hell out of Singapore and I mean fast."

"Your guy told me two hours."

"That is correct. There's a ship named the Sulawesi Maru anchored out in the harbor. It has already been cleared by the harbor-master. It will sail with the tide. You've already met Imdad. I trust him completely, Jack. We have some history. He will get you to the ship, after that you are on your own."

"Where is it headed?"

"First to Phuket and then Madras. I've got local transportation set up for you from there to Mumbai and an open ticket to Heathrow."

"What the fuck is happening, Charlie? I got the disk without a snag."

"Forget the disk. You may have just started World War Three and I'm not exaggerating. Did you show those documents to anyone? I mean anyone?"

"Nobody saw them but me and I don't know what the fuck was in them."

"Where are they now?"

"I flushed them."

"OK. It would have been a hell of a lot better for you if you had scanned them and then left the briefcase somewhere intact, but then you had no way of knowing. Did you find anything else?"

"Yeah, the guy had a digital camera but I couldn't download it. I have the memory card. There was also some kind of retinal scanner. At least I'm pretty certain that's what it was. I don't have it anymore. It was in the room and I assume they got it. I didn't have time to take anything. What's going on, Charlie? What's in the documents?"

"I'm getting to that. It turns out the face you sent me belongs to one Kwong Shen. He is not just some academic freelancing for the MSS. Mr. Kwong is a Major in the Peoples Liberation Army. We believe he is an intelligence officer but he is probably about to become very dead if he hasn't shot himself already. He screwed up big time and this is not something you recover from. The CIA station chief I deal with nearly had a heart attack when he read what you sent me. By the way, he told me to thank you for your good work."

"Fat lot of good that's going to do me. Next time tell him to send a check."

"In any case, Washington is going ape-shit. As far as we can tell, the Chinese still think you have the documents and they are trying very hard to find you. I don't read Chinese either. All my friend will tell me is that they are transcripts of some alleged conversations about a transaction between someone in the PLA and another party who is unknown at the moment. There is also suspected involvement with a terrorist group based in Indonesia. They believe it could be Jemaah Islamiyah."

"Conversations about what?"

"I don't have that information. Look, Jack, there is nothing you can do now but get the hell out of Singapore. If you get caught, there's not much I can do for you."

"I'll make it to the ship. One way or the other."

"Call me once you get underway. And Jack, hold onto the memory card for the time being at least. There may be something on it we can use."

"I need you to find out who killed Angel, Charlie."

"Listen to me, Jack. I know you cared for the girl but you need to forget about it, at least for now. Concentrate of getting out of there in one piece. There is no time for revenge as much as you may need it. You are in a world of shit. Just get to the damned boat."

5

The Sulawesi Maru was a 20 thousand ton, coastal tanker. It was small enough to enter some of the tidal estuaries that emptied into the waters around the Indonesian archipelago, in places where there were no deep harbors. Most of the time the cargo was diesel oil. The ship had seen every port in the South China Sea and the Indian Ocean. Imdad had driven Jack down to the marina where they met one of his friends with a 23ft Mirage, stern drive. There were so many ships anchored in the harbor it looked like the invasion of Normandy. It took them twenty minutes to locate the Sulawesi. It was a long way up the pilot ladder and the Mirage took off as soon as Jack started to climb, leaving him dangling like a drunken spider. The ship rocked gently in the calm waters. It wasn't the most sea-worthy vessel he had ever seen and it probably wouldn't be too long before it would be run onto the beach at Chittagong for the ship breakers to do their work. There was a long, horizontal crease a few feet above the waterline that looked like someone had tried to take a can opener to the hull. It was more rust than steel. He could feel the heartbeat of the ship as the engines idled, waiting for the command to make turns. There was a crewman waiting for him on the deck and he was escorted to the bridge to meet the captain. They weighed anchor as soon as he was on board. The captain was a Turk by the name of Sadik Batur. He was busy getting under way but he turned and took a long look at Jack.

"I will be with you in a few minutes, my friend. Mr. Musa will show you to your cabin."

The cabin was on the saloon deck, one deck below the bridge. It was small and smelled like a gas station. There was a bunk with some storage lockers underneath and a metal desk and chair. There was also a toilet and a small basin, both coated with rust. Everything was painted white, or at least it had been white at one time. Jack sat back on the bunk and tried to center himself. One thing experience had taught him was once you are on the run, no place is safe and no one is your friend. In this business, everyone has a price. He kept the Glock tucked in his waistband under his shirt along with the spare mag. If he were searched, they would find it. The sat- phone was another story. He had it taped to the inside of his ankle. Sometimes, once they found your weapon and emptied your pockets they didn't search you all that thoroughly. It depended a lot on who was doing the searching, and why. The phone was his only lifeline and he didn't want to take the chance of stashing it somewhere and not being able to get to it. He kept a few hundred dollars in his wallet. The rest of the money was rolled tightly and wrapped in a condom. If they got to searching him there, he wasn't going to need it anyway. At the shophouse he had covered the memory card with some plastic wrapping and taped it closed. He slid it into the inside of his shirt collar by means of a small slit he had cut in the fabric and closed it off with a small piece of tape.

He wondered how much time he had. The Chinese had a reputation for being thorough.

Sooner or later, when he didn't turn up in Singapore, they would be looking at the ship sailings and there was a chance they might be boarded. If that happened, he would take his chances in the sea. Better to drown than to be tortured to death. He started to think about Angel again but he forced it out of his mind. He had just started to doze off when there was a knock at the door. The captain entered and closed the door behind him. He was smoking a foul smelling black cigarette and he looked like he hadn't had a bath in a week. His trousers had once been khaki but were now covered in a dozen shades of grime. His black shirt had a small tear at the shoulder but the captain's cap looked clean and was perched at a jaunty angle over his thick, curly gray hair. He was tall and thick-boned and he had the face of a seaman. The sun and the wind took their toll to be sure, but it was the sea itself that carved lines in a man's face. Jack sat up on the bunk and they stared at each other for a few seconds. Finally the captain smiled and held out his hand.

"Sadik." He said. His voice was a thick baritone.

Jack shook his hand. "Jack."

The captain spoke at a slow, measured cadence as if he were giving commands to his crew. As he talked, his dark eyes studied Jack's face.

"I look at you and I see trouble, my friend. But then again, that is why they reward me so handsomely."

"I'm just taking a little boat ride, Captain."

"As are we all. Are you a poker player, Jack?"

"Sure, why not."

"Perhaps we will have time for a little competition later. My first mate claims he can play but I feel guilty taking his money. The rest of them, well, let's just say they swear I cheat and they refuse to play anymore."

"Sure. I'll play a hand or two with you."

"I have learned over the years not to ask questions, when men like you come aboard from small boats. The answers only make me unhappy, even if they are true. Except that I am fascinated by the men I find moving quietly in the night around these islands. So I ask them one question only. You see, I believe there are only two kinds or men, Jack. Men who choose to be where they are and men who find themselves where they are. It is a game I like to play, guessing which man I am talking to."

"And which man am I?"

"You, my friend, have not chosen to be here. Of that I am sure. Do you deny it?"

"No. Does it make a difference to you?"

"Most certainly. Any man who would choose to be here has some kind of craziness I do not comprehend. It makes me suspicious of him. On the other hand, I can almost always beat him at poker. Men like you. Like me. Men who are past choosing." He shrugged his shoulders. "We play the hand that is dealt us. If we survive, we learn to play well. Perhaps we will live long enough to be friends, Jack. Are you armed?"

"Yes."

"Keep it close."

With that he turned and opened the door. "Join me up on the bridge in an hour or so. We will see how fortune regards us on this night."

Jack tried to sleep but his dreams wouldn't let him. Every time he dozed off he saw Angel lying on that bed. He wondered if he would ever

55

be able to remember her the way he wanted to; purring like a black cat on his lap, lightly stroking his face with her claws. He gave up trying to sleep and decided to get some air. He needed to check in with Charlie, anyway. The narrow passageway was badly lit with two yellowed lamps recessed in the overhead between the runs of armored cable. It made the paint look like mustard. The passage ran amidships and ended in a sea door at both ends. He pushed open the starboard door, sending the sound of groaning metal echoing down the passageway. It was a calm sea and a clear sky except where it was darkening behind a blanket of cloud pushing in from the west, still low on the horizon. The warm breeze tugged at his shirt and jostled his hair. He closed his eyes for a moment and felt the deck rising under his feet. There was just enough moon to make out the Malaysian coast slipping by to the starboard. The breeze carried the fragrance of the jungle. Moist soil and nutmeg and the smell of things returning to the earth. He imagined what it had been like to sail these waters in earlier times when the land was inhabited by cannibals and such monsters and demons a sailor could conjure in the dark. Under different circumstances he could have stayed out on deck all night. There was something about the sea that made him feel the shape of the earth as it turned beneath the stars. It took hold of a man and said, 'ignore me at your peril'. He went down on one knee and removed the tape holding the sat-phone. It rang for a long time. He was about to hang up and try later when he heard Charlie's voice.

"Where are you, Jack?"

"I'm on the ship. We're heading up through the Malacca Straits."

"Well things are moving pretty fast. They found your friend Mr. Kwong in an ally with a knife in his chest. He had your passport in his pocket. Pretty sloppy work but that's what panic will do for you. Needless to say, there is an all-points out on you and they are turning over stones. I wouldn't plan on going back to Singapore any time for the rest of your life."

"I don't have any reason to go back there now."

"What's your ETA in Phuket?"

"The mate said about 28 hours if the weather holds. That would put me there around 0200 the day after tomorrow."

"We're going to take you off the ship in Phuket, Jack. With this much heat we don't want you stationary for too long. We're still working on transportation from there, but it will be ready by the time you arrive."

"Whatever works."

"Listen, Jack, the CIA doesn't want anyone to know they have seen the documents. Not yet anyway. Washington wants to handle this thing as quietly as possible. For the time being, the Chinese will be working under the assumption that you have the only copies. I know that's not good news, but I can't do anything about it."

"They'll kill me either way, Charlie. It doesn't really matter."

"Yeah, well they are pulling out all the stops trying to find you, Jack. How's the captain."

"I think he's OK, but who the hell knows."

"Well, keep your head down. Contact me in six hours. I should have more information for you by then."

In spite of the darkness he knew he was a sitting duck. The ship felt like it was crawling and he needed to run. He realized he was tapping his foot against the deck and forced himself to calm down. He looked over the side. It was a long drop, but at least it wasn't the long drop at the end of a rope. He was lost in thought and didn't hear Sadik come up behind him.

"We are making good headway, my friend. Twelve knots with a following sea."

Jack turned and nodded to him. "You know these waters well?"

"They have been my home for more than ten years."

"But you are not from here."

"No. For many years I sailed the Black Sea and down through the Bosporus and the Dardanelles to the islands of the Aegean. Some say the world is all just one big ocean, but they are wrong."

"So how did you end up here?"

Sadik didn't answer right away, and Jack turned to look at him.

"I had a fine ship, Jack. A ship that loved the sea. Not all of them do you know. It was a night like this one. Calm, warm, a sky full of stars. Like dust. We hit something in the water. Perhaps a large tree or a partially submerged wreck. Sailors say they sometimes rise up from the bottom to swallow souls. I, however believe it was an overdue payment on some quantity of my forgotten sins. Who knows why things rise to the surface to interrupt a man's life. The board of inquest said I was drunk, which was a lie. I wasn't even half drunk."

"Did your ship sink?"

"No. If it had, I would have been content to ride her to the bottom. We were hulled, but not badly. The pumps held and we made it into port."

"How long with this ship?"

"Eighteen months I think. I no longer count time in years. I count only in hours. Thirty hours to here. Twenty more to there. Two hours before the tide."

"So why don't you retire?"

"I am a condemned man, Jack. Condemned to live the rest of my life at sea. If I spend too much time ashore, I feel like the earth is swallowing me. It is the stillness I think. Many of us are the same. I need to watch the stars rise from the sea. The same stars that have stood over us since men were men. I find I need their reassurance. That, and the company of my crew, such as that may be, doing their familiar things. At this moment I know that Mr. Musa is on the bridge. I know who stands watch in the engineering spaces. I know that the cook is in his bunk, conspiring to serve us an indifferent breakfast in the morning. Everything is in its place. The stars. The ship. The men."

"Everything except me." Jack said.

"Yes, but you see that is also as it should be. It should be that from time to time someone stands on this deck because his journey has intersected with ours for a short time. We become a part of that journey for a few turns of the earth, to some purpose that is not given us to know, but fills our heads with imaginings, and stories to tell ourselves on the long night watch when the rest of the world is sleeping. Spice for the stew as they say. In any case, I think we must save our poker game until tomorrow. I will need more rest before I am ready to separate you from your money. Do you need anything?"

"No, I'm fine."

"Good night then, my friend. Dream well."

He awoke from a fitful sleep to the sound of running in the passageway. He sat bolt upright and felt for the Glock. There was gunfire coming from somewhere aft of the cabin and men were shouting. He assumed it was the Chinese. It took him a few seconds to calm down and orient himself. He opened the door and moved quietly down the passageway to port, holding the Glock in front of him. He met the Captain coming down the gangway.

"We are being boarded by the stern, my friend."

"Are they military?"

"I'm afraid we are not so lucky as that. Pirates, I am sure."

"Can we fight them off?"

"I could if my men would fight, but they will not. Some of them probably are friends of those who have come to visit us. Possibly even complicit. Listen, Jack, you have three choices. You can go over the bow and swim. I would make certain there is a life jacket thrown over in the excitement. Or you could fight them and I would join you with perhaps one or two others. I have two UZIs and some side arms. We would fight heroically, most likely lose, and be executed on the spot. Or you can surrender, which is my choice. They will hold you for ransom in some place that God has overlooked and perhaps cut off one of your fingers. Of course you may survive. The other option is that they may kill us on sight, which means we make no choices. What hand do you wish to play, my friend? Are you the kind of man who must have his honor, or will you chose to suffer some indignity for your survival?"

"I'm not much for dying heroically, Sadik. I'm going for a swim."

"As you wish. Come this way, quickly."

Sadik led him down the passageway and they made for the port sea-door. "We are still making about eight knots. The engines are stopped but she will sail another quarter mile, maybe more with the tide. The screws will not be making turns so there will not be too much turbulence. We are about 6 miles off the Sumatran coast to the port side. How far can you swim?"

"Until I reach something to stand on."

"Good luck, then, my friend."

"What will happen to you?"

"Again, there are several possibilities. Probably they will force me to open the ship's safe, which I will, take anything they can find of value and go back to their hovels. If they are more ambitious, they may force me to sail to one of the sheltered coves that capture these waters, where they will be prepared to offload my cargo. At least some of it."

"And then what?"

"Then, if I am fortunate, I will get my ship back. If not..."

Jack started to turn, but as Sadik pushed the sea-door open they were greeted by the muzzle of an AK47. They were pushed backward into the passageway. A short brown man, naked to the waist but wearing a headscarf was screaming at them in Malay. There was a short sword tucked into a hemp belt around his waist. He was crazy-eyed and wired and Jack couldn't stop looking at the sword. It felt like a hallucination. Sadik back-pedalled a few steps and then stopped. Jack had the Glock in his hand. The adrenaline was surging through his body and he had already made up his mind to drop the guy when two more came in on the starboard side and it was game over. He put the Glock back in his waistband but kept his hand on it.

Sadik gathered himself to his full height and began shouting orders in Malay. Or at least Jack thought it was Malay. The pirates were mostly young fishermen from small villages who subsidized their income with a little theft on the high seas. They were not much accustomed to being ordered around by large white men in uniforms. Even such as this captain wore. They seemed to cower before him and were looking at each other in confusion when another one stepped through the sea-door. The three in the passageway immediately froze in place. He was older and hard-looking with a deep scar across the right side of his face. The muscles under his skin were like braided wire. A look of contempt came over his hard face as he regarded his men. He shouted something in a fierce voice, and pointed a pistol at them. They winced. Finally, he took three strides forward, put the pistol to Sadik's head and pulled the trigger, all the while shouting at his men. Sadik's body slumped to the deck with a sickening thud. It was all instinct and adrenaline now. Jack threw his left arm around the closest man's neck and held the Glock to his head. The man started to struggle but Jack pushed the muzzle of the gun into his temple and the man went still. The one with the pistol said something to Jack in a mocking voice and then he raised the gun and shot the man Jack was holding right in the middle of his face. The insides of his head sprayed all over Jack's face and shirt. Jack let go of the man and dropped his pistol on the deck. He raised his hands.

"Insurance. My company has insurance on my life. They will pay you if I am not harmed."

The leader came up to him and snarled in his face. "I don't give a shit, they pay for you or not. I wasn't kill you yet anyway." He put the gun in Jack's face and then kicked him in the groin. Jack slumped to the deck in agony.

He was blindfolded and frog-marched over to the gangway. They took his wallet and knife. He couldn't stand upright and the two men holding his arms dragged him down the stairs. The pain in his groin was making him nauseous and he was fighting hard not vomit. There was nothing he could do but submit. They took him down two decks and along a passageway to the port side. The hull side door was open and he could feel the sea air against his face. He knew they were taking him off the ship but there was no way he could handle a ladder. They were screaming at him but he didn't know what they were saying. Finally, the two men let go of him and someone kicked him in the back. He tumbled over the side of the ship, hitting the water hard. He could feel himself slipping into unconsciousness and he fought against it. The blindfold had come off when he hit the water and he could see land in the distance. He started to swim. The pain in his groin was easing and for a moment he thought they were just going to leave him to drown. He managed about ten strokes before a Zodiac pulled up beside him and he was hauled aboard. They re-blindfolded him and tied his hands behind his back. He was forced to lie down on the bottom, which was awash with spilt fuel and seawater. The engine burst into life and the small boat careened off into the darkness. Jack tried to lay still but he was being bounced all over the boat. He took in a couple of mouthfuls of water before he found a way to support his head. It was difficult to anticipate what would happen next. They hadn't found the sat-phone and it was watertight. He decided to submit, at least for the time being. If they were just a bunch of pirates they would probably keep him alive, for a while anyway, until they could find out what he was worth. If they were working for the Chinese, he was as good as dead, but not before spending some bad time tied to a chair. All in all, his future was not looking too promising. Of course Sadik didn't have a future anymore and neither did Angel.

It was difficult to keep track of time, but it seemed like they had been at it about an hour when he felt the boat start to lift and could hear the surf pounding against the shoreline. They ran the boat up onto the beach and Jack was spilled out onto the sand by the impact. They hauled him to his feet again and started to march him up the beach. He could smell the jungle and the ground began to feel harder under his feet. They started climbing a fairly steep grade and Jack concentrated on his breathing and on the sounds of the jungle that had enveloped them. Some macaques screamed in the distance and he could hear movement in the trees. After about fifteen minutes they stopped and he heard the sound of a chain being moved, followed by the metallic squeal of a rusty door. Someone pushed him in the back and he slammed into something hard and metallic. They went through his pockets again and patted him down. They removed his watch. There was some excited conversation when they found the sat-phone, followed by a slap on the back of his head. Someone grabbed him and he was pushed forward. The door slammed closed behind him and he stood still for a moment, trying to get a sense of where he was. The air was stale and foul smelling. He was not alone.

He sat down on what turned out to be a dirt floor and managed to slip his hands over his legs so that he had them in front of him. He lifted the blindfold. The only light was coming from some cracks in the wall near the door. As his eyes adjusted, he could just make out some forms in the darkness. He moved toward them and heard some muffled groans. There appeared to be five or six people seated against the back wall of the structure, which was some kind of storage shed. Jack knelt down and tried to get a better look at them. They appeared to be young women. They were bound and gagged and they pulled away from him in fear, as he got close. He was trying to figure out what to do next when one of them spoke in a harsh whisper.

"Who the hell are you?"

"I'm Jack, who are you?"

"My name is Annie, what are you doing here?"

"You mean this isn't part of the tour?"

"That's very funny, Jack but in case you haven't noticed we're in a shit state here. You're not part of a rescue party by any chance?"

"Sorry, I just got lifted off a ship by Blackbeard and his merry men."

"Well that's just bloody brilliant. You don't have any water or something useful like that I suppose."

"I've got a small knife. It's hidden in my belt buckle."

"Super, maybe you can get my hands loose."

"Maybe not. How often do they check on you?"

"They'll be drunk in another hour and we won't see them again till morning. Now will you please cut these bloody ropes?"

Jack managed to slide the small blade out of the buckle and began sawing at the ropes binding Annie's hands. It was difficult with his hands tied.

"How did you get here, Annie?"

"Ever hear of sex slavery? Well, we're auditioning."

"Where are you from?"

"Colchester."

"They kidnapped you in England?"

"No, Jack. They didn't kidnap me in bloody England. They kidnapped me in Jakarta."

"And what were you doing there?"

"I was working as a hostess in one of the clubs. It's a long story. Can you go a little faster?"

Jack accidentally nicked her arm and she flinched.

"Save a little skin, will ya love?"

"What about these others."

"Mardi and Sakina are from Manila. They signed a contract to be lounge entertainers in Jakarta and they didn't read the fine print. The part about being a whore until you pay back your plane fare. The other three are Indonesian. Eidah and Lyana were sold off by their families. Dasima was a stray. Lyana is only ten years old. It's a beautiful world, Jack."

He managed to cut through the ropes and she immediately started to rub her wrists.

"Can you get mine now," he asked.

She took the knife and began sawing at the ropes binding his hands.

"How did you all get to this place, Annie?"

67

"They bundled me up in the boot of a car and dropped me in some shit hole in Jakarta for a day and a night. Then they did the bloody rounds and got the rest of this lot except for Eidah and Lyana. They were already here. They dumped us into the bottom of a fishing boat and sailed us up the coast of Sumatra to this lovely fucking place. We've been here two days. I think they plan on dumping us on another boat to God only knows where. Probably someplace in the Middle East."

"Are any of you hurt?"

"No, but Lyana is scared silly and the two Filipino girls won't stop crying. They didn't touch any of them because they are all virgins. The big poobah would have their knackers if they tried anything."

"What about you?"

"You mean am I a virgin? That's not a proper question to ask a lady on the first date."

"No I mean..."

"Let it go, Jack." Annie started working on the other girls. "Listen, Jack, can you handle yourself? I mean are you out here studying plants or something useless like that or are you some kind of a player?"

"I'm a bird watcher."

"Fucking marvellous."

"Why?"

"Because Eidah knows where we are. Her village is only about a three-day walk from here. If we can get past those lovely boys outside we might be able to get out of here."

"How many are there?"

"Last night there were three. One of them stays by the door. They have a bungalow up the path a bit."

"How did you figure on getting out of this shack?"

"We're almost out now. They didn't tie us up at first. Eidah dug under the wall. She's like a bloody ferret. Yesterday, Sakina threw a fit and started punching the night watchman. That's when they tied us, but they didn't find the hole."

"How long would it take to finish it?"

"Hold on. I'll ask. Mardi, ask Eidah how long to finish digging."

Mardi evidently knew some Malay and an animated discussion ensued.

"Maybe an hour."

"Tell her it has to be deep enough for this man."

More discussion. The one called Eidah leaned forward and took a closer look at Jack."

"Maybe two hours."

"That's cutting it kind of close." Jack said. "It must be near morning already."

"Listen, Jack, I don't think they'll be keeping us here much longer. If we don't get out tonight there might not be another chance."

"OK."

"OK what?"

"OK, I'll do it. Just get them moving."

"Are you sure you can handle it?"

"I'm not a virgin either."

7

Jack hated killing, but he had done enough to be proficient at it. Just not lately. Once it got started there was no going back. So far he had survived, but every time it devoured a little more of his soul. He had to find that place inside himself where the hatred was so strong, no vestige of humanity could stand against it. He summoned up the image of Angel, lying in her own blood, and felt the rage come over him. He knew he couldn't leave any of these boys alive. He and the girls would be on the run, and they would need all the time he could buy them. Besides, he was pretty sure he would only end up facing them later when they would have the advantage. The way he figured it, they had committed suicide when they decided to threaten his life. It was a tight fit but he managed to crawl under the wall of the shed. At least he didn't have to bother with blackening his face. He crept around the side of the shed and found the guard sitting with his back against the wall with an AK across his lap. He was sound asleep. Jack cut his throat and held him down until he stopped moving. The AK was tempting but he didn't know how many more of them were around and he couldn't risk a fire fight. He decided to get it on the way back. He unlocked the door but told Annie to keep them inside unless he didn't come back in fifteen minutes.

There was music coming from somewhere further up the trail. The sky was starting to lighten and he knew there wasn't much time. It was a two-room shack with a palm leaf roof. The jungle was alive with the sounds and Jack wondered what else might be lurking out there. He knew there were tigers on Sumatra, not to mention some very nasty snakes, and spiders the size of hubcaps. He took it as a good sign that it hadn't gone silent. One of them was out cold in a hammock on the lanai and Jack finished him quietly. He could hear a generator running in the back somewhere. He crept up to the window and slowly raised his head. A small lamp sat on a desk next to an ancient radio set that was tuned to a station playing native music. The place was frozen in time. He almost expected to hear an announcement from Tokyo Rose. There was also a Royal typewriter that looked like it had been pinched from a museum, and a bunch of empty beer bottles. The radio operator was asleep, slumped over against the wall. He was wearing a sidearm that looked like an old Enfield revolver. Jack saw the sat-phone on the desk next to the radio along with a partially assembled AK that someone had been cleaning. There was no door, just some mosquito netting. He crept forward. The other room appeared to be empty. He knew he should check it out but he didn't want to lose the advantage. The floor was covered with a Tatami mat that crunched under his weight. He had just reached the radio operator when the man awoke with a start. Jack lunged forward and caught him as he started to stand. There was a brief struggle as the man went for his weapon but Jack managed to pull him to the floor and snap his neck.

He was trying to free himself from the body when a fourth man burst out of the other room, yelling at the top of his lungs and swinging a

71

parang. The blade sliced down but deflected off the desktop and missed him by inches. Jack lunged out with his foot and caught the man in the kneecap. He fell screaming. Jack scrambled to his feet and moved toward the man but he wasn't quick enough. The man jumped to his feet and came forward again, swinging wildly. Jack moved backward avoiding the blade until he lost his footing and fell. As the man moved in for the kill, Jack grabbed the end of the Tatami mat and pulled it with all of his strength. The man fell backward and hit his head, momentarily stunning him. A woman screamed. Jack leapt up and took hold of the typewriter. He slammed it down on the man's head repeatedly until he went still. He turned and saw Annie staring at him.

"Pretty smooth, Jack. What do you call that? Taekwon-typo?"

The women were clustered around the doorway, staring at him in horror. Mardi had her hands covering Lyana's eyes. Jack got his first good look at Annie. She was wearing a pair of men's trousers, which didn't fit very well with a red, spaghetti strap top. She was tall, about five nine, he thought. Despite the ill-fitting clothes, he could see she had an athletic body. Her hair was blond and about shoulder length. She had a nice face with wide lips and hazel eyes, and a few freckles across her nose, but she had some bad bruises and it looked like she had been given a rough time. The rest of the girls were dressed in jeans and tee shirts. They were all dark haired with light brown skin. The two Filipino girls wore their hair long, almost to their waists. They were both beautiful.

"Way to stay put, Annie. Look, we have got to move fast. Tell the girls to search the place for any food or water or anything useful and tell them to move it. I don't know how much time we have."

Jack was out of breath and his hands were shaking, but he needed to move. He quickly searched the bodies, taking the Enfield and the parang along with butane lighter he found in the radio operators pocket. He removed his watch from the radio operator's wrist. He put the sat-phone in his pocket. Next he smashed the radio and threw the pieces of disassembled AK into the Jungle. He tucked the long curved magazine in his belt. One of the girls came out with a spray can of insect repellent and handed it to Jack. He smiled at her.

"Good find." He sprayed her arms and legs and then her hands, indicating she should rub it on her face and neck. Next he sprayed Annie's arms and legs and then did his own and each of the girls except for Eidah who refused. The other girls had found some canned food and bottled water. Not enough but better than nothing. He opened one of the bottles and went over to the little girl. She backed away from him. He looked at Annie.

"What's her name?"

"Lyana."

"See that she drinks as much of this as she can. Tell the rest of them to drink as much as they can and then refill the bottles. Did anyone find a metal pot or even some empty beer cans?"

Mardi answered. "There's a coffee pot and some cups."

"Great. Go get them, would you? Now we need some way to carry this crap."

As if she could understand him, Eidah went into the other room and took a sheet and blanket from a cot. She tore the sheet a few

73

times and tied some loose ends together, creating a carrying bag. The rest of the girls got the idea and soon they were all more or less ready to go. Jack took a look in the other room and found another AK and what looked like a wooden ammunition box and some empty magazines underneath the cot. He pried the top off with the parang but instead of ammunition, he found four, British L2A2 fragmentation grenades. He carried the box out and put it on the desk.

Jack looked at the group of women and wondered if they had any chance at all. It was then that he noticed that Annie was bare footed.

"What happened to your shoes?"

"I didn't think a pair of six inch heals were proper attire for the tour."

"Well, hell, you have to have something on your feet."

"Got any suggestions?"

Jack pointed to the dead radio operator. "Take his boots. It looks like you could fit into them."

"No bloody way, Jack. Who the hell knows what that bastard has growing on him."

"OK, just remember, the scorpions with the huge claws are the least poisonous. It's the ones with the little claws you need to worry about."

Annie looked at him for a second and then went over to the body, removed the boots and slipped them onto her feet.

"OK, listen Annie. Are you sure this girl knows how to get us out of here?"

Annie spoke to Mardi and she jabbered something at Eidah.

"Eidah says she knows the way but it will be difficult until we get up into the mountains."

"Get Eidah to take the girls into the jungle. We need to stay off the trail for a while at least. I'll catch up with you. If you hear a whistle, that will be me. Just let me know where the hell you are."

"Where are you going, Jack?"

"I just want to leave a little thank-you gift for our friends. Annie, you and Eidah lead the way." He handed her the Enfield. "Can you handle this?"

"I suppose."

"Well, don't shoot anything unless I tell you to. And don't shoot me under any circumstances."

"Great. If a tiger comes at me, I'll send you a bloody memo. You're no fun at all, Jack. Is it OK if I just hit you with it?"

"I've got the hammer on an empty chamber so it won't go off accidentally. If you need to use it, just point at your target and pull the trigger until there are no rounds left. Keep Mardi with you to translate. What are the other one's names?"

"Sakina and Dasima."

"OK, ask those two to take care of the little one. I'll catch up. It should be light enough to travel now and we have to get moving. Tell the girls not to drop anything near the trail. Got it?"

"Aye Aye, Capitan. Anything else?"

"Yeah, tell them all to keep quiet."

"Hah, fat chance."

The two Filipino girls looked terrified but whatever they faced in the jungle was going to be a lot better than what they were in for if they didn't get away. Jack moved quickly. He dragged the two bodies into the sleeping room and went back for the one in the hammock. He went around the back of the building to where

75

the generator was mounted and found a partially full gas can. Back in the radio room, he took the chair and put it on its side in the doorway along with some other debris from the fight. He propped the gas can just inside the doorframe so that it would fall over if the chair were moved. Next he slid one of the grenades under the gas can so that the spoon remained depressed, and he carefully pulled the pin. He took the rest of the grenades and went back down the trail to the shack. He dragged the guard inside and set another trap just inside the door. Finally he chained it shut. He clipped the remaining grenades onto his belt and shouldered the AK. With any luck, the traps would take out a few of them and make the rest cautious enough to slow them down a bit. The sun had come up but as soon as he entered the high canopy it became difficult to see more than a few yards ahead. Jack took a last look at the shoreline a few hundred yards below the camp. The turquoise colored rollers were breaking hard against the beach and he listened for any motor noise above the deep rumble and hiss of the surf. It was quiet and he couldn't see any boats. He hoped they had a few hours, but he wasn't optimistic.

It wasn't hard finding the girls. They were about a hundred yards in and huddled in a group like they were trying to stay warm. Jack caught up to them and indicated to Eidah they had to get moving. She started off at a brisk pace. There was a heavy mist clinging to the floor of the forest and, in places where the light penetrated, it was breathtakingly beautiful. The rich smell of, living, fertile soil enveloped him, immediately erasing any vestige of the civilized world. Everywhere he looked, insects scurried across the forest floor. There were a dozen varieties of orchids, and blossoms of every color, some as large as beach umbrellas. The trees were alive with flying squirrels, macaques, and other primates chattering to each other as they searched the high canopy for food. The foliage was every shape and shade of green and some of the plants seemed to fluoresce with there own internal light. But for all of its beauty, it was an alien place, dark and brooding. Passing silent judgment on them as they passed. Testing them with every rock and thorn. He moved along behind the women in silence, as he tried to get adjusted to this new nightmare. It felt like a death march but there was nothing else for it. Nowhere to go but deeper into the gloom. Images of Angel played through his mind in an endless loop and it was all he could do to keep his feet moving.

Eidah proved to be a good guide. He had to use the parang in a few places but all in all it was better than he had feared. He was thinking ahead to where they might camp at the end of the day. They would need a small fire or the girls would never get any sleep and neither would he. It would be a gamble. The men would be looking for a fire. Jack knew that most of the jungle predators hunted at night and he wasn't particularly worried about being attacked before sundown. At least not by animals. They moved through the jungle for almost an hour but the going was getting tougher and Jack asked Eidah to find the trail. It only took her a short time. It wasn't much better than the jungle but at least he didn't need to hack his way through. The humidity was so high that the moisture wouldn't evaporate from their skin. Their clothes were soaking wet, but it did nothing to help cool them. The girls were all miserable and he wondered again if they would make it. It was hot, but not as hot as it was going to be and the air was stifling.

If they were lucky, the bodies back at the camp wouldn't be found for a few hours, but probably no more than that. The girls were making a lot of noise but, for now, it was better that way. The last thing they wanted was to surprise a tiger in the bush. Most predators would shy away from a group of humans, unless they were very hungry or protecting their young. He was more concerned about snakes and scorpions, and some of the girls looked terrified. They needed to make time. The little one was having a tough go of it and finally Jack slung the AK under his arm, picked her up and put her up on his shoulders. He told Sakina and Dasima to move faster. In a strange way, carrying the little girl made his load seem lighter. Annie turned around and watched him for a moment. She smiled and quickly turned away.

8

After about three hours on the trail, they came to an area that had been clear-cut by a logging crew. Everyone needed a break and Jack wanted to contact Charlie. The girls stayed at the edge of the forest just out of the sunlight and finished the remainder of their water. Sakina handed out some fruit. There was finally some air to breathe, but it was hard to find any place to sit that wasn't crawling with ants. The jungle had gone silent at first, aware of their presence. After a short time, as if on cue, it came alive with a cacophony of whistles and shrieks and the sound of things moving in the trees. The breeze helped keep the flies and mosquitoes at bay. Jack ventured a short way into the clearing and punched in Charlie's number. It took a while to get a signal and at first he though he might not get through. Finally he heard the familiar voice on the other end of the line.

"Christ, Jack where the hell have you been? We completely lost track of the ship. We thought the PLA had you."

"We were boarded, but not by the PLA. They were pirates. They killed the captain and held me for a while. They had the sat-phone so I wasn't able to check in."

"What is your current situation?"

"I got away. I'm on Sumatra headed west across the north end of the island. I haven't seen any signs of pursuit but I've only been at it for three hours."

"Listen, Jack, it's possible we may be able to send a chopper in to get you. We have contacts in the Indonesian government. I'll work on it."

"Well make sure it's a big bird, Charlie. I have some company."

"What are you talking about?"

"I have some girls with me."

"Jesus Christ, Jack, can't you keep it zipped up until you're rescued at least."

"They were being held at the camp. They broke out with me."

"How many?"

"Six."

"No way. I can't do that."

"Well I can't leave them in the jungle. Listen, one of the girls comes from a village a few miles from our current location. I think we can get that far and then I can drop off the girls. I'll keep you up to date."

"What about your captors?"

"I took care of four of them. I don't know how many are left."

"Send your position and re-contact in six hours."

"Roger that. Any news on your end?"

"From what I hear, the Chinese are denying any contact with Jemaah Islamiyah or any other terrorist group. I doubt I will get any more information at all, Jack. My contacts have clammed up on me, for obvious reasons. Let's just get you home and let the Company worry about it. Do you still have the memory card?"

Jack hadn't thought about it since back on the ship. He felt his collar. "Yeah, I still have it. I don't know what kind of shape it's in."

"Try to take care of it, Jack. My contacts seem to feel it's important. If you think they are going to take you though, destroy it."

80

The girls looked beat but Eidah hadn't even sat down. She was walking a semicircle through the forest, digging in the ground and picking leaves and plants. Annie got up and walked over to him.

"So tell me that was rubbish. The part about being a bird watcher."

"I like birds. Sometimes I watch them."

"So what are you really doing here, Jack?"

"I'm trying to get home."

"Presumably at some point you were trying to get here. I don't mean the back of beyond, just the general neighborhood."

"I'm what they call a contractor."

"A building contractor?"

"More like a business consultant."

"So you just happened to be taking a cruse in the middle of the night, or don't they pay for airfare?"

"Something like that."

"OK, so you're a spy. Whose side are you on?"

"Is this the part where I say 'my side'?"

"Well, you're not CIA and obviously not SAS."

"How do you know?"

"Too clumsy."

"And you would know about these things, how?"

"Because I've met quite a few."

"Horizontally or vertically?"

"I'm a hostess, Jack, not a prostitute."

"Which means what? You hang all over them for a couple of hours and then protest that you're a good girl?"

"Pretty much, although I give them a good referral to girls I know who are more horizontally inclined."

"God save the Queen."

"Look, let's not play games with each other, Jack. We may need a little trust before this thing is over."

Jack looked at her. There was something behind the sarcasm that he wasn't getting yet. He didn't think it was insecurity but there was something else there. She wasn't just some club hostess. His thoughts were interrupted by the sound of branches cracking in the jungle across the clearing. Jack grabbed Annie by the arm and started to move back into the cover of the trees until he saw Lyana jumping up and down and laughing. As he and Annie watched, a herd of elephants emerged into the clearing. They were smaller than the other Asian elephants he had seen and there were no bulls among them. The cows sniffed the air and examined the clearing. A couple of calves ran along between their feet. Evidently they did not like what they found and they turned back into the bush. It seemed like the entire jungle went still to watch them pass. Finally, Jack turned to Annie. Whoever she was, she deserved to know what she had gotten herself into.

"OK, listen. I work for a private security agency. I was doing a job in Singapore and it went bad. I was on my way up to Phuket when we were boarded."

"Did you kill somebody?"

"No, but they think I did."

"So you're wanted for murder?"

"Worse than that. I accidentally lifted some documents and it appears the Chinese government is a little unhappy with me at the moment."

"Accidentally?"

"Yeah, I just couldn't resist, you know?"

"Well that's bloody brilliant, Jack. What did you do with the papers?"

"I flushed them."

"What were they about?"

"Damned if I know. I'm pretty sure it wasn't the Star Spangled Banner in Chinese."

"So they think you still have them."

"That would be my guess."

"Have they been trying to find you?"

"They probably are by now."

They were interrupted by the sound of a low rumble coming from the east, like distant cannon fire. It was followed by a second one, moments later. Jack looked at his watch.

"That would be the door bell. Whoever isn't dead is going to be very pissed off. We've got three hours on them and it will hopefully take a while to find our trial and get organized. Let's say three and a half. We need to get them moving."

Eidah seemed to know exactly what was going on. She had a brief discussion with Mardi. Mardi ran over to them.

"Eidah says we should leave the trail now and go north."

Jack interrupted. "Ask her how bad the jungle is up ahead?"

Mardi spoke to Eidah who answered rapidly and made some indecipherable gestures with her hands. "Eidah says it is bad in places but if we keep climbing it will be clearer."

Annie joined Eidah and they headed off into the jungle. Jack let the little one walk a bit to save his energy. She seemed to be doing better. They were climbing steadily as they moved to the northwest. Jack had to take the coffee pot away from Dasima. It was banging around like a mad tinker. The ground was firm but the vines were thick in places and Jack had to move to the front to do some clearing with the parang. It was hot, heavy work and after an hour he had to take a break. They all slumped to the ground and tried to catch their breath. Without a breeze, the insects swarmed in as soon as they stopped moving. After a few moments, Jack noticed a shadow move in the trees. He stared up and saw a large, male Orangutan eyeing him curiously. Two more came swinging in. They were quiet. Eidah yelled something at them and the big male responded by urinating. It splashed all over them and the girls all screamed in disgust. The Orangutans were not aggressive but they were curious about what the group might have in their bags. Eidah indicated they should get going. The jungle did start to thin out as they gained altitude and a fine mist hung in the air.

Eidah seemed to be totally at home. She was gathering plants and fruit as she led them along. She continually rubbed the leaves of one plant on her skin and Jack asked Marti what it was. Eidah pointed to it and said Pokok Jermin followed by a long speech, which Mardi didn't try to translate.

"She says it keeps the mosquitoes away."

As they gained altitude, the ground became rockier and there were more openings in the canopy. They were more or less scrambling over rocks when Eidah suddenly froze. Jack moved to the front to see what the problem was and he found her staring down the biggest cobra he had ever seen in the bush. Sakina screamed and Lyana buried her face in Annie's legs. Eidah remained completely still for a moment and then slowly she sat down in front of the snake. She began to make slow rhythmic

84

motions with her arms. She was singing some kind of rhyme in a low soothing voice. The snake followed her hands and seemed to be mesmerized by the motion. When it happened, it was so fast Jack wasn't sure he actually saw it. There was a blur of motion and suddenly Eidah had the cobra gripped just behind its head. She held it against the ground and crushed its head with a rock. She said something and Mardi turned to Jack.

"She wants to use the knife."

Jack handed her the parang. Eidah deftly chopped the head off and then cut the snake open to remove its entrails. Then she wrapped the body in some large leaves and put it in her bag. She looked at Jack and smiled.

"Cena." She motioned with her hands to her mouth.

Eidah headed off through the jungle as if she had merely stopped to take a pebble out of her shoe. The girl had nerves of steel. The rest of the girls were spooked and they were eyeing the ground as if it were going to come alive and devour them. Jack looked at Annie.

"Remind me to get her number. I want to take her with me next time I'm in the jungle."

Annie laughed. "I doubt she has ever made a phone call in her life. Besides, she's not your type."

"Oh, yeah. What type is that?"

"If I had to guess, I would guess horizontal."

Jack just looked at her. She was starting to get under his skin. "I hope I get to meet her father'" he said, after a while. "I think I'll kill the bastard for selling her."

"He was doing her a favor."

"What the hell do you mean?"

"There are probably fifteen kids in her family. Most of them will live in poverty for the rest of their lives. If they survive to be adults."

"Better than being sold off to be a whore."

"That's not what her father thought he was doing. They probably told him she would be going to school and learn how to make a lot of money in the big city. In return she would send money back to her family. He was trying to give her a better life."

"Somebody ought to clue him in."

"Well, I think you're just the guy to set him straight, Jack. Just wait until I get a safe distance away. Oh, and by the way, her great grandfather was very probably a cannibal."

They took breaks several times through the afternoon. Eidah stopped at one point to climb a tree and knock down some fruit. She told Mardi it was called Jambu Bol. They looked a little like apples and were tart but they seemed to raise everyone's spirits. There were no more encounters with snakes but Eidah did have to stop Lyana from touching a strange looking tree. She told Mardi it was called the pain tree and could kill you just by touching the leaves. As they moved through the forest, Jack became aware of a feint roaring sound which grew louder the farther north they went. In a while, they emerged from the forest and found themselves at the edge of a deep gorge. Even though it was still the dry season, there was a fast flowing stream at the bottom, which was about sixty feet below them. A heavy vapor was rising up at them and it felt like steam. Eidah stopped and looked around. She spoke to Mardi, who translated for Jack.

"Eidah says there is a good crossing to the east of here. Maybe a one hour walk she thinks.

She says there is another way if it is still open, not far from here. It is a rope bridge. It is what the hunters used before the new bridge was built. She asks which way you want to go."

"How far to the rope bridge?"

Mardi asked Eidah.

"She says it is very close. Just a few minutes."

"Let's see what it looks like."

Eidah headed west along the edge of the gorge and after a few minutes they came to the hunter's crossing. It was really just a thick rope; about three inches in diameter with two smaller ropes on each side at what would be waist height. They were laced together by thin cords spaced at three foot intervals. The rope looked pretty rotted and Jack had his doubts. Eidah indicated they should wait and she ventured out on the rope, bouncing slightly to see if it were sound. Jack stopped her after she had gone a few yards. He told Mardi to call her back. He was the heaviest and if it wasn't going to hold his weight he didn't want to find out after some of the girls had crossed. Eidah complained but she did as she was asked. Jack ventured out on the rope, holding the guide ropes as tightly as he could manage. It was not much to walk on, but he worked his way out to center span about thirty yards from the bank. He bounced up and down a little to get the rope moving, expecting to be dumped into the gorge at any second. The mist had cleared and without the protection of the trees, the sun burned into his skin like a hot iron. The rope made some ominous creaking sounds but it held. He rejoined the women on the bank.

They went two at a time. Eidah went first with Sakina and they made it across without incident. Next he sent Annie with Dasima. About three quarters of the way across, Dasima lost her footing. She was holding on to the guide rope with both of her hands and her feet were kicking in the air. She was screaming in terror. The rope was swaying and Annie almost lost her balance. Jack moved as quickly as he could. Annie held on to Dasima's arm but they were both losing their grip. Jack reached her and grabbed onto her other arm just as she let go of the guide rope. The bridge twisted toward them until the other guide rope was directly over their heads. Annie had to let go of Dasima to prevent herself from falling. Jack managed to hook his knees over the main rope and then grabbed Dasima's other wrist. They were swinging in the air like some kind of a circus act gone wrong. Jack couldn't pull from the position he was in and he didn't know how to get her back up onto the rope. The water rushing past below them was disorienting and he tried to fix his eyes on something that wasn't moving. Dasima was screaming in terror. A flock of birds soared past below the bridge and his head began to spin. The bridge was swaying and it was all Jack could do to hold on. The pain in his legs and arms was excruciating. Eidah started to work her way toward them. She had some vines looped over her shoulder like a mountain climber. As she came closer the bridge made an ominous snapping sound and seemed to drop a few inches. Jack yelled at Annie.

"Go across, Annie. There's too much weight out here."

For once Annie didn't argue and she worked her way to the far bank, nearly slipping as Eidah passed her and worked her way out to Jack. Eidah moved on the rope as if she had done it all of her life. When she reached Jack, she looped a length of vine into a snare and dropped it down below Dasima's legs. She managed to loop it over and then raised it until it was under Dasima's thighs. She pulled and the loop closed tightly. Next, she took the other end of the vine and looped it over the guide rope and began to pull. Gradually they were able to pull Dasima up to the main rope until she was sitting on it. The bridge righted itself and the three of them clung there out of breath and unable to move. After a few minutes Jack stood and pulled Dasima to her feet. Her knees were shaking and she was still crying hysterically. Eidah held on to her and helped her to the other side. Jack returned for Mardi and Lyana. He had to take a few minutes to regain his strength.

Mardi looked down into the gorge and became terrified. She didn't want to go. Lyana was crying and refused altogether. Finally Eidah came back across and took Lyana. She carried her over on her back. Jack spoke to Mardi.

"We have to do this, Mardi. There isn't time to go around."

"I can't do it. I'm afraid of heights. I'm afraid I'll fall."

"It'll be OK, I'll keep a hold of you. We'll go across together."

Mardi was nearly as rigid as a board and whimpering. Jack had to push her forward as he held on to the waist of her jeans. They inched their way across. When they finally reached the other side they collapsed on the ground exhausted. They had wasted a lot of time but everyone needed to rest a little. After a few minutes, Jack looked back at the bridge. He took the parang and walked over to the tree that served as an anchor. He raised the parang over his head but Eidah ran to him screaming and grabbed his arm. She was yelling at him and he could see the fear in her eyes. Mardi came over.

"Eidah says you must not cut down the bridge. The penalty is death. The hunters will track you and kill you."

"If those men are behind us, Mardi, they are going to kill me anyway."

Jack looked at Eidah and she slowly took the parang from his hand. She walked over to the bridge and swung it downward, cutting through each of the guide ropes, leaving the main rope intact. The guide ropes fell slack. It would keep anyone from crossing easily from the other side but could be repaired without too much trouble. She handed the parang back to Jack and walked away without saying another word. Late in the day Eidah stopped and had a discussion with Mardi. Jack and Annie looked on, waiting for her to translate.

"Eidah says we should stop soon to make camp. She says there are some caves up ahead and maybe we can use them."

He liked the idea. They could have a small fire without giving away their position and hopefully there would be fewer insects. Of course there were the vampire bats but he wasn't about to mention it. The sun was starting to set behind the mountains and there would not be much light left. They were near the equator and the sun seemed to sink like a rock at the end of the day. He had come to trust Eidah, though, and he followed along with the group. Several times during the day he had let the girls get ahead of him and he stopped and listened to the forest for any signs of pursuit. As soon as the girls were out of sight, everything seemed to close in on him. It was almost overwhelming, being alone in what looked like primeval forest. It was like a single, living beast. You could feel it envelope you, and study you. Deciding were you stood in the food chain. At one point, he thought he heard someone shouting but he couldn't be sure. He hoped he was wrong.

After about twenty minutes of hiking, they came to an escarpment. Several caves were cut into its face. Eidah scrambled up and started to investigate. A small waterfall had cut a channel into the rock nearby and Jack had everyone fill their water bottles, but he told them not to drink. They did anyway. After a few minutes, Eidah indicated they should come up. Jack had to carry Lyana on his back. The cave entrance was small but once inside it opened up to a fairly large space. There was only a small amount of guano on the floor and no bats that he could see in the dim light. Just some geckos and a few whip scorpions, which were not poisonous. Best of all, the cave had been used by people before and there was a fire pit and some wood lying about. Jack got a fire started right away and had the girls start boiling water in the coffee pot. He went back out and gathered as much wood as he could find. When he turned to go back, he saw what looked like a spray of ink coming from one of the larger caves. Bats were emerging by the thousands. He stood transfixed as they circled outside the cave in a swirling toroid waiting for it to empty. There numbers were countless. Finally, as if by some signal, they headed out over the forest in an enormous black cloud. He was happy to get back to the fire.

Eidah said something to Mardi and then she took the parang and went out into the jungle. It was getting pretty dark and Jack almost stopped her, but he guessed she knew what she was doing better than he did. It seemed like a long time had gone by. He was beginning to get worried about her when he saw her emerge from the trees with an enormous bundle of palm leaves tied together with a vine and slung over her back. Back in the cave, she quickly went to work spreading them out on the cave floor for the girls to sleep on. When she was done, she took the snake out of her bag. Jack watched as she sliced up the meat and put it on skewers she had formed from the palm stalks. The girls looked disgusted by the idea of eating it but it smelled pretty good and in the end they all had some. While they were eating, Eidah took some leaves and roots from her bag and started grinding them up with a stick. Once she had a good handful she dumped it into the coffee pot, which was boiling next to the fire. Dasima whispered something to Annie and she nodded her head. Annie indicated she wanted to talk to him alone. They got up and walked toward the mouth of the cave.

"The girls would like some privacy for a few minutes to clean up. Would you mind?"

"No problem. I'll be out on the door step."

He watched the darkness fall over the forest. There was less noise coming from the tall trees but the forest floor was alive with sounds. He wondered what was out there searching for its dinner. All in all it had been a good day. He was even starting to feel a little more optimistic about their chances. He knew they wouldn't have fared so well without Eidah. She had no idea how valuable she was. He couldn't imagine her being used as a prostitute. She was pretty enough, in a native kind of way, but she probably would skin anyone who tried to touch her. He laughed to himself at the thought of it. The mosquitoes were starting to swarm and in a while he stood up to get back to the fire. Just before he turned he noticed something out of the corner of his eye. He looked off to the southeast. It was just a faint glow of light out in the forest but he knew right away what it was. Annie came up and stood beside him. She looked at him for a moment and then followed his eyes. Jack heard a slight gasp.

"Is that them?"

"That would be my guess."

"How far?"

"It's kind of hard to say but I would guess a mile, maybe a little more."

"What are we going to do?"

"Nothing for now. They aren't going anywhere tonight but you better get the girls bedded down. We're going to need to get an early start in the morning."

"Can we stay ahead of them, do you think?"

"No."

"How soon then?"

"Half a day if we're lucky. I need to talk to Eidah."

9

Jack put some more wood on the fire and then sat on the floor opposite the girls. Annie brought Eidah and Mardi over to sit with him. She handed Jack a metal cup with some of the tea Eidah had been brewing. It had a strong, spicy odor and tasted a little bitter but it lifted his energy almost as soon as he took the first sip.

"Mardi, I need to know where we are going, how long it will take and how hard it will be to travel. Can you ask Eidah?"

Mardi began conversing with Eidah but Eidah was watching Jack as if she could understand him. She said something to Mardi, who looked back at him.

"Eidah asks if they are coming."

Jack nodded and looked at Eidah. Mardi looked like she was going to lose it and Jack put his hand on her shoulder to try to reassure her. The last thing he needed was to have the girls in a panic. Eidah took in a deep breath and then got up and took a twig from the woodpile. As she spoke she drew a crude map on the cave floor. When she had finished, Mardi took the twig from her and looked at Jack.

"Eidah says her village is here. She thinks we can get there in one long day but we may need to camp one more night. She says the ground will continue to rise if we go this way and there are many large rocks but the forest is not difficult."

Jack looked at the map, trying to figure out what to do. He spoke to Mardi again. "Ask her if there is anyplace we could climb."

After a brief exchange, Eidah took the twig from Mardi and indicated a place on the map about a third of the way to the village. She spoke rapidly and was watching Jack's face.

"She says there is a road here. It can be reached from this point with a short climb. It is possible but a little difficult. It is not a good road but it is wide enough for trucks. It's not used too much and never in the rainy season."

"How long to get there?"

"She thinks maybe three hours."

Jack turned to Annie. "That's cutting it close but it may be the only hope we have."

"What? Are you guessing there'll be a car rental by the side of the road, Jack?"

"Listen, any time you have a better idea, feel free to chime in. If there is a road there may be some traffic along it. That's the best I can do for the moment. I don't know how many are behind us but we can't outrun them. If I am going to have to fight them I want to pick my spot. You are going to have to get everyone up onto the road. I think I can buy you enough time to do that at least."

"Then what?"

"I don't know. Stick out your thumb."

Jack turned to Mardi. "Tell Eidah I want to be ready to move at first light. And tell her thank you, Mardi. For everything."

Eidah listened, and then turned to Jack and held his eyes for a moment. She smiled a slow smile, and then turned away. Annie whispered in his ear.

"Maybe I was wrong about her not being your type."

Once the girls settled in, Jack picked a spot between the fire and the cave entrance. He didn't think they needed to post a watch. The girls were too tired anyway and he was going to need some rest. He checked the chamber on the AK and placed it within easy reach before lying down on the floor. He had just started to drop off when Lyana came over to him and crawled between his arms without saying a word. He brushed her hair back out of her face and held her until she fell asleep. He hadn't thought about the little girl much during the day, but there, in the stillness by the fire, he remembered another time and place and another little girl that he hadn't known and would never know. The urge to protect Lyana arose from a place deep within himself and he vowed that he would not let any harm come to her. His dreams were troubled, as they always were when he was forced to improvise. Jack was a careful man and he normally always had an out. This time he didn't see one. It was going to get bloody.

Sometime later in the night he awoke with a start. The hairs were standing up on the back of his neck and there was a musky smell in the air. He knew something was wrong. He lifted his head slowly and saw, at the entrance of the cave, a pair of large, pale yellow eyes, staring back at him. It looked like some demon from hell. He reached over slowly and took the AK. He pulled back the charging handle letting it return easily and moved the selector to semi-automatic. The big cat was creeping on its haunches. He could just make out its shape, hunched down and crawling forward. He could hear its breathing. It was going for the little girl. The last thing he wanted to do was discharge the weapon and give away their location. It would echo like a cannon-shot in the cave. It didn't look like he was going to have another choice. The cat crept forward and Jack held its eyes. Its stare almost had him paralysed and at that moment he knew what an animal felt, just before it was taken. It would only take a moment of hesitation and it would be too late. The cat rocked back ready to pounce. It was panting and he could feel the heat of its breath. Jack lifted his head and took aim. Suddenly there was a flash of light and a flurry of sparks. The cat hissed and then quickly retreated toward the cave entrance. It turned one time and looked at Jack as if to say, 'you were lucky this time'. And then it was gone. Jack turned and saw Eidah standing over the fire. She had thrown a log on it just in time. The rest of the girls stirred but didn't wake up. Eidah came over to him noiselessly and picked up Lyana. They didn't speak a word but as she picked up the girl she leaned over and kissed Jack on the lips, lightly. She smiled and carried the girl back with her.

His watch had stopped and he didn't know what time it was, but his heart was pounding and there was no way he was going to get any more sleep. He popped the magazine out of the AK and examined it. It was a full 30 round clip. There were eighteen rounds in the spare and he still had two grenades. He thought about what he needed to do. If they had enough time he would take them from ambush. The AK was somewhat accurate out to about 300 yards, but not accurate enough to insure a single shot kill. The barrel was so short that it made the sights almost useless. He couldn't take them at a distance. It would have been a lot easier if he knew their numbers, but for now he had to guess and he decided on a dozen. Ideally he wanted to find a spot near the road but far enough so that the girls would have a chance if the men got by him. He didn't think they would be harmed. Aside from taking revenge on him, they were coming after the girls to recoup their investment. Annie, he wasn't sure about. She would have the Enfield and her bluff and not much else. He decided he would walk with them for an hour or so and then look for a spot where the trail narrowed and would force them to come through one or two at a time. He tried the action on the AK. It felt a little gritty, but he had seen these things fire with sand spraying out of them. It would work. It had to. He took the parang and started carving some short wooden stakes. It helped to be doing something with his hands. He was lost in thought when he felt someone come up behind him. He turned and saw Annie. She sat down beside him. Neither of them spoke right away.

"Not done busting on me?" he said, finally.

"I'm sorry, Jack. It's just the way I am. I was wrong about you."

"Oh, yeah? How?"

"I had you pegged as just another out-for-yourself loser down here slowly drinking and screwing yourself to death."

"You must have read my resume."

"No, I don't think so. I think that's what you pass yourself off as, but that's not who you are."

"You mean like you pass yourself off as a hostess?"

"I am a hostess."

"Maybe. But my guess is it's just a part time job."

She stared at him for a moment, as if trying to decide what to say. "Look, Jack, there is a lot involved here that you don't know. For the time being, at least, I have to keep it that way. It's better for you anyway. It's better for all of us."

"So, what? You are some kind of spook or something?"

"Let's just say I know how to handle a weapon. If you need help tomorrow I'd be happy to pitch in."

Jack looked at her and wondered who she was really. Still, she would just be in the way on an ambush unless they choreographed every move and there wasn't time for that. He didn't want to have to choose between saving her and getting his ass shot off.

"OK, sure. I'll give you a yell if I need you."

"Do you want to tell me what the plan is, Jack?"

"I'll pick a place to set up an ambush. We'll see how it goes."

"Are you afraid?"

"Now? No. I'm saving that for tomorrow."

"Does it bother you, Jack? The killing I mean."

"Some. When it's over." He stopped and looked at her for a moment. "Last night, up close and personal like that. That turns my stomach. I've never gotten used to it."

They sat together in silence for a while, looking out into the night. Finally, Annie spoke.

"What if they get by?"

Jack didn't answer right away and he really didn't want to think about it. After a moment, he answered. "Don't shoot at them unless you have to save your life or one of the girls. Almost anything is better than dying, Annie. These guys aren't all that smart. You'll find another way."

"What about you? You could take off. You could get away if you didn't have to take care of us. They probably won't do anything to us. We're too valuable to them. I wouldn't blame you, Jack. You know they're probably going to kill you."

"I thought about it."

"And?"

"I don't know. It's just what needs to be done. Besides, I really don't have much choice. They're coming after me. On this Island, without help from someone, I can't outrun them. Sooner or later they'll find me. At least this way I get to pick my spot. If these are the same assholes who took me off the ship, I have a score to settle with them anyway. He turned and looked at her.

"Did you ever have one of those times in your life, Annie, when something happens and you know your life will never be the same again?"

"Sure."

"Well, this is one of those times for me. I've come to the end of something. Every time I go through one of these, there's a test. It's always pass or fail, no in between."

"Remind me to ask you about your death wish some time. I mean, why you, why now?"

"I don't know. I don't ask 'why me' anymore. I really don't want to know."

She started to get up to leave when he grabbed her arm.

"Listen, Annie, maybe there is something you can do. If they get through on me I'll be busting it up the trail. It would be nice to have some cover from the road if I make it that far. How good are you with that pistol?"

"Well, it's old and worn but I think it works. With a proper weapon I can place a 50-millimeter group at ten meters, depending on the load of course. I've only got five rounds."

"That's good enough."

"Listen, Jack, I don't suppose you would let me use the satellite phone for a moment."

"What? You dying to tell Aunt Millie about your vacation in the jungle?"

She just stared at him.

"OK but make it quick. I don't know how much longer the battery is going to hold out."

"I'll use it in the morning after we get going."

He leaned against the side of the cave and managed to doze off a little. Sakina awakened him once. She evidently had felt something crawling on her and went crazy for a few minutes brushing off her clothing. It was just starting to get light when Eidah rousted the girls and got them moving. They all had some water and the remainder of the fruit. It was probably all they were going to get for the rest of the day. They were all pretty grumpy, and Jack had to carry Lyana again. He gave Annie the sat-phone and she hung back behind the group and made her call. Eidah had them moving at a quick pace and the going wasn't too bad. He gathered some thin vines as he moved along and began twisting them into a cord. Annie finally caught up with the group and she took Lyana from Jack. He asked her to hold onto the phone. Almost two hours had passed and Jack moved up next to Mardi and asked her how far to the road. Mardi checked with Eidah and then told him it was just up ahead, maybe fifteen minutes. It was time to pick his spot. A little further along they came to a place where the trail pinched between a large Banyan tree and the face of the escarpment. There was a dense thicket on the other side of the tree and no good way to get around it without going pretty far down into the forest. He moved up the trail and identified his primary firing position and two good fall back positions. Annie came back to join him.

"This is it then?"

"Yeah, I think I can make it work. How are you doing?"

"I'm alright, except my feet are killing me. I'd give my left arm for a pair of socks. Are you sure you don't want me to stay?"

"No, thanks, Annie. But if you see me humping up the trail, you shoot anything that's behind me. Even if it's an elephant."

"Take care of yourself, Jack."

He went back down a little past the choke point, and found a place where the underbrush was thick and partially covered the trail. He pushed a stake in the ground on each side and ran his makeshift cord between them, tying it fast at one end and covering it all with brush. He took a grenade and set it on the ground against a large rock to direct its energy toward the trail. He placed a smaller rock against it to keep the spoon in place and then tied the other end of the cord around the grenade. He made sure the spoon was secure and then carefully pulled the pin. Then he retreated to the firing position and imagined how it would unfold. It felt good to have some rock around him. A lot better than being out in the jungle. He struggled to control his breathing. If they were observing good trail discipline they would be spaced out at intervals and the trip wire might only get the lead man. If luck was with him, they would be bunched up and the blast could take out two or three. The rest would hit the deck and look for cover.

They would probably wait for a while to see what was coming next but he wasn't going to fire on them. Not right away. Hopefully, after a few minutes they would begin to creep forward a couple at a time. He guessed they might split their force and send some men around through the jungle. That would bring some of them east of his primary firing position. He had a good field of fire from that point on both the trail and the forest below. There was a natural, shallow bowl below him, which would slow them down and force them to bunch up. If these were professional soldiers he would be overrun in short order but he was counting on them being just a bunch of thugs with guns. If he got enough of them in the initial attack, he had a chance. Once the party was really rolling it would be maneuver, cover and fire as he worked his way up to the road.

Another half hour went by and he began to think they weren't coming. He assumed the girls had made it to the road and he thought about cutting out and joining them. If they were still being pursued though, it would be better to face them where he was, rather then up on a road that might not provide good cover. He thought he might go a little farther up the trail just to see what his escape route looked like but something stopped him. The forest had gone still. No birds, no movement in the trees. Then he heard them. He took a peek around the side of a large rock and saw a group of men moving together about fifty yards from where he had set the trap. They had their weapons slung and did not look particularly alert. Jack took up his position and waited. His hands started to tremble and his mouth tasted like sand. He could feel his heart beating and he forced himself to go quiet inside. A few minutes passed and he thought they had stepped over it. Then all hell broke loose. The grenade went off and he heard screaming. Suddenly there were bullets flying in all directions, chopping through the brush and singing off the rocks around him. He heard more shouting and men running. He lay still and waited. Someone yelled out a command and everything went quiet except for one man who was screaming in agony. He heard a single shot and then silence.

It seemed like an eternity but it was probably no more than three or four minutes. He began to hear movements on the trail. He took a peek and saw them creeping forward. There looked to be at least a dozen men, possibly more. They were just on the other side of the choke point and had their eyes to the ground looking for more tripwires. He let three of them come through and then he stepped out into the trail and opened up with the AK, taking all three before they managed to fire their weapons. He dove back behind the rocks and listened. It was hard to control the rate of fire on fully automatic but he figured he had spent about twelve rounds. Someone began shouting commands and he started to take covering fire on his position. Keeping to the rocks, he managed to fall back to his next firing point without exposing himself. As he had expected, there was now a group of men down in the forest below his position working their way around the thicket in an effort to out-flank him. The rest of them continued to rake his original position with sporadic fire to keep his head down. He waited until the group in the forest had made their way around and entered the bowl beneath him. As soon as they started moving up toward the trail he took the last grenade and pulled the pin. He let the spoon go and lobbed it down to where they were advancing. It went off and there were more screams. Two men came up over the side of the trail right in front of his position and he cut them both down. He stepped back into the trail and caught two more coming at him. He emptied the remainder of the mag on them and ran as fast as he could up the trail, not stopping until he found cover.

He took a quick look down the trail. They weren't coming yet. He tried to slow himself down but his chest was heaving. He dropped the empty mag, slapped the new one in place and pulled back the charging handle. He figured he had taken out at least ten but he didn't know how many were left. There was half a mag left, and then it was going to get interesting. He waited. He couldn't hear any movement at all, which didn't make him happy. He ventured another look and his heart fell. There were at least five or six more of them and they were working their way forward keeping to cover. He waited unit two of them were exposed and he fired, getting one but missing the other. It was time to make a run for it. He waited a few seconds and then jumped out of his position. He shot by reflex at the first exposed man he saw but missed. He bolted down the trail running like a mad man. Fortunately the trail curved off to his left, which kept him out of the following fire for a few critical seconds. They were in hot pursuit. He dropped behind a rock and counted to five before stepping back into the trail. He caught a group of them rushing forward and emptied the mag on them. One of them got through and Jack caught him in the head with the stock of the AK, nearly breaking it loose from the barrel. He dropped what was left of his weapon and ran, taking a quick look over his shoulder. There were two of them left and they were firing as they came forward but without taking aim. The rounds were kicking up dirt at his feet and he heard a few whine past his head.

He was a strong runner and he knew he could out-distance them but there was no way he was going to be able to make the climb up to the road without being cut in half. The trail turned left again and he saw the girls standing at the top of a wash that looked to be about fifteen feet high. They started to cheer and then quickly scattered as they saw what was happening. He didn't see Annie. It was game over. He stopped at the bottom of the wash, stooped down, picked up some rocks and started throwing them. He recognized one of the men. He was the one who had kicked him in the groin on the ship. They came forward with their guns levelled and he waited for the inevitable. When they were about ten feet away, they stopped and the leader sneered at him, levelling a pistol at his head. It was his Glock. He started to say something to Jack and then stopped as he sensed movement to his side. Before he could react, Annie stepped out from behind a tree and fired twice. Jack leapt backward, stunned. There were two dead men lying on the trail in front of him. Finally, he regained his composure. He walked over to one of the bodies and picked up the Glock.

"Thanks for returning my weapon, asshole."

10

It was an old road that had once serviced a rubber plantation, but it didn't look like anything had travelled on it recently. The jungle pushed in against it, hungry for the open sky. In places it was covered over completely, forming a tunnel of green leaves, and woven with thick vines finding their way to the top of the canopy. Still, it made for easier travel. They had gained a good bit of elevation during their trek and the air was cooler. Jack was happy to have the Glock tucked in his waistband. It was a lot better than humping the AK through the bush. Everyone was much more relaxed now that they were not being pursued but Annie was quiet and looked a little shook up. She may have been a good shot, but Jack guessed it had all been paper targets until now. A stray bullet had grazed Jack on his side. It wasn't bleeding badly but Eidah insisted on treating it before they moved on. She made him take his shirt off. Annie watched the procedure absently, not making eye contact with anyone. Eidah applied a poultice made up of some leaves and flower petals, which she chewed into a paste. She applied it to a leaf and attached it with a bit of vine wrapped around his torso and up over one shoulder. When they started moving again, Annie walked along beside him.

"Are you OK, Annie?"

"Yeah, I'll be alright. It's just that...."

"I know. It's always tough the first time."

"How do you know it was the first time?"

"Just a guess. Anyway, thanks, for what you did back there. I've seen a lot of guys freeze when they had to do it for real. You did great."

"I feel badly about just leaving them there on the trail."

"Well, there's not a lot we can do about it. If we wanted to burry them all we would be here for days. The jungle will take care of them. There won't be anything left of them inside of a week."

"That's what I mean. Anyway, I guess they deserved it. That wanker with the pistol was the one who tried to knob me when they took us off the boat. Did you notice his left ear?"

"No, I was busy looking for rocks."

"Yeah, I enjoyed that part. How many were there anyway?"

"I don't know, but two more than I had rounds for."

"Anyway, nice one. I'll see if the Queen wants to give you a medal."

"Where did you learn to shoot like that?" Jack asked. "Was it part of your training?"

"No, my dad taught me. He was in the Regiment."

"SAS?"

"Yes. He was killed a couple of years ago."

"That must have been tough."

"Yeah. I still miss him. He was away a lot. Sometimes when I'm home I half expect to see him show up at the door."

"Would you like to tell me who you are, Annie?"

"That wouldn't be my preference. All I can tell you is I work for the British Government and I am here trying to get any information I can on illegal trafficking in the region."

"So what? MI6?"

"I couldn't say if I was but no I am not employed by the SIS. All I can tell you is that I am assigned to this region by an agency that looks out for the commercial interests of the UK. This is not something I normally do. I just happened to be in a position to get close to someone who was of interest to my government."

"So how did you end up with Blackbeard back there?"

"I pissed somebody off and I got myself lifted out the back of a nightclub."

"What did you do?"

"I'd rather not say."

"Look, if you're going to clam up than so am I."

She stared at him for a moment. Jack suspected her curiosity about him had been growing since their first meeting and he was prepared to use it as leverage to find out more about her.

"OK, Jack. But if you ever tell anybody I'll kill you, I swear I will. My current assignment is to investigate allegations of the harvesting of human organs in China. We had set up a meeting with a man who claimed to have first hand information about it. He wanted to speak to me because I have met other members of their group and they trust me."

"Harvesting?"

"Yeah, I know it sounds unbelievable but there is evidence it's happening. The Chinese labor camps are crammed full of political prisoners. Almost half of them are practitioners of a religious practice called Falun Gong. Something like sixty percent of the alleged torture cases involve people arrested for being involved with or practicing that religion. The

110

man I was supposed to meet claimed he had had a kidney taken while he was a prisoner. He claims it is happening on a routine basis. He escaped from China and has been working with a group of Chinese ex-pats who are trying to get the truth of the situation to the outside world. If his story is true, it will be one of the most egregious examples of human rights atrocities in Asia since Pol Pot and the Khmer Rouge. In any case, I never got the chance to meet him."

"Why, what happened?"

The night before I was to meet with the guy, they asked me to get close to this big shot businessman. Apparently I was his type, or so they told me anyway. One of the other areas my agency has been investigating is illegal arms trafficking in the region and we had information this guy was a player. Our sources believed there was a deal getting ready to go down at a nightclub in Jakarta. We work through a service that provides hostesses for events and private parties. It's big business down here. Tall, European women are in demand. The people who run the service are sympathetic to our government and they are in a position to gather some excellent intelligence for us. When they identify someone they think we would be interested in, they let us know and one of us gets assigned to play hostess for the evening. Before you get the wrong idea, Jack, it doesn't involve anything more than conversation and at worst a bit of bum patting."

"What were you supposed to do?"

"The idea was to get a miniature radio device onto the guy's coat. We have these marvellous little things, no bigger than a button. They don't have very good range but if you are close enough, you can here everything the target is saying and most of the other conversation in his immediate area. It just sticks onto almost any kind of cloth and you wouldn't notice it unless you were really looking. Even if you found it you probably wouldn't think it was a bug."

"So did you get the thing on him?"

"Yeah, but it all went bad after that. This guy I was assigned to was the biggest Indonesian I've ever seen and he thought he was God's gift. He was chatting me up hard all evening and he got really plowed. He started to chase me around the room but fortunately, I managed to stay ahead of him. Finally, he unzipped his fly and whipped it out like it was some kind of monument. He had this tiny little pud and I started to laugh. I mean it wasn't the first undersized weenie I've ever seen. It's just that the bloke was so bloody huge. Anyway he went unhinged and I thought he was going to kill me. I think he paid your friends back there to get some revenge."

"Tough line of work you're in."

"It isn't usually like that, Jack. Normally the guys I get assigned to just want to waffle on about themselves. They know the rules."

"So did you learn anything at all?"

"Not really, although hopefully the bug worked and our people were able to get something. Anyway, the illegal arms trade has been going on for centuries. It's not an area I care all that much about. Tying somebody down and forcibly removing a kidney, that's a different story. I really wanted to help expose it."

"Well, it doesn't look like you're in a position to do anything about it now."

"We'll see."

"So, what next?"

"I've got transportation arranged from Medan. All I need to do is get there."

"Headed where?"

"Can't say."

"OK, sorry I asked."

"No, I mean I don't know. They haven't told me yet. What about you, Jack?"

"They're trying to arrange an out for me. I'm going to be checking in soon. Hopefully I'll know more then."

"So it wasn't the Chinese who were coming after you after all."

"I don't know. My guess is they're still looking. Those boys back there in the woods were pretty motivated. Somebody must have made it worth their while."

"Maybe they were just coming after us."

"Maybe. Listen, Annie, I need to make that call. I'll catch up with you."

The battery indicator on the sat-phone was low and Jack figured this would be his last call for a while. It took a while to get a signal. Finally, Charlie picked up.

"Where are you now, Jack?"

"We're in the mountains, headed for a village somewhere. That's all I can tell you."

"What about the pursuit?"

"Eliminated. Listen, Charlie, this phone is almost dead and I don't know when I'm going to be able to check back in. One of the women I'm with works for the Brits. She's got transportation arranged in Medan. I figure I'll go there, too. It may take a couple of days, I don't know."

"What's she doing out in the bush?"

"She was picked up with the rest of the girls. She's been doing some Intel work for her government down here. Do you think you can get me something out of Medan?"

"I'll see what I can do, Jack, but you are still a hot commodity and you better keep your head down. It's probably not safe for you to travel by commercial air. I might be able to get you on a ship out of Belawan."

"Christ, that's all I need. I just got lifted off of the last scow you put me on. What about a bird, Charlie?"

"That's a little dicey that far north. The Indonesian government is fighting an active insurgency by a group called the Gerakan Aceh Merdeka out of Banda Aceh. I don't think we can risk it without clearance and that could take a month."

"Alright but see what you can do for me, Charlie. I want to get the fuck off this island."

"I'm working on it."

"Any more news on the crisis?"

"Yeah and it isn't good. They're not sure but they think that was not just a run of the mill digital camera you found. They think it was set up with a short focal length lens to be used to photograph documents. What you sent me was a transcript of a conversation but the critical information is probably on that card."

"Critical information about what?"

"They are keeping pretty quiet on that front but I can tell you what I think from my recent conversations. You may be carrying around the operating manual for a small nuclear device."

"What the hell!"

"Yeah, I know, Jack. Like I said, you really know how to get the shit flying. Right now the suspicion is that someone in the PLA is helping to broker a deal to get a nuke into the hands of

Jemaah Islamiyah, or some other terrorist organization."

"What's the target?"

"Nobody knows. Or at least they aren't saying. Like I said, this is still speculation but listen, Jack, it gets worse."

"I don't see how that's possible."

"It's been suggested that the documents on that memory card may also contain the initiation code and possibly an abort code for the nuke."

"Well, then why don't I just smash the damned thing, Charlie, and be done with it?"

"You can't do that, Jack. If it's destroyed they have the original documents to go back to, or at lease we assume they do. On the other hand it's damned sure this is going to be our only chance to get our hands on the abort code it there is one. If it all goes bad we may need that."

"I don't know if the memory card is still good, Charlie. It's been a little exciting around her lately."

"Well, there's nothing we can do about that. Just try to keep it as safe as you can and only destroy it if don't have another choice. Whatever you do, don't let anybody get their hands on it."

"OK, Charlie. See what you about getting me off this island, will you? I'll check in when I get to Medan. It will probably be on a land line."

"Be careful, Jack. The last thing the PLA wants is evidence to get out that they have their hands in this thing."

Jack caught up with the girls but he suddenly felt like the all of the energy had drained out of him. He wasn't sure he could take another day on the trail without some decent food and some sleep. The girls were dragging, too, and they were nearly out of water. He was just about to suggest they stop for a while when he heard a vehicle coming up the road behind them. He checked the chamber on the Glock and stepped off to the side where he couldn't be seen. It was an old stake-body truck filled with rice sacks, and just the driver. It was draped over with leaves and branches it had shorn off along the way. The driver stopped the truck when he saw the girls. Eidah walked up to the door and started talking to him. Jack stepped out on the road and watched. After a few minutes Eidah said something to Mardi.

"Eidah says he will give us a ride."

Eidah sat up front with Lyana. The rest of them climbed into the back among the rice sacks. The road was rough and nearly washed out in places. Sometimes the truck was so close to the edge that one of the tandem rear tires was spinning in the air. The driver didn't seem concerned. He was having an animated discussion with Eidah and not paying much attention to the road. The air felt good and, after a while, Jack fell asleep.

When he awoke the truck had come to a stop. He had expected to see a village but there was just more jungle and a trail leading off toward the west. The truck pulled away, leaving a blue cloud of exhaust fumes. Eidah pointed to the trail and said something to Mardi.

"Eidah says this way. Only a short distance."

He wasn't sure what Eidah thought a short distance meant but he felt a little better after the nap. After about fifteen minutes they entered a clearing at the edge of a river. On the other side he could see acres of terraced rice paddies and some water buffalo. A little beyond the rice paddies there was a village. It was a

Batak village and the roofs of the wooden houses had tall peaks at the front and rear, like horns. There were several open fires burning and a lot of people milling about. There was also what looked like a church, with a cross above the roof.

On the other side of the river some women were furiously slapping their laundry against some stones. A little farther down stream, some young boys were jumping off rocks into the river. Apparently they hadn't discovered bathing suits yet. Jack wondered if they were going to have to swim across but Eidah lead them a little way upstream to where a large dugout canoe was pulled up on the bank. It was attached to a rope and pulley system that stretched across the river. It took two trips to get everyone across. Eidah went first with three of the girls. By the time Jack and Annie got across there was already quite a commotion going on. Eidah's father had been summoned and he was none-too-happy to see them. Eidah's whole demeanor had changed. Jack was so used to seeing her strong and confident that it was a shock to see her cowering in front of someone. Jack's anger started to rise and Annie sensed it. She grabbed him by the arm and shook her head. She was right. If he did anything it would just get worse. They waited and watched. After a few minutes, Eidah's father went marching back toward the village with Eidah in tow.

The remainder of the people turned to the group and suddenly there were smiles and hands extended. They were led into the village and immediately taken into one of the larger buildings and invited to sit. The interior was decorated with elaborate woodcarvings and colorful fabric wall hangings. There were cushions on the floor. Women started appearing with food and drink. Jack didn't know what it was but it was all good. Eidah had apparently gone home with her father and Jack wondered how she was being treated. Annie and the rest of the girls were in high spirits and it was the first time he had heard any of them laugh. It looked like Mardi was providing a blow-by-blow description of their trek through the forest and everyone was paying rapt attention. Occasionally they all would turn and look at him, nodding their heads and smiling. He suddenly became aware of what a foul state he was in. He still had dried blood all over himself and his clothes needed to be thrown out, except he didn't think he would find anything in the village that would fit him. He caught Mardi's eye and asked her to come over.

"Mardi, could you ask them if there is a place I can go to get cleaned up?"

Mardi spoke to one of the women and she shouted something to a group of boys who were hanging around admiring the new girls. One of them came over to Jack and indicated he should follow. Jack drew a lot of attention as he walked through the village. People were pointing and some laughed. They were mostly short in stature and he was beginning to feel like Gulliver. Some of the log and frame houses were small but others looked like they were big enough for several families. They all seemed to have window boxes, brimming with colorful flowers. The wooden fronts were elaborately carved. They passed the church he had seen from the other side of the river. He had thought Indonesians were all Muslims, but apparently this place was the exception. They stopped at a house and the boy indicated he should wait. A moment later he reappeared with a towel and some soap. Jack followed him down to the river and they walked a little down stream to a place where some rocks blocked the view of the village and created a pool away from the current. The boy nodded to Jack and pointed to the river. Evidently this was where they bathed.

Once he was alone he removed his shirt and trousers. He carefully extracted the memory card from the collar and examined it. It didn't look damaged and he hoped it had remained dry. He put the card in his shoe along with his watch and the contents of his pockets and placed them next to the Glock within easy reach. He had liberated the rest of his money back in the jungle and he still had eighteen hundred Singapore dollars in case he had to bribe his way out of the country. The water was surprisingly cold. He stripped naked and waded in, leaving his clothes on the bank. His side hurt a little but not enough to keep him from swimming and he ventured out toward the center of the river. As soon as he was in the current it started to take him down stream at a pretty good clip. He had to work a little to get back to the shore. He washed himself and then did the best he could with his clothes. After a half hour or so, he climbed out and dried himself off with the towel. He wrung his clothes out before laying them on the rocks to dry and then spread the towel on the ground. He lay there in the shade and closed his eyes. Disturbing images were passing through his consciousness like some kind of a macabre slide show. He was still pretty wired. It would be a while before he would be able to relax again, but he was exhausted and eventually he fell into a fitful sleep.

He awoke with a start and found Annie staring down at him, smiling. Her hair was wet and she was wearing some kind of flowered wrap that looped over one shoulder and tied on the side. He forgot he was naked for a second and when he remembered it was too late any way. Annie didn't seem to mind.

"Integrating the men's locker room are we?"

"You left the door open. Listen, Jack, I think we can get a ride out of here tomorrow morning to a town called Rantauprapat. They tell me a bus runs between there and Medan."

"I'm not sure we should be travelling together from this point, Annie."

"Why not?"

"Because whoever is looking for me is pulling out all the stops. I'm not real optimistic about getting off this island in one piece."

"I don't get it, Jack. What in the world did you steal from these guys?"

"Hold on a minute, will you?"

He got up and went over to where his clothes were drying. He turned his pants and shirt over and put on his shorts. They were still a little wet. He went back and sat down next to Annie.

"How's your wound?"

"It's fine. Whatever Eidah put on there did the trick. Anyway, those papers I told you about. I did destroy them, but first I scanned them and sent them on to my handler. At the time I had no idea what was in them. It started a world class shit storm and I'm right in the middle of it."

"Why? What was in the documents?"

"Nobody is saying, except that they contain details of a conversation between somebody in the PLA and a weapons supplier. They think a terrorist group called Jemaah Islamiyah is involved."

"You're joking."

Jack reached over and took the memory card from his shoe. He handed it to her.

"What's this?"

"It's a memory card I took from a camera that was with the papers. Nobody knows what's on it for sure, but all of a sudden it has become a hot commodity. They think it contains some information the Chinese do not want to see the light of day. My handler thinks it involves a small yield nuclear weapon. They found the guy I took it from dead in an alley with a knife in his chest. He had my passport in his pocket."

"Jesus, Jack. That guy I was assigned to in Jakarta? My government thinks he has been brokering arms to the same group. I wonder if there could be some kind of connection."

"Who the hell knows? Nobody is sure of anything at this point."

"I need to contact my people about this. Can I use the phone?"

"No good, the battery is dead and I doubt there is a charger within a thousand miles of here. Besides, my guess is they already know."

"How?"

"My government is involved, which probably means yours is, too."

She put her chin down on her knees and started chewing her bottom lip. Jack watched her turning things over in her head.

"So what do you intend to do, Jack?"

"I'm still working on that. If I can get to Medan there is probably a place where I can buy a camera. Those flash memory cards are pretty much universal. Then, if I can find someplace to get on the Internet, I can upload the data to my handler and destroy the card. After that I just need to get out in one piece."

"Why in the world would the Chinese be involved with a terrorist group?"

"Who knows why they do anything. Governments have been guessing wrong about China for a thousand years. Besides it might not be the government. It could just be a splinter group of some kind."

"Even so, it's hard to believe it would do them any good. Certainly not in the long run."

"To tell you the truth. Annie, I really don't give a damn. I just want to get rid of that card and get the hell out of here."

"So you don't think it's your problem if somebody sets off a nuke down here?"

"Nope."

"How can you be like that? It could kill thousands of innocent people."

"Yeah, it would be a horrible thing. I just don't see that there is anything I can do about it, beyond getting whatever is on this disk to somebody who can."

11

That evening there was some kind of celebration in the village. Jack wasn't sure what it was all about but he was feeling rested and relaxed for the first time in days. Mardi told him it was an Adat ceremony. The central meeting area was lit with torches and a large fire was blazing in the center. There were spirited speeches that went on for hours, and music from a gong and drum orchestra. They served a dish made up of banana leaves, rice and coconut juice all cooked up in a piece of bamboo. It was worthy of the menu at the IndoChine. Annie was enjoying herself with the girls and Jack sat with a group of men just taking it all in. After the speeches, there was a kind of puppet show with life-size wooden characters dressed in various elaborate costumes. He was told it was called a Gale-gale. All of the villagers were paying rapt attention and they were laughing like children. Suddenly, everyone seemed to be dancing and having a good time. Someone passed him a cup and he took a drink. It tasted like coconut milk but there was some kind of alcohol in it and it was strong. He sipped it slowly but after a while he began to feel its effects and he decided not to overdo it. He couldn't afford to let his guard down too much. Later in the evening, Mardi came over to him.

"Eidah asked me to come talk to you."

"How's she doing?"

"Her father is angry with her. He thinks the man who paid him will come back and demand his money back."

"Doesn't he know what was going to happen to her?"

"He doesn't believe it."

"What about you and Sakina?"

"We've been invited to stay here for a while. All of us. They'll get a message to the police and then our embassy will be contacted. Eventually our families will arrange to get us home."

"You've been a big help, Mardi. I don't know how we would have gotten along without you translating for us."

Mardi blushed, and looked down at her feet. "It was nothing. But thank you for saving us. We all owe you our lives." She reached over and gave him a hug.

Jack held her for a while and then broke away. He felt a little awkward. Finally, he broke the silence. "So what did Eidah want you to ask me?"

"Eidah wants you to stay here in the village with her. She wants to marry with you. I know that's not what you want, but I promised I would talk to you."

"That would never work, she has to know that."

"Eidah thinks you are a great warrior. She says you were sent by God to save her. She says she belongs to you now. Even if you don't stay with her."

"Eidah is an amazing woman, Mardi, but she's not for me."

"What do you want me to tell her?"

Jack was silent for a few moments. He didn't really know how to respond without hurting

Eidah's feelings, and he was really grateful to her for her help.

"Could you bring her over to talk to me, Mardi? Maybe tomorrow morning some time?"

"I think I can do that. If her father will allow it."

The girls all seemed to have been adopted by some of the families, even Annie. They didn't seem to know what to do with Jack. He was starting to get tired and as much as he was trying to push it out of his mind, the reality of his situation was digging at him. People were starting to drift back to their houses and Jack wondered where he was going to sleep. After a while a man came over to him and extended his hand.

"My name is Waluyo. Did you enjoy the festivities?" He spoke with a slight British accent.

"Sure, it was great."

"Yes, they are always enjoyable but too much talking for me." He smiled, revealing teeth that were blackened by Betel nut.

"The women have made a place for you to sleep in the meeting house. I can take you there now if you wish."

Jack followed him through the village. The people were a little more used to seeing him now but the story had gotten around and they were looking at him with something like awe. It made him a little uncomfortable.

"Where did you learn to speak English, Waluyo?"

"I worked for many years at the Swiss Belhotel in Banda Ache. I met many Westerners there."

"Why is there a church here? I thought Indonesians were all Muslim."

"Most are Muslim, sir, but this particular area was settled by the Dutch missionaries many years ago. I think they are called Methodists, but I am not certain."

"Is there a minister in the village?"

"No, sir. He visits every few weeks to gather with the people."

"Waluyo, can I ask you something?"

"Of course. What do you wish to know?"

"How much was Eidah's father paid by the man who took her away?"

"I don't know, sir. Usually the price is around one million rupiah."

"A million? Do you know how much that is in dollars?"

He thought for a moment. "It is about 60 British pounds, I think. I don't know what that is in dollars."

They entered the main gathering area of the meetinghouse and then Waluyo lead him to a small room off to the side. A bed had been prepared for Jack and there was a container of water also. It felt good to be in a bed again. As he lay there in the dark, his thoughts ran back to the fire-fight in the forest and he felt his muscles tensing. He forced it out of his mind and tried to concentrate on something else. The image of Angel kept intruding on his thoughts. He felt like something had been cut out of him. He had known for a while that she was the only reason he was still in Asia. What he hadn't realized was how much of what he liked about this part of the world was somehow connected to her. With her gone, it felt like an alien planet. After a while the fatigue and the alcohol put him into a deep sleep.

He awoke with the first light of dawn and he was startled for a moment, not yet aware of his surroundings. The memories started flooding in again and he felt the tension rising. He tried to force himself to relax. He lay in the bed, listening to the sounds of the river and the jungle beyond. He was trying to come up with some kind of a plan to get off the island, but there were too many unknowns. In a while, his thoughts turned to Eidah. He really didn't know what to say to her. He was thinking it over when the door opened and Annie stuck her head it.

"I see you got a private room. Sleep well?"

"Like the dead. You?"

"Wonderful. I want to come back here for a holiday some time. These people are just super."

"Do you know when we'll be leaving?"

"They said around ten. It depends on when the truck shows up."

"Did you meet Waluyo? He speaks English."

"No. Listen, Jack, I'm going to spend some time with the girls before we have to leave. I'll meet up with you when the truck gets here."

"Are you sure you want to travel with me, Annie?"

"Well, we have to get to Rentauprapat no matter what and I'm not walking. Let's talk about in on the way down."

After Annie left, Jack dressed. He was looking out the window at the people walking by, when one of the women of the village came in with a tray of fruit and some tea. He ate absently, too distracted to enjoy it. When he had finished, he took a walk through the village. In a while he heard someone call to him. He turned and saw Waluyo smiling at him.

"I am to ask if there is anything you require, sir."

"You can call me Jack. There is something you could do. I would like to talk to Eidah's father. Do you think you could translate for me?"

"Certainly, sir. Please wait here."

He sat on a split log bench and watched the people moving about the village. They all smiled and bowed to him as they passed. He didn't know how to handle it exactly so he just smiled back and waved occasionally. Finally, Waluyo returned and he had Eidah's father with him. Waluyo introduced him and he bowed but he was not smiling. Jack figured he was not too happy to be talking to him.

"Would you tell him that Eidah is a very brave woman and we could not have gotten back safely without her?"

Waluyo translated but got no reaction. Jack took some money out or his pocket.

"Tell him I want to give him this money in case the man who took Eidah away returns and wants his payment back."

Waluyo translated again and Eidah's father lit up like a Christmas tree. Jack counted out two hundred Singapore dollars and handed it to the man. He started rambling on in a singsong voice and smiling as if he had just won the lottery. Finally he turned and just ran off.

"Saudara Sukarnoputri has accepted your offer, but I believe you have overpaid, Mr. Jack."

"Not the way I figure it."

Waluyo stood, and shook Jack's hand.

"It was a pleasure meeting you, Mr. Jack. Unless you need me for something else, I have some duties to attend to."

"No. Thanks for your help."

Jack watched Waluyo walk away. He sat back down on the bench and waited. The village

128

was not large and he was sure Mardi would find him but he was dreading the conversation. In a short while he saw Mardi and Eidah walking toward him. Mardi looked a little tense, but Eidah seemed happy. Eidah stopped in front of him and bowed slightly. She looked him in the eyes and smiled. Jack greeted them both, then he turned to Mardi.

"Mardi, would you tell Eidah I have given her father some money, in case he has to pay back the man who took her away."

"She already knows that, Jack. Her father has spoken to her. I don't think it was a good idea to do that."

"Why?"

"Because her father thinks you have bought her now. He thinks she is going away with you."

He looked at Eidah and she peered into his eyes with an intensity that made him look away. He was way out of his depth and now it looked like he had made things worse. With all the trouble he was in, this was the last thing he wanted to have to deal with, but he was determined not to hurt Eidah's feelings. In the end, he decided that the best way to handle it was to be completely honest with her. He turned to Mardi again.

"Mardi, this is going to be a little embarrassing for you but I need you to translate for me. Do you think you can do that?"

"I will try."

"Tell Eidah that I think she is a wonderful young woman but she is not the right woman for me."

Mardi translated. Eidah looked down at her feet for a moment and then looked at Jack. He could see the disappointment on her face. She said something to Mardi.

"Eidah says it is not necessary that you love her. She says she knows you would not hurt her and that you are brave and kind. She wishes to help you on your journey. She says you have saved her life and she belongs to you now."

"Tell her I have to leave here and return to my own country and that it would be too dangerous for her to come with me."

Mardi translated again.

"She says she is not afraid."

Jack was becoming more and more exasperated.

"Tell her that I like her very much but that I do not love her. I would not take her away from here unless I was in love with her and wanted to spend the rest of my life with her. I don't feel that way."

After Mardi translated, Eidah was silent for what seemed like a long time. Jack didn't know what else to say. He suddenly wished he was back in the jungle getting shot at. At least he knew how to handle that. Finally, Eidah spoke. Mardi listened but didn't translate right away. Eidah stood and faced Jack and she bowed again. There were tears in her eyes. She reached down and kissed him on his cheek and then she turned and walked away.

"What did she say, Mardi?"

"Eidah said to thank you for setting her free."

He spent the rest of the morning walking around the village. It was amazing to see small boys leading enormous water buffalo around by their nose rings as if they were sheep. The village was from another time and it had a feeling of completeness about it that he had not experienced before. Everywhere else he had been in Asia was just one big hustle. Making money was an open obsession. It wasn't just the desire for material things. It was the currency itself. Holding it, counting it, looking at figures in the books. Here, there was a different rhythm to life. The people seemed deeply content and so relaxed that they walked around with smiles on their faces and laughter in their voices. He was watching the women washing their laundry in the river. It was hard manual work but you wouldn't have known it by the way they interacted with each other. They lived their lives together as human beings had always done, before modern civilization began to drive people into isolation. He was beginning to feel calm inside for the first time in weeks, but with the calm came remembrance, and with the memories came rage. He knew his life would be in danger as long as he remained in Asia, but somewhere out in these islands was the man who killed Angel. Snuffed out her life as if she mattered for nothing. He didn't know how, but he knew his life couldn't move forward until that man was made to pay. Even if it was the last thing he did on this earth.

The truck was similar to the one they had ridden in on the plantation road. There was a driver and two other men. Jack and Annie would be riding in the back on something that looked like coconut husks. The girls were all in tears and they spent some time hugging each other. All except for Eidah, who had not come out to see them off. The girls all hugged and kissed Jack. The little one came up to him shyly and gave him a flower. Jack reached down and gave her a hug. Many of the villagers had come to see them off and they were smiling and waving. One of the women gave Annie a bag of fruit. Jack was about to climb into the back of the truck when he saw Eidah and her father walking toward them. The crowd parted to allow them to come through. Eidah's father was angry. He started yelling at Jack and waving his arms in the air. Eidah looked embarrassed. She looked at Jack briefly but then looked away. She whispered something in Mardi's ear.

"Eidah say she is sorry, Jack. Her father is not being reasonable. He insists you must take her with you. She says not to worry, he is just saving face."

Annie started laughing at him.

"What's the problem, Jack? Buyers remorse?"

Jack glared at her.

"How about a little help here or we are never going to get out of this place."

"OK, Jack, but it's going to cost you."

Annie took Mardi aside and spoke to her. Mardi nodded her head and then turned to Eidah's father and translated. He listened but did not respond right away. He was clearly thinking things over. Finally he nodded to Jack and said something to Mardi. Then he turned and left. Eidah walked over to Jack and put her arms around him lightly. She kissed him on the cheek again and then stepped back and bowed. She said, "dalam kehidupan yang lain", then she turned and walked away.

Mardi came over to say her final goodbyes.

"What does that mean, Mardi?, what Eidah just said?"

"It means 'In another life'."

12

The truck pulled away and they tried to get comfortable. They had expected a rough ride but it was a lot worse than they imagined. The road was laced with deep furrows that had been carved into the surface in the last monsoon and never repaired. They were being bounced around the back of the truck like a couple of rice sacks. There were some hair-raising drop-offs and not many straight stretches. They were following the slope of a mountain and it got really dicey when there was something coming in the other direction. At one point they had to back up to a wider stretch to allow another truck to pass, removing a large swath of their trucks remaining paint to the music of groaning metal and cursing men.

There were still islands of fog below them, like blankets of white cotton, draped across the high canopy. The terraced rice paddies, luminous in the late morning sun, and the farmers with their straw hats and teams of oxen were like something out of an Ukiyo-e woodblock print. In too many places the view was marred by clear-cut patches of teak forest and eroded earth. Jack was trying to adjust to the feeling of being swept along by events he couldn't control. It was an uncomfortable place to be, but there was no choice but to try to stay calm and go with it. Annie was being pretty stoic, but he could see she was having a tough time. He tried to get her mind off of it.

"So what did you promise Eidah's father?"

"I'm not telling."

"Seriously, what did you tell him?"

"It will be my secret until the day I die."

"Which may be today if you don't tell me."

"It may be today in any case the way this trip is going. Anyway, are you ever going back there?"

"Not on purpose."

"Then it doesn't make any difference does it? All I can tell you is, if you ever go back again, you better have your tuxedo and a water buffalo."

"Eidah knows I'm not coming back for her."

"Yeah, but her father doesn't. Listen, I've been thinking about what you said. About not travelling with you, and I've decided you need my help."

"What if I decide I don't?"

"Come on, Jack. Don't go macho on me. You know it's better if there are two of us on this thing."

"What thing? We don't even know what this is all about. All I know is that I have to get whatever is on this card to somebody who can do something about it. After that, I'm out of here. Besides, I'm being hunted and it'll be a lot easier if I only have to look out for me."

"Yeah well, I'm involved in this thing, too, and besides, I can look out for myself."

"That's not the point. It's just that if the shit hits the fan, I only want to be worried about me."

"Yeah, well who saved who back there on the trail? Besides they are looking for a single guy. If we are travelling as a couple we might be able to pass ourselves off as tourists."

He knew she was probably right. Still, he didn't like the thought of it. There was no way he could walk away if she were in trouble. He had never turned his back on anyone. They travelled in silence for a while. After about an hour, the road became wider and they passed a few trucks and a battered Range Rover. Finally, Annie broke the silence.

"So, what happened to you, Jack? I know there has to be a story hidden in there somewhere."

He looked at her. "No, now it's your turn."

"OK," she said finally, "but it's not much of a story, really. I wanted to travel, get to see the world. I liked the idea of working for the government."

"But you didn't sign up for this."

"No, this is a little beyond the worst I could have imagined. But it's not the first time I was ever in a cock-up."

"I don't doubt that. So what else can you do?"

"I have a black belt in Akido."

"No, I mean can you cook, sew, that sort of thing?"

She punched him in the arm. "Yeah I can do that to, wanker."

"So where did you pick up the attitude?"

"Attitude? If I were a man you'd be calling it self-confidence. Anyway, I had three brothers. I used to play rugby with them."

"Do you think they're going to keep you on the job?"

"This job? I doubt it. I'm sure it's way beyond me now. They'll probably send somewhere else. I'm hoping Hong Kong."

"You mean as a reward for the fine work you did on this assignment?"

135

"Yeah, Jack. I mean, after I tell them how I saved your life, and rescued five virgins from a life of slavery, they'll love me."

"I think it has to be seven virgins."

"Well, I could try passing you off. I don't think they would believe me. That's it. Your turn again, Jack."

"What else do you want to know?"

"I want to know how you ended up in the middle of nowhere being chased through the jungle by a bunch of pirates."

"I don't know," he said. "Shit happens."

"Why not some nice safe job back in the States?"

"I tried that. It didn't work."

"Why not?"

He didn't answer right away. It was a question he often asked himself, and he was never really satisfied with his own answers. When he spoke he was staring down at his feet.

"I'm not much for kissing ass, Annie. I never minded putting in the long hours and I always gave it my best shot but sooner or later I always ran into some jackass who thought he was some kind of a god. It didn't bother me if the guy was actually capable. Most of them were just empty suits with inflated opinions of themselves. Sooner or later I always ended up giving them a little personal evaluation, one way or another. It's amazing to me how full of themselves a lot of people are. They don't seem to have the capacity to take an objective look at what they've actually accomplished as opposed to what's been handed to them by somebody."

"Well, you have to have self confidence, Jack. Otherwise you get walked on."

"Self confidence is one thing. Thinking you're actually worthy of the history books should require a little evidence."

"So what is it, Jack? Most of the guys I've met in your line of work have been adrenaline junkies, but I don't think that's you."

"I like a little excitement now and then, but I don't really enjoy getting shot at, if that's what you mean. I don't know. Somewhere along the line I got off the bus."

"Did you not like where it was going, or do you just not like busses?"

"It's hard to explain. I had this neighbor for a while, back in the world. His name was Leonard. I was thinking about him when I was down there in the rocks waiting for Blackbeard to show up. It's funny, some of the things you think about before a fight. He was one of these guys who spent his whole life climbing the ladder. He worked for some aerospace company and he used to leave the house at 4:30 in the morning. Most of the time he didn't get home until after nine. I talked to him once in a while but it was like listening to a promotional spot for his corporation. His wife Carol was a nice person but she was like a Stepford wife. Their house was impeccable. They were like a couple of cardboard cut-outs. For a while, I thought they were in the witness protection program, or maybe a couple of spies trying too hard to look normal. They invited us over a few times and I could never find any evidence that their place was lived in. He had two daughters, but I don't know if he was actually aware of it."

"They had this huge lawn and on the weekends, instead of doing things with his wife and kids, he would wheel out his ride-on mower and orbit his house like an obnoxious little green moon. All day Saturday. He must have gone over every square foot of that place at least twenty times. The noise almost drove me to murder. Sunday afternoon he would have at the flowerbeds with this rack of implements that he wheeled around in a little custom cart like a surgeon. They moved away after five or six years, to a bigger house with a bigger yard. A few years later I heard they found him dead on his lawn from a heart attack. I think I disliked that guy more than anyone I had ever met, and I've run into some real scumbags, believe me."

"I thought you were going to tell me you shot him off his lawnmower."

"No, but I really did think about it. It's not that he was a bad guy. I mean he was the model of the solid American citizen. I don't know. It's like he'd arrived at this place in his life where he had achieved success, and all he could think to do with it was to mow the damned lawn. I have this theory that houses are actually alien beings that capture humans and turn them into slaves."

"Are you planning to go back some time?"

"I don't think so. I can't handle the States anymore. There's no soul left in it.
It's starting to look like they're doing the 50's all over again, but in color this time.

It's just one endless advertising campaign. They've taken all the music I used to like and they're using it to sell cars."

"What happened to your wife?"

"We split up a long time ago. I think down deep she wanted a guy like the lawnmower man and that just isn't me. I don't know how it is for most people but it seems like they never ask why."

"I don't know if that's true, Jack. I think everyone has doubts."

"Yeah, but I'm not talking about having doubts. When it comes right down to it, it's all just a lot of smoke. Politics, religion, all of it. What did Shakespeare call it? A tale told by an idiot, full of sound and fury, signifying nothing."

"Did you read that or did you just hear it on the telly?"

"I saw it in a Superman comic book."

Annie laughed, and shook her head. "Surely you have to believe in something, Jack?"

"I believe in survival."

"That's a pretty dismal view of the world."

"Spoken by someone who was about to be sold off as a sex slave. I mean, have you taken a look at how most people live out here. Have you been to Bangladesh? Have you seen what's going on in Burma? People in the developed world are in denial about it. Civilization is just a thin veneer, Annie, and it looks to me like it's beginning to flake away. When we really start running out of oil and clean water, when we can't grow enough food to support the population, it's going to get ugly."

"Sure, I admit most of the world is a pretty sad mess, but you have to have hope. At least I do."

"OK. While you're hoping, hope I can find an Internet connection in Medan."

The truck dropped them off at a small building that looked like a post office. Rantauprapat was a gritty little town and there were a lot of men loitering on the streets doing nothing in particular. Surprisingly, there were also a lot of abandoned cars and too many kids running around half naked, without any kind of supervision. He hoped whatever malaise had

139

come over the place never reached Eidah's village. They couldn't find anyone who spoke English but they were able to get a couple of tickets to Medan by pointing to a map. Jack exchanged some of his Singapore dollars into rupiah. They had a little over an hour before the bus was scheduled to arrive. There was a street market nearby with fruit and coconuts spread out on blankets along the street. The milk tea sellers were performing their long pour. There were booths selling monkey meat, flying squirrel and even bats. Women were walking about with four-foot high stacks of baskets balanced on their heads. Jack and Annie picked up some clothes and toiletries and two small carrying bags. Jack couldn't find pants that would fit but he got a new shirt and a baseball cap. He also bought a cheap watch and a pocketknife. It had been a few days since he last shaved, but he decided to let it grow in for a while, despite the streaks of gray he didn't want to own up to. Annie had picked up some new clothes at the village but she wanted some things that looked a little less native. They were drawing more attention than they wanted and when they were finished at the market, they got a quick bite to eat and then tried to stay out of sight. Westerners were not a common sight in this part of the island and although they didn't feel threatened, not all of the faces were friendly.

The bus was an hour late. They picked seats about half way in. The rear was a smoking section and there was a bathroom. It only had a squat toilet and a basin and it smelled pretty foul. The driver had on a set of headphones and the music was turned up so loud they could hear it from their seats. The bus careened off down the road like they were in some kind of

140

death race. The road was a series of loops and switchbacks and the bus rocked so violently on its springs that they were sure it was going to tip over. It was pretty hard to have a conversation and impossible to sleep. Jack got tired of looking out the window and he turned to Annie.

"Do you have someone to contact when we get to Medan?"

"I just have to get over to the British Consulate. Why don't you come with me? We can probably upload the memory card from there."

"That wouldn't be my first choice."

"Why not?"

"Because I think my handler would be a little upset if I gave it over to you Brits without giving our guys the first shot at it."

"Oh, come on, Jack. Since when did you become a patriot?"

"I'm just making sure my bread stays buttered."

"Well, if this thing is as hot as you seem to think, you ought to be taking care of it the fastest way you can, instead of wandering all over some strange city trying to find an internet connection."

"If I can't find another way, I'll go to the consulate with you. It will probably be too late to go there today anyway. I'm hoping I can get this done tonight."

"Then what?"

"I'm not sure. I'll be contacting my handler for a way out. I don't have a passport so it may take a little creativity."

"Maybe my government could help. In light of your recent service to the Queen."

"What service?"

"Rescuing one of her loyal subjects from a fate worse than death. I'm sure I can get somebody to listen anyway."

"Thanks, but I'm a wanted man at the moment and your government may feel obliged to return me to Singapore to face a trial. That isn't going to happen."

"So what are you going to do? Run for the rest of your life?"

"The person they are looking for in Singapore doesn't exist any more. He never did exist. I'll go back to being who I was before, and get the hell out of Asia."

"So who are you really? Is your name really Jack?"

"Yup."

"Jack what?"

"Jack B. Nimble."

"Come on. How am I going to send you a Christmas card if I don't know your name?"

"You're an optimist. I go by Jack Lawrence."

"OK, but seriously. Where will you go?"

"Maybe Germany. I like it there, down by the Bodensee or maybe London."

"Do you know any people in those places?"

"I know some people in Europe."

"It sounds like a pretty lonely life, Jack."

"I guess, but in the end we're all alone anyway. We just pretend we're not."

13

The bus arrived at Amplas Station Central late in the afternoon. Again, they couldn't find anyone who could speak English. There were pay phones by the street-side exit and after some failed attempts Jack got through to Charlie.

"Where are you now, Jack?"

"We just arrived in Medan."

"Who's we?"

"I have the British woman with me. She making a call to her consulate and they'll be taking care of her."

"How much does she know?"

"She knows I'm dangerous to hang around with."

"OK, listen. My contact is arranging for one of his guys to meet you. I don't know what the agenda is. This thing has gone way up the tree. Do you understand?"

"Yeah, I get it."

"He will be there by tomorrow night. Just find a place to keep your head down and we'll get you out of there. Do you still have the memory card?"

"Yeah, I've got it. I still don't know if it's functional."

"Just keep it safe, Jack. Where will you stay tonight?"

"Don't know yet."

"Well, call me when you get checked in. And, Jack, it would be an excellent idea to see if you can get that sat-phone charged."

Annie was just hanging up when Jack walked over to her. "So are they sending a limo over for you?"

"No such luck. The consulate is only open until noon. I won't be able to get anything done until tomorrow morning."

"Well, I have to stay here tonight anyway. We may as well find a place to stay for the evening. Got any ideas?"

Annie pointed to a poster on the wall. The Novotel Soechi Medan looked like a half decent place. She jotted the name down on the back of a discarded ticket and they made their way out to the street. Jack flagged down one of the motorized becaks that was buzzing the station and Annie showed the driver the name of the hotel. He looked confused for a moment but then brightened up and indicated they should get in. The drivers were worse than in Bangkok. There were traffic signals but red lights didn't seem to mean anything. The city itself was sprawling. There was a huge cylindrical water tower that dominated the skyline and what looked like an enormous Mosque stood out among the mostly two and three story buildings. There was a lot of tin roof squalor but some of the city looked modern and interested in attracting tourists. There was the typical line-up of open shop fronts but here and there a Western business was tucked in with some of the more upscale stores. They passed a Dunkin Donuts and a Pizza Hut and reached the hotel after twenty minutes of breathing exhaust fumes.

"You're going to have to buy, Jack. I'll reimburse you as soon as I get some cash."

"Can we do a double or do you want your own room?"

"Don't worry. I'll try to control myself."

He lay down on the bed and closed his eyes. He was trying to figure out his next move and eventually he fell asleep. When he awoke it was dark and he checked the clock. It was after eight. Annie came out of the bathroom.

"Do you know how you're getting out of here yet, Jack?"

"They're sending someone to meet me. Tomorrow night sometime."

"Any more news about what's on the card?"

"Nope."

"Listen, I have an idea. How about we find out what's on the bloody thing first. I mean we ought to see if it works before you go to all the trouble. After we see it you can decide whether it's worth the risk of trying to use a public Internet connection."

"How do you propose we do that?"

"Well, back in the UK they have these picture stations in the camera stores. You can just put your memory card in and it will give you prints while you wait."

"Yeah well that doesn't sound like the safest thing to do either."

"It's better than hanging out in some Internet café. Come on, Jack. You know I'm right."

"The curiosity is killing you, isn't it?"

"No worse than you. I know you, Jack."

"You think so? How do you know we can even find one of these picture stations?"

"We don't know until we try."

145

"Jack looked at her for a moment. She was ambitious and her enthusiasm was starting to get the best of her. That could be dangerous. For a moment he considered not getting the prints made, but she was right about making sure the memory chip was still functional. He decided to go along with the idea. The first shopping area they found didn't have a photo store but after an hour of searching they found one with a Fuji film store and it had a photo station. At first it didn't look like the card was any good, but after some help from a clerk they got the images to appear. They popped up on the screen as a group of small thumbnails. It was impossible to make out any detail. Annie kept lookout and shielded the view of the machine while Jack finished the eight by ten prints. He put them into a folder as soon as they came out of the machine and they left the store quickly. Back at the hotel, Annie spread the photographs out on the bed.

"What the hell is all this, Jack? It looks like it's written in Korean."

Jack was looking at one of the prints, which had some kind of a diagram on it. "If I had to guess, I would say we are looking at the design of a small yield nuclear device. I can't read it either but the units are metric. This mass in the center of the device here is labelled PU-239, which is Plutonium. The whole thing looks like it could fit in the back of a van or small truck."

"Christ. How big would an explosion be from something like this?"

"I don't know. We were briefed about a year ago by the CIA on what they were calling a suitcase nuke. It used about 10kg of plutonium and the yield was supposed to be around one kiloton. There was a lot of worrying going on about supposed Russian suitcase nukes that had gone missing. It turns out those things have a pretty short shelf life. Maybe only six months or so because the plutonium core is constantly emitting radiation and is starts to loose its shape. To explode one of these things you have to compress the whole mass evenly with a shape charge. The consensus was that any of these things that were still out there would be useless. At least, for a nuclear explosion. You could still use the fuel for a dirty bomb, but plutonium isn't a great choice for that either."

"Well, this isn't any suitcase bomb. It's too big."

"Yeah it's too big and it is apparently Korean. For years the nightmare scenario has been that the North Koreans would build a small bomb and get it into the hands of a terrorist group. The worry was about something that they could put in a missile warhead but that is apparently pretty difficult to do. This looks like it could be plan 'B'."

"Do you think this thing has actually been built?"

"Beats the hell out of me, but apparently somebody thinks so."

"Let's go through the rest of these photos. Maybe we can find something else."

They split the pile in half and carefully examined each one.

"Maybe we could find someone who can read Korean."

"Slow down, Annie. If we are right about this, we need to get this information to somebody who can do something about it and the sooner the better. I don't want to be screwing around playing Sherlock Holmes with this crap."

"Right. Which is why I should take these photographs to the British Consulate as soon as possible. I wonder if I could reach someone tonight."

Jack studied her face for a moment. "We can talk about that, but let's see if there is anything else here we can figure out first."

They went over each remaining photograph. There were a few technical diagrams but it was mainly text, written in Korean. Jack put all of the photos back on the bed except one.

"Did you find something else?"

"I'm not sure but this page has two lines of numeric code. Charlie told me the initiation code and possibly an abort code could be on the card. This could be it. Do you have a pen?"

Annie found a pen and a note pad in the desk drawer. She handed them to Jack. "What are you doing?"

"I'm going to write down these numbers and memorize them in case we have a problem." Jack studied the numbers for a few moments and then he tore up the paper with the rest of the pad. He took the scraps into the bathroom and flushed them down the toilet.

"OK, Jack, so what are we going to do now?"

"Well, let's walk back the cat. We think the Chinese are involved in this thing because the guy I lifted this stuff from was PLA. The bomb, if that is what we are looking at, is Korean. No doubt North Korean. I think we can be pretty sure they didn't just give this thing away. They are in desperate need of cash and my guess is they wanted a pretty hefty price. I doubt that this Jemaah, whatever it is, group has the money, so if I had to guess I would say the

Chinese are trying to finance a little chaos without getting their hands dirty."

"Christ, if this gets out it's going to cause the biggest international incident since the cold war."

"Exactly. Which means right now a lot of people are trying very hard to find me."

"So what do you think we should do?"

"Well, we have a few choices, none of which are very good. We can stay here but we can't be sure we haven't been spotted. If they get to us in this room it could get dicey. I've only got four rounds in the Glock. On the other hand, if we move now it will probably buy us some time. We could probably move around the city for a few hours without raising too much attention but the later it gets, the more difficult it will be."

"Why don't we see if I can get the home number of someone at the consulate? If I can reach somebody maybe they can bring us in."

"That might work, but I don't think we should use this phone. We would need to locate a pay phone somewhere out of sight."

"What about your contact, Jack? Charlie you said? Maybe he could get you a number to call at your consulate."

"I could try it, but my government doesn't know me from Adam's house cat. I think you have a better shot at being listened to. I mean, think about it. All we have are some details of what we think is a Korean nuclear device. Somebody could have downloaded this stuff on the Internet for all we know. At least you are employed by your government and are known to be missing. You have a lot more credibility than I do. Besides, it's dangerous talking on an unencrypted line."

"Maybe we could find a charger for the satellite phone."

"Maybe, but I'm not real optimistic about that."

"Well, we have to do something."

Jack stood up and started pacing the room. He looked out the window at the street below and tried to decide their best move. Finally he turned to Annie."There's another possibility."

"What?"

"We could burn these photographs, smash the memory card and just lay low until the morning. At least we wouldn't be holding any evidence if they nab us."

"We also wouldn't have any proof."

They were interrupted by a soft knock on the door. Annie froze and was about to say something but Jack put his finger up to his lips. He put his arm around her and whispered in her ear.

"Douse the lights and go into the bathroom. Lie down in the tub and keep quiet."

She started to balk, but then she did what she was told. Jack checked chamber on the Glock and crept over next to the door. The knock came again and he could hear some muffled conversation. There were at least two of them.

He knew it wasn't the police. They would have announced themselves. After another few minutes he could hear a metallic scraping sound. He bent his knees and prepared himself. Whoever it was, it was taking them a long time to pick the lock. He waited. Finally there was a click and the door opened a few inches. From the light coming through the window by the street he could see a hand holding a pistol and then the door started to open. Jack stepped back and slammed his whole weight against the door. He could hear the sound of bone breaking and a sharp scream. He crouched and pulled the door open. There were two men standing in the hall and one down, still screaming. Jack put two rounds, center chest into the closest man. The other one opened fire but Jack dove across the doorway and kicked the door shut as he passed. He hit the floor just as rounds starting coming through the door and the adjoining wall. He could hear screaming and running. He pulled open the door again and saw two men retreating down the hallway, one slouched over and holding his arm. Jack hit the lights and ran into the bathroom.

"Get your stuff, Annie, and don't forget the prints."

They quickly gathered their belongings and Jack took a look out the door. There were some people peeking out of some of the other doors but no sign of the two men. He quickly searched the pockets of the man he had shot and took his pistol and his wallet. Then he grabbed Annie by the arm and they ran down the hall in the opposite direction. They reached the fire stairs and ran down the three flights to the street entrance. Jack opened the door just enough to stick his head out, and then they ran. They crossed the parking lot and up a small side street. Jack stopped and pulled Annie into an alley next to a garage and they waited. They were both too out of breath to talk. Jack watched the street. There was no sign of pursuit but there were sirens screaming and he could see flashing lights over in the direction of the hotel. He turned to Annie.

"Are you OK?"

She nodded, her chest still heaving. He handed her the Glock. "There are only two rounds left. If the police spot us, get rid of it. We need to get as far away from here as we can, but we can't run."

They walked down the alley and crossed another street. There were a lot of cars parked along both sides and no people. Jack kept them to the shadows and they ducked into a doorway when a police car came by with its lights flashing.

"Where are we going?"

"I don't have a clue. We can't risk another hotel."

"Well, we can't just walk all night."

"Just keep moving. I'm working on it."

They walked for another half hour, keeping to the back streets and ducking into the shadows when cars passed. Finally, Jack stopped. Annie looked around and gave him a questioning look. They were in front of a florist shop and there was a driveway along the side that curved behind the building. Jack took her by the arm and they walked behind the building. There were two vans parked in the back. Jack checked the rear door on one of the vans and it wasn't locked. He climbed in and motioned for Annie to follow.

"Why did you pick this place?"

"I wanted to find you someplace that smelled like Lotus blossoms."

"No, seriously, why here?"

"Because they usually don't keep anything in these trucks overnight and they are normally pretty clean inside. I figure we'll be all right here until first light. You should try to get some sleep."

"And then what?"

"It's time for us to split up, Annie. In the morning we'll find you a cab and get you over to your consulate. Take the pictures and have them contact MI6. Tell them we suspect there is a small yield nuclear weapon either on its way down here somewhere or maybe already here. They probably already know. Whatever you do, don't mention anything about the Chinese being involved in this. As far as you know this is a deal between the Koreans and Jemaah Islamiyah."

He handed her the wallet he had taken from the dead man at the hotel. "Don't let the local police get their hands on this, but see if you can get it to one of your spooks. It may give them a starting point to help track down the nuke."

"What shall I tell them about you?"

"Tell them I have the memory card and I'm trying to get it to my government."

"Why don't you come with me, Jack? I'm sure they will be willing to help you."

Jack looked at her and smiled. "You really believe that don't you?"

"Of course I bloody believe it. Why wouldn't they want to help you?"

"The problem with you is you still think we're the good guys."

"We are the good guys."

"There are no good guys, Annie. Not when it comes down to something like this. Your government, my government. They both may want me dead as much as the other people who are trying to find me. I am what is known as an expendable asset."

"Why would they want you dead?"

"Because they play this game at a whole different level than the rest of us. Think about it. What would happen if it got out that the

Chinese government was complicit in supplying a nuclear device to a terrorist group?"

"They would be condemned by virtually every nation in the world. It could even start a new war."

"Do you think my government wants that to happen? China virtually owns our national debt and we are one of their largest trading partners. We may not like each other but we are joined at the hip. There may be a lot of cat and mouse going on but nobody wants something like this to see the light of day. My guess is the Chinese are now trying just as hard as everyone else to locate this bomb and bury it. They also want to bury anyone who may even have a whiff of their involvement. It's too late for me but you can't let on you know anything about that. Do you understand?"

"What are you going to do?"

"I'm going to try to download this card and get it transmitted to Charlie. Then I have to figure a way out of here."

"I thought they were sending someone for you."

"They are. But I'm not going to hang around."

"Why not?"

"Because there's a better than even chance they're sending a magician."

"What do you mean, a magician?"

"Somebody who makes people disappear."

"You think Charlie would do that?"

"No, but this is out of his hands now. He told me so. He knows the score as well as I do and he knows I won't be trusting anyone they send for me."

"Jesus. What are you going to do?"

"What I always do. I'm going to try to stay alive."

14

Jack woke as soon as the sky began to lighten. Annie was still sleeping quietly. He looked at her and wondered how she was going to be treated when she got back in. Hopefully she was smart enough to keep her mouth shut. He had started to enjoy her company. She was so different than any of the other women he had been around and had more guts than a lot of the guys he knew. He quietly took stock of their situation. They were safe for the moment but they would have to move soon. The first priority was to get Annie to her consulate. Once she was safe he could go about trying to get off the island. He needed a charger for the sat-phone. Charlie would help him but he couldn't talk to him on an unencrypted line. The pistol Jack had picked up in the hotel hallway was a SIG P229 with a full 13 round mag. He had fired one once and it was a good weapon but there was no external safety. If you didn't shoot off an entire magazine it had to be manually de-cocked or you could blow your foot off. His Glock had too much history now and he needed to dump it. Annie stirred and opened her eyes. She was disoriented for a moment but then she realized where they were and she sat bolt upright and looked around. He looked at her and smiled.

"Good morning. I'm afraid the butler forgot the tea."

"I drink coffee in the morning, Jack. Strong enough to melt a spoon. What time is it?"

"It's six thirty. What time does the consulate open?"

"Not until 9:00. Do you think it's alright to stay here for a while?"

"We probably have another hour or so, but I'm not waiting."

"What are we going to do?"

"I'm going to hot-wire this thing and drive us somewhere else?"

"You're going to steal it?"

"Yeah why? Your conscience bother you?"

"No, but if you're going to steal something, let's go for a Lexus."

"Sorry, Your Majesty. You're going to have to travel steerage on this voyage."

"Where are we going?"

"Someplace as far from here as we can manage. Someplace we can find a cab when the time comes."

"How did they find us so fast, Jack? I mean this is a pretty big city."

"I don't know. Maybe they picked us up at the bus station and followed us to the hotel. Or maybe the hotel manager was paid off to make a call if he spotted us. We've shaken them off for the moment but you need to get to the consulate as soon as it opens."

He climbed into the front and pulled the wires down from under the dash. It took him just a few minutes to get the engine started. They drove slowly out of the driveway and down the street. He had no idea where they were but it didn't really matter. He wanted to get far away from the general area of the hotel. There were not that many places you could go early in the morning without being noticed. The transportation centers were no doubt being watched and the malls weren't open yet. After driving around for a half hour he found a restaurant in one of the better sections of the city that looked like it was serving breakfast. He pointed it out to Annie.

"I think that's got to be it. I don't want to be driving this truck around too much longer. It will probably be reported stolen soon."

Jack parked the van a few blocks away and wiped down everything he had touched. Annie took control of the rear view mirror and tried to make her hair look presentable. Finally, she gave up in disgust. Jack reached over and wiped her prints from the mirror. After she got out, he finished wiping the door handles. He pulled his cap down lower on his brow and took her by the arm. They walked away at an unhurried pace. On the way to the restaurant he found a dumpster near the street.

"Let me have the Glock, Annie. I don't think you are going to need it now and they'll be able to trace it to the dead guy back at the hotel."

He ejected the two remaining rounds and tossed them into the sewer. Then he wiped the gun down and threw it in the dumpster.

They picked a table in the back near the kitchen, with a good view of the front door. They ordered breakfast and then headed for the restrooms to clean up. Jack was on his second cup of coffee when Annie returned to the table.

"Look, Jack, I know you don't think you can trust anyone right now but you can trust me. I still may be able to help you. I don't know where they'll be sending me but you can reach me through the FCO. That's the Foreign & Commonwealth Office. Ask for Annie Blake. If you contact any British Embassy or Consulate they can get a message to me." She handed him a piece of paper. "This is the number of the

British Consulate here in Medan. I will probably be here a couple of days at least. Call me, even if you don't need help. Please, just let me know what's going on."

"OK, I'll call you if I get a chance. Look, make them put you up in the consulate if you can. At the very least, make sure they provide you with some security if you have to go to a commercial hotel. I don't think anyone will be looking for you but it's better not to take the chance."

"Is there anyone you want me to get in touch with, Jack? To let them know where you are? Somebody back in the States maybe?"

"Not really. Not anymore. But I'm going to give you a number to contact Charlie in case I don't make it. Let him know what's going on."

"OK, I'll do that for you, but I don't get you, Jack. How can somebody grow up in a place and not have a connection to at least somebody?"

Jack looked at her for a moment. He was pretty sure it was the last time he would ever see her and somehow it felt OK to talk about it. "Am I talking to Annie Blake or to Her Majesty's government?"

"This is just us, Jack, really."

The waitress brought over their food and he waited while she refilled their coffee cups. "I had a friend, Brad, from the war. I mean I had a lot of friends but we all went our separate ways. Brad was more than that. He was the guy I trusted to watch my back. We went through a lot together and he saved my ass more than once."

"Which war?"

"The first Gulf War. We spent a lot of time together on recon out in the desert. I ran into

159

some of your dad's guys out there. We had some fun, blowing stuff up and raising hell. They were a good bunch. I could never get used to them sitting down in the middle of all the shit and brewing a cup of tea. Brad was always half crazy. I mean, when it got serious he was right there with you but the rest of the time he was a wild man. I guess we were all a little nuts. The thing is, he never was able to adjust to being back in the world. He got pretty heavily into gambling. Mostly sports betting. He ended up owing some money to the wrong people. I bailed him out a few times but there's only so much you can do. I tried to get him to go to a gamblers anonymous meeting but he wouldn't do it. In the end, it all caught up with him."

"What happened?"

"They picked him up one night and started cutting his toes off with a pair of bolt cutters. He made it over to my house and I got him to the hospital. He stayed at my place for about a month after that but Melissa wasn't happy about it. When he had healed up I gave him some money and a plane ticket out to the West Coast."

"How bad off was he?"

"You mean physically? He had a slight limp after that, but that wasn't the worst of it. It did something to him inside. It's that moment you know? When you realize it could really happen to you. Up until then, I don't think he really believed it."

"What became of him?"

"He ended up in Las Vegas and got himself into some more trouble out there. Finally he came back. He still owed a lot of money. I tried to get him a job but he just couldn't concentrate on anything. I'm sure he had Post Traumatic

Stress Disorder but it was almost impossible to get any help for him. He tried to stay out of sight but eventually they caught up with him. Some hunters found him in a field with the back of his head blown off."

"Oh, god, I'm sorry, Jack."

"Everyone knew who did it but they weren't able to prove it. Brad was a nobody to them, and somebody was getting paid off. I raised a lot of hell about it but it didn't do me any good. I nearly got locked up for threatening the prosecutor."

"So what did you do?"

Jack was silent for a moment; it wasn't an easy thing for him to talk about. He looked at Annie for a few seconds, unable to begin.

"What is it, Jack?"

"I killed them all."

Annie seemed stunned. "You killed them? How?"

"I knew where the boss of the operation lived. I watched the house for a few weeks. I found out they had a meeting every Thursday morning. This guy had two daughters and his wife took them out to a dance class every Thursday and that's when they did their business. There were seven or eight guys. It varied from week to week. I got my hands on some C4. It isn't that hard if you know the right people. The night before, I broke into a FedEx office and stole a uniform and a truck. I hid the truck in an old barn overnight. The next morning I waited until I saw the wife's car leave the house and I drove up to the door. I had the package rigged to go off when I called a number on my cell phone. One of the thugs came to the door and I just handed him the box. I made him sign for it. I waited about thirty seconds and then I called the number. I was already out on the road. Every window on the first floor blew out and then the house collapsed in on itself and burned." He looked away, unable to continue.

After a time, Annie broke the silence. "Men like that, Jack, they always die bloody. If it hadn't been you it would have been someone else. They got what they deserved."

Jack started to say something but the waitress came over with the coffee pot and, when she had left, the moment had passed and he said no more. They finished their breakfast in silence. Annie didn't seem to know what to say and Jack was lost in his thoughts. At 9:00, Jack paid the bill and gave the hostess some money to arrange a cab. He didn't want Annie to be riding in an open becak. They waited inside until the cab pulled up to the curb. Jack walked her out and opened the door. He handed her some money.

"Take care of yourself, Annie. It's been a real hoot. You're a hell of a girl."

She put her arms around him and held him for a few moments. "Thanks, Jack. I know I can be a smart ass sometimes, but I realize what you did for me. I owe you." She pulled back and looked in his eyes for a moment, and then she kissed him on the lips.

Jack kissed her back and he suddenly realized how much he was going to miss her. He stood on the sidewalk and watched the cab drive away. Annie waved through the rear window. He suddenly felt very exposed and he started walking. They had passed a mall on the way over, and he headed toward it. He didn't like being out on the street but very few of the becak drivers spoke English and he didn't know the name of the mall anyway. It took about twenty minutes. He was hoping he would find a camera store and not have to go looking somewhere else.

The mall was open when he arrived but the individual stores didn't open until 10, so he went to the restroom and waited in one of the stalls. He had the memory card hidden in his collar again. He needed to buy a digital camera. It wasn't likely he could find a charger for the sat-phone but it was the only way he was going to contact Charlie, unless he had no other option. He was sure they would be listening to his phone conversations, especially when he didn't show up to meet their errand boy. He waited until ten after and then headed out into the mall. He found a Sony store just a few doors down from the rest room. The clerk spoke English and tried to sell him a top-of-the line camera but Jack settled on a low-end model. It didn't matter; he just needed to be sure the memory card was compatible. He showed the clerk the sat-phone but he didn't have a charger that would work with it. He did, however, know the location of an Internet café and he wrote the address down on a slip of paper. Jack checked out the rest of the stores, hoping to find something like a Radio Shack but he didn't have any luck. It was nearly eleven AM when he walked out into the parking lot.

Immediately he sensed someone was watching him. There were some people getting out of their cars and no one seemed to be paying any attention to him but it just felt wrong. He crossed the parking lot, heading for the street. There was a good bit of traffic and it took him a while to flag down a becak. He felt exposed and it was good to be moving again. He showed the driver the address of the Internet café and he made an abrupt u-turn, to the sound of honking horns and squealing brakes. There didn't seem to be anyone following, but it was so chaotic it was difficult to tell. It was a short ride. Jack paid the driver and headed for the café. Just before he reached the door someone grabbed his arm from behind and spun him around. Jack brought the edge of his hand down hard on the man's neck but before he could get away he felt a tremendous shock and his muscles locked up. The man with the stun gun grabbed him by the shirt as he crumpled to the ground. Someone hit him on the back of the head and everything went black.

15

It was a small room with one narrow window high up near the ceiling. It appeared to be a basement in the back of a small building. The window was covered with a security grate and the windowpanes were painted so he couldn't see outside. He tried the door but it was locked from the outside and was too solid to kick through. The walls were stone, covered in places with flaking stucco. There was a cot and a metal table with two chairs. A squat toilet occupied one corner and a rusted faucet protruded from the sidewall. The dripping water had carved a narrow channel in the stone floor. The air was damp and stale and the floor was crawling with roaches. Aside from the fact that he was locked up, they had not mistreated him. In fact they had gone out of their way to be polite. Shortly after locking him in the room they had returned with some food and bottled water. He wondered what would come next. They hadn't found the memory card in his shirt collar. He thought about Annie. He hoped she was able to get the photographs into the right hands. He guessed at some point they would kill him but his options were limited. He forced himself not to think about it.

It had been several hours and he was pacing the room for lack of anything else to do, when the door opened and a tall, brown-skinned man entered. Another man with an AK remained by the door. The one who entered was dressed in khaki slacks and a blue, madras, short sleeve shirt. He had thick, black hair and wore a close-cropped, dark beard. The wire-rimmed glasses he wore had thick lenses that made his eyes look overly large. He approached Jack cautiously and did not extend his hand.

"My name is Amir. My friends tell me you are called Jack. Is this correct?"

"Yeah, that's right."

"I would like to have a conversation with you, Jack. I do not wish to have armed men present while we talk. Will this be necessary?"

"That depends on what kind of conversation you're talking about, sport."

"We have no desire to harm you. We have been asked to hold you here for a short while. There are some other people who also wish to have a conversation with you and, for the moment at least, we are honoring their request. So, may we talk?"

"Sure, why not."

Amir took a seat at the table and Jack sat down across from him. Amir studied his face for a moment.

"You are American, and I would guess from your accent, East Coast, perhaps?"

"Canadian."

"I do not think this to be so, Jack."

Jack knew it really didn't matter now that the passport was gone. "I grew up in Baltimore."

"Yes, I have visited the Inner Harbor. They have improved the city quite a lot I would say."

"I haven't been back there in a long time. Are you from the States, Amir?"

"No, but I attended university there. Princeton and then Columbia in New York City. And where have you been spending your time?"

"Mostly Hong Kong, South Asia."

"So, which is it? CIA, military intelligence or something even more in the shadows?"

"I'm a contractor."

"Which means?"

"Which means I work free lance for anyone who wants to pay me."

"Doing what, please?"

"Mostly surveillance for corporate customers."

"Surveillance of what kind?"

"Usually we are paid to get evidence of industrial espionage, theft of trade secrets, that sort of thing."

"But you are ex-military."

"Yes, but not for a long time."

"Special Forces perhaps?"

"No."

"So you have chosen to live in this part of the world. For what reason?"

"It's where my work takes me."

"Do you miss the States?"

"Once in a while. I miss football."

"Did you play?"

"A little."

"College?"

"Yeah, Syracuse."

Amir smiled. "Yes, I know of this institution. The orange men. It is an interesting image." He sat back in his chair and regarded Jack for a moment. He tilted his head and smiled. "So, I will accept that some of what you have told me is true. At the moment, I do not need to press you on these issues. But let us put that aside for the moment. I would like to find out what you believe, Jack. You are a Christian I assume?"

"I was raised Christian. But I wouldn't call myself one now."

"And what would you call yourself?"

"A cynic."

"But cynic is not a religion."

"It is for me."

"So you believe in nothing?"

"I believe in survival."

"Survival for yourself, for your friends, for your countrymen, perhaps?"

"For everyone."

"Ah, so there is something. So you believe in survival for even the pitiful masses you find in this impoverished part of the world."

"Sure."

"And yet presumably you are paid by the very corporations which have contributed so greatly to the deplorable poverty we find here."

"Poverty was here long before there were American corporations."

"So you do not agree that some American companies are at least complicit in what you see here?"

"I think it comes down to greed, Amir. But not just by corporations. There has to be hands on both sides of the table."

"Yes, I admit that we have been our own worst enemy in this regard. We are working to change that."

"Who's we?"

"Let us say the people of my country."

"So are you a terrorist?"

"Here they are called freedom fighters. But, no, I am an economist."

"That's interesting. I'm sure everyone will be shocked to find I've been captured by a band of economists."

Amir laughed. "That is actually quite amusing, Jack. I am glad you have a sense of humor. Your present circumstances are a regrettable consequence related to your particular disposition on this island. I assure you I have taken no part in your imprisonment."

"So then why are you here?"

"I have been asked to talk to you. To gain what information I can. I believe they feel I can relate to a Westerner better than they. Actually, you are very lucky I was here. I was visiting some friends."

"Otherwise?"

"They would not be as amicable, I'm afraid. I told them I could get more information from you if you were well treated."

"So you are co-operating with them. That must mean at least that you support them."

"The only thing we have in common is that we both want the same result."

"Which is what?"

"Which is a country that is able to take hold of its rightful destiny and become properly compensated for its labor and resources. And to be free of the corrosive influence of powerful countries like yours."

"It seems to me you took advantage of some of the trappings of power in the US."

"Yes, I received an excellent education in your country. That does not obligate me to believe in your politics."

"So, tell me, Amir, do you feel some complicity for all of the innocent people who have been slaughtered by these terrorists you cooperate with."

"I do not support violence. There is no way to keep them from what they want to do. At least, not in the short run. Probably much longer."

"You could speak out about it."

"And so I do. But not in an armed camp. Are you a hero, Jack?"

"No."

"Nor am I."

"So, I don't suppose you would consider helping me get out of here."

"Actually, I would like to help you free yourself, but unfortunately that does not seem practical at the moment."

Jack sat back in his chair. He really wasn't interested in a philosophical debate but it was better than staring at the walls. It was also possible Amir could help him in some way. He decided to press the conversation.

"So I assume you are Muslim, Amir?"

"Yes."

"Are you a devout Muslim?"

"There are only devout Muslims."

"So you believe it is your obligation to kill the infidel?"

"Only if attacked by him."

"Your friends seem to believe it."

"If a Mullah told them it was Allah's will that they chop down trees, there would be no more forests."

"So they are being manipulated."

"Of course they are. But then are not your countrymen being manipulated?"

"How?"

"By allowing their government to wage an unjust occupation of a Muslim country."

"I wouldn't call it an occupation, and they are not being encouraged to fly planes into buildings."

"No, they only turn the other way when your forces drop bombs on Muslim women and children."

"We don't deliberately drop bombs on women and children."

"I am sure that is quite comforting to their families. But let us not dwell on those things that will make us angry. I would like you to understand what we see in this current state of the world. When it comes to natural resources, the world economy is becoming more and more a zero-sum game, Jack. Everyone knows the US is in Iraq and must stay there because the Middle East is where much of the oil is. It is becoming more and more expensive to sustain the kind of bloated lifestyle Americans have been enjoying. The balance of wealth in the world is shifting in many ways. We are trying to insure that some of it comes our way."

"By means of terror?"

"That depends on who you are talking to. For me, no. Aside from being brutal and immoral, I do not see it as necessary. In fact, I think it is greatly hindering the natural economic forces, which are currently working in our favor."

"It isn't going to stop unless people like you start speaking out against it."

"Come, Jack. You are not as naïve as all that. You know that it will stop, only when it is no longer effective. Your country once dropped two atomic bombs on cities in Japan, but has not used these weapons since. Why?"

"We haven't had cause to use them."

"I do not think that is correct, Jack. I think the answer is that using them would create more problems for your country than not using them. Still, you have the threat to use them and this is their only value now. The same is true of terrorism. As yet, it remains a useful weapon for some. Even when it is no longer used, the threat of its use will still provide leverage. It is the nature of power, is it not?"

171

Jack had to make a decision. Either Amir had skilfully turned the conversation to the subject of nuclear weapons as a ploy to find out what he knew, or it was the opening Jack needed to get his help. Something told him to go for it.

"What if I told you some of your countrymen had gotten their hands on one of these weapons, Amir? What if they planned to use it to advance their cause?"

"A nuclear weapon? I do not think so. Of which countrymen do you speak?"

"I am told they call themselves Jemaah Islamiyah."

"I can assure you, this group does not have the sophistication required to do such a thing."

"Maybe not by themselves. Maybe they have some help."

"Are you telling me this is so?"

"If it were so, would you be willing to do something to stop it?"

"I do not believe this is true. I must also ask how a 'contractor' as you describe yourself would have knowledge of this."

"Let's just say it is true, for a moment. What do you think the consequences would be if they used a nuclear weapon?"

"No good would come of such a thing. That is why I do not believe such a thing will happen."

"There is evidence that this is so."

"What evidence. Do you have such evidence?"

"No, but that is why I am being held."

"Have you seen such evidence?"

"I am told this evidence exists."

"Then for now, at least, I must refuse to believe you."

172

"Think about it, Amir. If it is true and these terrorists succeed in detonating a nuclear weapon down here, or anywhere else, there will be hell to pay. Whatever you are trying to accomplish peacefully will be lost."

"I admit this is a disturbing idea, Jack. I do not believe it, but I will attempt to see if there is any truth to it."

Amir looked at his watch. "I must depart now, Jack. Is there anything you would like me to tell them. Something to make it easier for you perhaps?"

"Just tell them I'm a tourist and I got lost in the jungle."

"The ones who have requested these people to hold you seem to know who you are. I am afraid it may not go well for you."

"Can you do anything, Amir?"

"I do not believe in torture, Jack. If I can imagine something, I will try. I give you my promise."

"I'm just trying to get home, Amir. I don't suppose you would agree not to mention our conversation about nuclear weapons."

"I do not believe there is a nuclear weapon. Therefore, I have no reason to mention it." This time Amir smiled and offered his hand. "Thank you for exchanging your thoughts with me. I found it very enjoyable."

He wasn't optimistic Amir was going to give him any help and it didn't look like anyone was going to send in the Marines. It really didn't make a lot of difference if Amir mentioned the nuclear weapon. They already knew he had seen the documents. Even if he claimed he couldn't read them, they wouldn't believe him. He decided his situation was too precarious to risk keeping the memory card intact. Flushing it

173

down the squat toilet was one option, but in the end he decided it would be better to damage it enough to make it useless but keep it so that he would have something to hand over if the going got tough. He removed it from his collar and placed it under the leg of the chair and then pushed down until he heard a crack. It was still wrapped in tape and it didn't really look any different on the outside. He flexed it between his fingers and it felt like it had broken almost in two. So much for getting the pictures to Charlie. It looked like the Brits were going to have to handle it. He put the card back in his collar.

The hours passed and he tired of pacing the room. It wasn't the first time he had been held for questioning. They had held him for a week in China and interrogated him before the rescue by Charlie and his boys. It got a little rough but not so bad he couldn't handle it. Of course that was just about some commercial CAD files. This time, there was a good chance they were less interested in what he knew than in shutting him up, permanently. They would want to know if the contents of the briefcase had been shown to anyone else. If the answer was yes, they would want to know who saw it. If he told them the CIA, there would be no reason to question him further and they would probably get it over quickly. If the answer was no, they would probably administer a lie detector test with a cattle prod or something equally entertaining. He decided to tell them the CIA had all of it. They would kill him either way. If they left his hands free, he would see if he could choke the life out of one of them before he went down.

Back in China, what had bothered him most were the long hours of isolation. He had passed the time by building a house in his mind, board by board from foundation to roof. After a while he lay back on the cot and started digging the foundation again. The light from the painted window began to fade and soon it was so dark he couldn't even see his hands. The only sound was the steady drip of the faucet. He didn't want to go to sleep and wake up in the total blackness not knowing where he was. Lying there in the absolute darkness with only the sound of dripping water was disorienting. The sound seemed to grow louder and he could hear it echo off of the stone walls. After a while he could almost tell where the walls were by listening carefully. The images in his mind were no longer confined and they seemed to fully occupy the space he was in, as if the room were a place in his imagination. In time, sleep took him. He dreamt about Angel.

16

He awoke, disoriented, a bright light shining in his face. He raised his hand to shield his eyes. For a moment he couldn't remember where he was.

"Right, that's him. Come with us, mate, were getting you out of here."

Someone grabbed him by the arm and led him out the door and up a flight of stairs. They exited through another door into a small courtyard and he was maneuvered under the eave of a low roof.

"Hold it here for a bit, mate." The voice was low and confident sounding, not quite a whisper. He couldn't quite make out the face. Jack didn't know who they were but they were getting him out and he just did what they said. There was not a lot of light but he could see some other forms moving quietly up an outside stairway leading to a second floor room. Suddenly there was the sound of breaking glass and a loud bang, followed by blinding flash of light and the sound of a door being kicked in. He could hear a struggle but no shots were fired. In a few seconds two men exited the room, each holding a captive in front of him. A third man followed. He heard the crackle of a radio.

"That's two of two subjects apprehended, no serious injuries. No one else present."

A reply came from another part of the compound. "Team two, all clear. The rest of the building is empty. That's Tony and Al heading for the street."

176

"Roger. Everyone to the rally point."

Jack followed the group of men through a door and down a dark corridor. A door opened to a side street where two unmarked vans were parked. The three holding the captives entered the side door of the first van. Two more followed. He was led to the second vehicle and he jumped into the back. They drove off quickly but without squealing their tires. A light came on from the front and he saw Annie grinning back at him.

"How many times do I need to rescue you Jack, before you learn to behave yourself."

He smiled back at her. "Can't a guy get a decent nights sleep around here?"

"That's Danny sitting next to you and Phil up here with me."

Phil turned and waved. Danny offered his hand and Jack gave it a shake.

"Thanks for the rescue. How the hell did you find me?"

"That wallet you gave me last night. It had this address in it."

Danny interrupted. "Actually we have been watching this place for a while now. It seemed like a good time to pay a visit."

"It worked for me. Thanks. What's been happening, Annie?"

"I'll fill you in once we get back to the consulate."

It was called an honorary consulate. The ambassador resided in Jakarta but there were honorary consulates in the larger cities in most foreign countries. For the most part they handled travel visas and a variety of business issues. It was a small compound with a gated parking area. Somewhere along the way the other van had taken a turn and they arrived alone. Annie led him into the rear door, while Phil and Danny drove off with the van. They entered what looked like a library. It was like walking back into the nineteenth century. There was a stuffed leopard standing in the corner, a lot of well-polished mahogany and a cabinet filled with vintage hunting rifles on one wall. Even the telephone was from another time. Jack was admiring the guns when a door opened and a balding, portly man in a slightly dishevelled, navy, three-piece suit entered. His tie was carelessly knotted and slightly askew. He nodded to Annie and made his way over to where Jack was standing. His face was fleshy and red like someone who had seen the bottom of too many bottles. It was the face of a bureaucrat, except for the eyes. The eyes were intelligent and they didn't look away. Jack had met men like this before. In many ways, they were more dangerous than the physically imposing men they often sent to their deaths.

"Trevor Martin", he said, extending a clammy hand. "And you would be Jack Lawrence."

Jack nodded and shook his hand. Trevor's face showed no emotion but his eyes searched Jack's face for a moment like a police detective, trying to sniff out a lie. Jack knew he had already come to some conclusion. Finally, the man turned and took a seat behind the desk. He motioned for Jack to sit. Annie joined him. He examined some papers in silence for a moment. It was another way men like this had of making sure you knew who was calling the shots. Finally, he spoke.

"Quite a little adventure you've been having for yourself I hear."

"Yeah, it's been a little interesting lately."

"Interesting indeed. In any case I will get to the point. Miss Blake was kind enough to provide us with the photographs you acquired and she filled us in some of the details of your escape. She tells me you have destroyed the memory device. Is that so?"

"Yes."

"In any case, we are grateful to you on several levels, Mr. Lawrence."

Jack nodded.

"First, let me tell you that we have shared this information with your government and they are working with us on this."

Annie interrupted. "I contacted Charlie. He's up to speed except for your whereabouts. You'll have a chance to call him later."

Trevor continued. "Needless to say, this incident is on the top of everyone's list and there are a lot of hands at work. We don't normally share the kind of information I am about to divulge, particularly to a foreign national. However, in light of the unique circumstances surrounding these events and your involvement to date, I am going to brief you on what is known so far. We believe there may still be a part for you to play in this. I don't think I need to impress on you the sensitivity of this information and the absolute need for secrecy. I must ask for your word that you will not divulge any of what I am about to tell you to anyone. Your government is in possession of the same information we have so there is no need to communicate it with them. Do I have your agreement?"

"I guess I don't really see the need for me to be involved in this thing now. It seems like you have plenty of people to chase it down."

"That is true. There may well be no need for further involvement on your part but we can foresee a possibility that you could be of some help to us. On a voluntary basis, of course. Do I have your agreement to keep this in confidence?"

"Yes."

Trevor nodded and continued. "About three months ago, we received intelligence that a North Korean ship sailing out of the port of Nampo might be carrying medium range missile components. We were obviously concerned and, in conjunction with your country's naval forces, we monitored the transit of the ship. It sailed down the coast, holding to Chinese territorial waters and we were unable to board her. We did, however, manage a clandestine fly-over and to our alarm, detected the possible presence of fissile materials. The readings were somewhat ambiguous but it gave us enough justification to board her once she sailed into international waters. Depending on the type of material, these things can be devilishly difficult to detect, at least at any distance. A joint taskforce was assembled and we were prepared to board the ship in the South China Sea. Unfortunately, our plans were interrupted by that bloody typhoon and we were not able to initiate the mission. Worse than that, we lost track of the ship. We actually thought if might have been lost in the storm, until it turned up two weeks later in Da Nang. By the time we were able to get to it, whatever was on board had been off-loaded. The ship was empty."

Trevor paused for a moment, letting the point sink in. Finally, he continued.

"Needless to say we have been working vigorously to track down the cargo. We did actually locate at least some of the missile components on a fishing vessel preparing to embark for Yemen. The documents you provided confirm that there were more, but we have not had success in locating these, to date. Alarmingly, we have also not been able to find any sign of the fissile materials we suspected and, until those photographs surfaced, we were beginning to think we had been mistaken. I'm sure I don't need to impress upon you the kind of disaster we could be facing. We have got to find this thing, if it exists. At this point the consensus is this is a real weapon and it will at some point be detonated. When and where is anyone's guess. Indonesia alone is comprised of some seventeen thousand islands, Mr. Lawrence. Six thousand are inhabited. On top of that, there are many thousands of sheltered coves and inlets where a small ship could gain entry. Without some damned good intelligence, our chances of finding this thing quickly are not good. It could be anywhere in the region."

"How much damage would it do?"

"That depends on many variables. The documents do not tell us how much radioactive material is involved, but the design suggests it could be on the order of fifty or sixty kilograms. If this is so, it could produce an explosion on the order of the Hiroshima bomb. This, of course, assumes that the weapon fires properly. The firing mechanisms for these types of weapons are extremely complex and require frequent maintenance. The longer the maintenance is delayed, the greater the chances of a failed detonation. Also, at least in the case of this weapon, the firing mechanism requires an initiation code in order to prevent accidental or unauthorized use of the device. My people tell me it is virtually impossible to detonate a device like this without the proper code. The code number was included in the documents you photographed. Since you have destroyed the memory card, there is some question as to whether this weapon is useable in its current state. We do not know how easy it would be to re-obtain the code or how long it would take to get it into the hands of the people in possession of this weapon."

Trevor paused again and this time he walked over to a small table holding a decanter and some glasses. He poured himself a drink and held the glass up. "Scotch?"

Jack and Annie both declined.

Trevor returned to the desk and opened a folder. He removed a photograph and handed it to Jack. "Do you know this individual, Mr. Lawrence?"

Jack looked at the picture. "Yes. His name is Amir. I talked to him yesterday."

"What can you tell me about him?"

"Only what he told me. I'm not sure how much of it is the truth. He claims to be an economist, educated in the States. He speaks English well and seems to be on friendly terms with the people who were holding me. He also claims to have some knowledge of the Jemaah Islamiyah group."

"Do you believe he is working with any terrorist organizations in Indonesia or elsewhere?"

"He claims not to support terror. He comes off as a nationalist, although he told me he supports the same goals as these terrorist groups. He claims not to support their methods."

"Anything else?"

"Only that I got the feeling he was being up-front with me for the most part. Either that or he is a very skilled interrogator. The subject of a terrorist group with a nuclear weapon came up and he seemed disturbed by the idea."

Trevor raised his eyebrows, but otherwise his expression did not change. "And how did that subject come up?"

"We got into a discussion about the use of power. He mentioned our use of the bomb against Japan. I brought up the possibility that a terrorist group could get their hands on a small nuke."

"And he reacted negatively?"

"Yes. Actually he refused to accept the possibility. He claimed it would do irreparable harm to the goals of his country. He also did not think the Jemaah Islamiyah was sophisticated enough to pull it off."

"Interesting. The man's name is Amir Alatas and he is currently in our custody. He has been briefly interrogated and essentially he has given us the same information as you have just related. We aren't sure what to make of him yet. He told us he had met you and that he was trying to find a way to help you when he was picked up."

"Was he tortured?"

"Of course not. We do not engage in torture. I can tell you he is quite afraid that we might, however, which may or may not be to our advantage. We do not have much background on Mr. Alatas. Our current best guess is that he is acting as an unofficial economic liaison between his government and some of the terrorist groups in the region. He seems to have some connections with individuals in some of these groups. Just how, we are not sure. We suspect there may be family connections. He claims to be engaged in explaining the economic repercussions of terrorist activities in an attempt to dissuade these groups from further harming the economy of Indonesia. The recent bombing in Bali is a prime example. It did tremendous harm to the tourism industry down here. We frankly think he is wasting his time, if that is his agenda. These people value their Muslim faith far more than their attachment to any secular government."

"So what do you plan to do with him?"

"That is where we think you may help us, Jack. If you are willing, of course. We cannot force you to do anything, nor would we wish to do so. One hopes your loyalty to your country or, if not that, at least on humanitarian grounds, means you may be willing to expose yourself to some further risk to help us find this weapon so it can be disabled or destroyed."

Jack sat silent for a few moments. Trevor got up and topped off his drink. Annie had remained quiet through the entire conversation, but now she was searching Jack's face for a reaction. He hadn't been counting on any kind of thanks or reward. All he wanted was secure transportation off of the island. He had already had enough drama to last him for the rest of his life. It had even crossed his mind that Charlie might need a partner in his fishing tackle business back in the States. The last thing he wanted was any more to do with a nuclear weapon, or a terrorist group or anything else in Asia for that matter. Still, his curiosity was aroused and he decided to listen to Trevor's idea.

"Just what do you have in mind?"

"We were thinking a rescue might be in order. We, that is, both of our governments, have almost nothing in the way of human intelligence assets in Indonesia. At least, none within any of these terrorist organizations. If this man, Amir, has connections and can be persuaded to help us, it may be our best hope of finding this weapon. It occurred to us that were you to rescue this man, it might be enough to gain his confidence. Then, if he really is opposed to the use of this weapon, you may be able to convince him to help us find it."

"What kind of a rescue were you thinking about?"

"Well, at the moment he doesn't know who is holding him. If he knew the British Government was holding him, he would be suspicious of any rescue attempt by a Westerner. We thought we might play on his fears a short while longer. Let him think that the people holding him are mercenaries and not subject to any laws prohibiting torture. We might go so far as to rough him up a little. Nothing serious. We would not harm him in any way. At some point, we would orchestrate some theatrics. We haven't really played it all out yet. We thought perhaps if you showed up on the scene as some kind of person of authority. Demand his immediate release. That sort of thing."

"And then what?"

"And then get him to see what he can find out for us. Anything would be better than what we have now. If we had some idea of what part of the region we should be looking in, or which group has the weapon, that alone would be of great help. If we could find out what the intended target is, that would be even better. Anything on the timing of the attack or the means of delivery. Anything at all to get us headed in the right direction. Right now, we are at an almost total loss. Miss Blake has already agreed to work with you, should you agree to help us. She would act as your liaison with our government."

"How do you know he would be willing to help?"

"We don't. I'm afraid we are grasping at straws here."

"What about any involvement by the Chinese?"

"That, of course, is another area we are pursuing vigorously. We are in current discussions with the Chinese government at the highest levels. I cannot comment on these discussions except to say they strenuously deny any involvement in a terrorist plot of any kind and have, in fact, offered whatever assistance they can provide."

"Do you believe them?"

"We haven't ruled anything out but we feel it would be highly unlikely they would try something as foolish as this. Our current thinking is that, if there was any involvement at all, it may have been by a person or persons acting independently and without government sanction. Nothing else makes sense under the circumstances. Actually, if it were some kind of plot by the Chinese government it would be good news in a way. They certainly wouldn't risk following through with anything now that we are onto it. In addition, I can tell you there has been some back channel information regarding some sort of shakeup in the Second Department in Beijing. The Second Department being their intelligence apparatus. We have no further details at the moment. Whether or not it is related to this weapon is unknown."

Jack sat back and examined Trevor's face for a moment. It always amazed him how people like Trevor could sit back so calmly, drinking a scotch in a comfortable office while they asked people to risk their lives. He wondered if Trevor had ever actually ever had to brave anything worse than the morning commute. Finally Jack spoke.

"You guys knew this thing was going to happen eventually, didn't you?"

Trevor stared at him for a moment before answering. "We have always seen is as a possible if not necessarily likely event."

"And yet, in the end, it comes down to asking some civilian to risk torture and death to bail you out."

Trevor paused for a moment, staring off into a corner of the room. "That, of course, is one way of looking at things, Mr. Lawrence. I would be the first to admit that our efforts to infiltrate and gain intelligence from these groups have been almost entirely fruitless. We have been slow to understand the nature of the threat that now faces us. The most effective weapon at our disposal in the intelligence game is, and has always been, money. Somewhere, no matter how dedicated the organization, no matter how egregious the real or perceived grievance, there has always been someone we could turn with the right amount of cash. Surprisingly little, in many instances. This tiger we are hunting now is of an entirely different stripe. The most dangerous man in the world is the man who believes he is following orders from God with the promise of eternal reward. There is little one can offer or threaten to take away. Particularly if he has little or nothing to begin with."

"So why don't you get one of your spooks to rescue Amir. Somebody trained to do this sort of thing?"

"If you do not agree to help us in this, that is precisely what we will do, among many other ongoing efforts. We are asking you because you seem to have established a rapport with this man and because time is obviously of the essence. We understand you have been through a lot, Mr. Lawrence. We also fully understand your reticence in becoming further involved. We have been provided with your military records and what little additional information your government has in your file. You have an exemplary record, albeit with a tendency toward insubordination or at least, shall we say, toward speaking your mind. The willingness to speak truth to power is an admirable quality in a man. It is not usually a recipe for success or career advancement. That aside, we have no doubt that you can perform the task we are asking of you and perform it well. I would add just one more thing. There are no safe havens in the world we currently inhabit, as witness the events of nine-eleven. This is not some abstract, ideological struggle we are engaged in. These people aim to destroy our democratic way of life and replace it with a theocracy of the darkest, most repressive kind. You may be safely out of the way when, and if, this thing is detonated, but make no mistake, if we do not stop them here, now, we will eventually fight them in our own gardens."

Jack was barely listening. His mind had drifted back to that hotel room in Singapore and the vision of Angel lying lifeless on that bed. He looked over at Annie again and took in the expression on her face. He could see the courage and determination there, and it touched him somehow. She was young and naïve and full of righteous fire. She was Joan of Arc standing in front of her army, ready to offer up her life for her beliefs. For Jack, it had slowly turned into a different calculation. Someone involved in this thing had killed Angel. He really didn't believe he had a chance in hell to find the weapon, but if there was a chance it could lead him to Angel's killer, that would be reason enough. Working with the Brits would give him cover. What he needed most was the freedom to move around the region, and that would require a passport.

"Let's say I agree to do this. How am I supposed to get around? I don't even have a passport."

"We will provide you with suitable documents, whatever funds you require and whatever support we may otherwise be able to render. Our people will get your photograph when we are finished here. I'm afraid I cannot offer you any financial remuneration for what we are asking. I can only tell you that if you are able to help us locate and neutralize this weapon, you would have the sincerest gratitude of Her Majesty's government and no doubt of your own. I am certain it would open many doors for you."

"You mean if I survive."

Trevor studied his face for a moment. "Let us be direct with each other here, Mr. Lawrence. We are aware that what we are asking you to do could be dangerous in the extreme. If you are apprehended by Jemaah Islamiyah or any of the other terrorist groups, which may be involved, you will no doubt be treated badly. Possibly tortured and most probably executed. I would like to tell you that this concerns us greatly, but the truth of the matter is that the fate of any one individual pales in comparison to the catastrophe that would result from the detonation of this weapon. We will provide you with any kind of assistance we can manage. We have assembled a quick reaction force that, as of this morning, will be standing at the ready to deploy anywhere in the region at a moment's notice. If you are captured, we will make every effort to affect your release, by whatever means necessary. Beyond that, we would be trusting to your skills, which you have thus far ably demonstrated and, I am afraid, to your luck."

Jack remained silent. There were so many conflicting thoughts running through his mind, he was having trouble sorting it all out.

"I can understand your reticence, Mr. Lawrence. To be truthful, if the shoe were on the other foot, I don't know how I would react. I am not, by nature, a brave man. Lately, I seem to specialize in asking other, braver men to do things that would frankly get my knees to wobbling. In the end I am just a clerk, I'm afraid. I have often wished that I could have the courage to do what men like you are able to do. I suppose we are all born to our mission in life. As humble as that may be. If you choose to walk away from this, I can assure you there will be no consequences. At least, none that we would initiate. We would assure you safe passage out of Indonesia. Again, I can only reiterate our desperate need for your help and offer the opportunity to save, perhaps, thousands of lives. Whatever your decision, I am afraid I must ask for it now. We do not have the luxury of time."

Jack looked over at Annie again and he could see her pleading with him with her eyes. He stared at her for a moment before answering. "OK. I'll do what I can."

Trevor came around from behind the desk. He was smiling for the first time since he entered the room. He offered Jack his hand again. "That's a good lad. I knew I wasn't wrong about you. Let's get together tomorrow morning and orchestrate a rescue for Mr. Alatas?"

17

Jack and Annie were both given guest rooms at the consulate that evening. Jack was too exhausted to enjoy the monogrammed sheets. There was an elegant dining room on the main floor, obviously meant for entertaining VIPs. When Jack went down to get breakfast in the morning, a man was sitting at the table reading a newspaper. Jack hadn't seen him before. He wondered where Annie had gone. The man stood and offered Jack his hand. He was young, with a bad haircut and a boyish look about him, like a schoolboy grown suddenly larger. He looked at Jack briefly and then looked away.

"Jerry Eastland. I expect you would be Jack."

Jack shook his hand and nodded.

"There's some eggs and what-not under all these tin hats. Help yourself. Complements of the Queen."

Jack started piling food on his plate. He was starving and he took some of everything. Jerry watched him, smiling.

"Bit hungry, are we?"

Jack smiled, a little sheepishly. "It's been a while since the Queen cooked me breakfast."

"Trevor asked me to get with you this morning. I don't want to spoil your meal but we need to have a little chat about limited yield nuclear devices. Shall I wait until you're finished?"

"No, go ahead, but I'm not all that technical. If you're counting on me to take care of this thing we're all in deep shit."

Jerry laughed."Well, we all fervently hope that won't occur. But just in case you happen to find this thing lying under a bed somewhere, it would be important that you know a little about it. I'll try to keep it as straight-forward as I can."

"Be my guest."

Jerry slid his chair over next to Jack and opened a folder on the table. "You've seen these before. These are the photocopies of the materials you found. As you have correctly surmised, these are indeed diagrams of a low-yield fission type nuclear weapon. It is a single stage, asymmetrical Pit design. In this case the Pit is machined from Plutonium 239. The critical mass of a nuclear weapon is not so much a function of the amount of fissile material, although a minimum mass is required and this ultimately determines its yield, at least in part. The critical mass is a function of the amount of fissile material in a confined shape sufficiently dense to cause a chain reaction. In the case of weapons like this one, there is just less than a critical mass in the Pit. When it is evenly compressed by a controlled conventional explosive charge, it attains critical mass and we get a nasty little mushroom cloud, thank you very much. With me so far?"

"Yeah, I understand that part."

"As it turns out, fortunately for us all I might add, we know a little bit about this particular piece of work. It is actually an old Soviet era design with some significant upgrades. How the Koreans got their hands on this little bundle of joy is something we are quite interested in finding out, but it is obviously not our most pressing concern. You see this little box on the diagram? It is called the PAL and, believe me, it is our best Pal at the moment. PAL stands for permissive action link. It is an interlock device that prevents unauthorized or accidental detonation of the device. We think this is the equivalent of one of your Cat F Pals, which is a fairly recent evolution of the design. Also very interesting. It is basically an encrypted electro-mechanical arming switch. It requires a twelve digit arming code. Its normal use is in a bomb or missile system, but one supposes they used what they could get their hands on here."

Jack interrupted. "I saw some numbers in the diagrams when we first copied them. I assumed it was an arming code and maybe an abort code."

"You were correct about the arming code. I'll get to the other number in a moment. This is a strong link/weak link design. The weak link is environmental and it will prevent the weapon from detonating if it is tampered with or does not experience its design parameters. For instance, in a missile or bomb, the weak link would require a predefined, minimum amount of acceleration in order to activate. That way, if you were to accidentally drop it on the floor, the conditions would not be met and the device would not trigger. Some of these have what is known as a violent option, which means if an attempt is made to bypass the link, a small internal explosion occurs which distorts the shape of the Pit and makes the device inoperable, until the Pit is removed and re-machined. We think this device could incorporate that technology but we are not completely sure. Also, if the device were exposed to too much heat or moisture, for example, it would not trigger. If there were a fire or if the device fell into the ocean, it would not go off unless programmed to accept those conditions. The triggering mechanism is enclosed in a very tough, tamper resistant skin. If the skin is breached in any way, the device will not operate. It is virtually impossible to bypass the system without making it inoperable. Very good news for us at the moment, unless of course the people in possession of this device also have the arming code. There seems to be some doubt on that point. This device also incorporates a secondary security device. Your people told us that you found a retinal scanner along with these documents. It appears that, in addition to the arming code, only one designated person is capable of initiating the device. It seems like a prudent arrangement under the circumstances. We are assuming from the information we have been given, whomever has the weapon is now also in possession of the scanner."

Jack nodded his head

Jerry continued. "Just to be done with the technical points, the strong link is a motor-driven, rotary safety switch that allows the trigger to be electrically activated. This is done through a bank of capacitors that are charged by the on-board batteries if, and only if, the correct code is entered." Jerry sat back and looked at Jack, a slight smile on his face. "Any questions?"

Jack looked down at his coffee cup. He was silent for a few moments. "What's the time delay?"

Jerry's expression turned serious. "I'm afraid we don't know."

Jack looked at him in disbelief. "You don't know?"

"I'm afraid not."

"Can you find out?"

"I don't know that either. Listen, you must understand these triggering mechanisms are designed to be mounted on an active weapon. They are armed just prior to detonation. A bomb, for instance, is armed just prior to release. The delay is normally a matter of seconds or minutes, longer in a missile warhead, depending on its range. We just don't know."

"You mean to tell me once some idiot enters the arming code into this thing he has just a few seconds to live? Put your head between your legs and kiss your ass goodbye?"

Jerry laughed again."We don't think so, actually. It is possible there is a predefined delay built into the trigger. The documents are not clear on this point. It seems likely to us that, as this device was designed for some clandestine use, the desired delay period would be manually entered after the arming code." He pointed to the diagram of the display panel. "You see this small window here? This is a digital clock display. We are fairly certain that, once the arming code is entered, the device will sit idle until a delay interval is manually entered."

Jack shook his head. "How much of a delay can be programmed in?"

"Again, this is only a guess but, considering the projected yield of this weapon, we think anything up to twenty-four hours, but it is only a guess. Of course, we are presumably dealing with terrorists here. They may like the idea of turning themselves into sub-atomic particles. The diagram seems to show a split window with three groups of two digits. We believe this would represent hours in the first window, minutes in the second, and seconds in the third."

"Christ, this gets better all the time."

Jerry nodded his head. "I'm afraid that's not the worst of it, Jack. You remember the other number? The one you thought was an abort code?"

"Yeah?"

"Well, I'm sorry to say there is no abort code. Once the proper coded number is entered, this device will detonate after its predetermined or probably, in this case, programmed delay time. There is virtually nothing that can stop the sequence once that occurs."

"What about the safety interlocks you mentioned, like for fire and water?"

"They only prevent the sequence from starting. Once it starts, you could drop the thing straight into hell and it would go off on schedule."

"Well, what was the other number for then?"

"That's what is known as the training key. Normally these devises are incorporated into a missile or bomb system. These systems are made intentionally complex to prevent accidental or otherwise unintended launch. The people who are in charge of these weapons must continually train in the launch procedures to assure they will be able to function if they are ever required to launch. Otherwise they could lock up under the stress. The training key allows the arming sequence to initiate and the drill to be repeatedly practiced. Everything operates the same except that when the sequence is completed, nothing happens. Someone once told me the word 'bang' appears in the window but I personally doubt it. We really don't know why they would need a training key for this device, but as I said earlier, one assumes they used an off-the-shelf trigger, and this is what they ended up with."

The door opened and Trevor entered the room, followed by Annie. She smiled at Jack.

"Have you finished your briefing, Jerry?" Trevor asked.

"Almost done."

"I'm afraid I need to steal Jack away from you for a short time. Would you mind finishing up a little later? We shouldn't be more than an hour or so."

Annie drove him to the house in a rented Camry and waited in the car. It was a pretty tough neighborhood and Jack made sure the car was watched while he was inside. Danny took him to a room in the back of the house.

"Tony and Al are talking to him now. He's pretty shook up. They know what to expect so don't worry about hurting their feelings. Good luck, mate."

When Jack opened the door, one of the men was standing over Amir with a nightstick in his hand. He was slapping it, loudly, against the table. Amir wasn't wearing his glasses and he didn't recognize Jack when he entered. He looked terrified. They had one of his hands cuffed to the table leg and it prevented him from sitting up straight. He was rocking back and forth and moaning softly as they fired questions at him. Jack burst into the room.

"What the fuck is going on here? What are you doing to this man?"

Tony and Al backed away, looking like they had just been caught with their hands in the cookie jar.

"We have been instructed to question him."

"Is that what the club is for? I know this man. This man is not a terrorist."

Amir looked at him, squinting his eyes to make out his face. "Jack? Is that you?"

"Have these men mistreated you, Amir?"

"No. I mean, not yet."

"We haven't touched him. Tell him!"

"I want you to release this man immediately. If I find out he's been mistreated in any way, it will be your ass. Do you understand?"

They quickly removed the handcuffs and Jack took Amir by the arm.

"Come with me, Amir. I'm taking you out of here."

He walked Amir quickly through the house and out to the car. He opened the rear door and helped Amir get in. Amir found his glasses in his shirt pocket and put them on while Jack slid into the driver's seat. He started the car and drove away.

"Are you sure you're OK, Amir? I can get you medical assistance if you need it."

"No, I was extremely frightened but I was not harmed. Who are those men?"

"They are counter intelligence operatives. They work for my agency. I apologize for the way you were treated. It is not how things are supposed to be done. By the way, this is my friend Annie."

Annie reached over the seat and shook Amir's hand.

"I'm glad I was able to get to you in time, Amir. Everyone is in a panic down here and I'm afraid it could get a little rough. Is there someplace we can go to talk?"

Amir looked around. "Not in this area, Jack. It would not be good for me to be seen with you. I hope you understand."

"Sure. Listen, we have a room at a hotel downtown. Can we go there and talk for a little while?"

"Certainly. And thank you for helping me. Perhaps you will not believe me, but I was attempting to have you released when I myself was taken. I'm glad you were able to get away unharmed."

"We'll call it even, Amir. But is extremely important that we talk now. It's in your interest as well as mine."

They had taken a room in the Hotel Ankasa earlier in the day and put enough personal items around to make it look like they had been there for a while. Amir sat on the small couch and Annie joined him. Jack pulled up a chair facing Amir.

"Are you sure you're OK. Is there anything I can get you? A drink maybe."

"Thank you. I do not drink. Perhaps some water."

Annie opened the mini-bar and handed Amir a bottle of water. Jack leaned forward.

"Listen, Amir, I know you've been through a tough time, but I am hoping you will be willing to help us. You remember our conversation. About the nuclear device?"

"Yes, of course."

"Well, we are now certain a device exists and is somewhere in the region. We believe an attack is being planned. I'm hoping you may be able to help us find it."

"As I told you before, Jack, I do not believe this to be true."

Jack reached over to the bedside table and picked up a manila folder. He opened it and showed the photograph to Amir. "This photograph shows the design of the weapon we are looking for. It was found, along with other documents that indicate an attack is being planned."

"Found by whom, please?"

"I found them."

"What attack? Where would such an attack occur?"

"We don't know. That is why we need your help."

"But I have explained to you, I know nothing of such a thing."

Jack paused for a moment. "I'm sure you understand what's at stake here, Amir. If we are right and this weapon is used, it will be a disaster for all of us. Especially for your country. You have to believe that."

"All you show me is a photograph. Why should I believe you are telling me the truth?"

"It isn't just the photograph, Amir. I also found a retinal scanning device along with the papers. It's something needed to activate the weapon."

"You know about such things? How do you know about such things?"

"I examined it myself."

"You are sure? It could have been something else. Something quite innocent."

"I tried it myself. It wasn't the first time I've had a retinal scan. I know what they look like."

Amir was silent for a while. Finally, he looked at Jack. "Even so, such a thing must have many uses. How do you know it is for a nuclear weapon?"

"It was with the documents that described the weapon. Look, Amir, I don't know what else I can do to convince you. We are facing a disaster here."

"Perhaps, or possibly this is merely an elaborate ruse."

"Why would I bother trying to trick you?"

"Perhaps you are interested in locating members of the so-called terrorist organizations we discussed. Perhaps this is merely a ploy to see if I will lead you to them."

"I don't know how I can convince you, Amir. I can only tell you that the reason I was being held was because your people knew I had these photographs."

"They are not my people. I am not a terrorist."

"Yes. I'm sorry. I believe what you are telling me is true. However, I also believe you know some people in these groups. I am not asking you to betray anyone. I am not asking you for names. It would have been easy to let those men beat you until you told them everything you know. I didn't want that to happen to you. All I am asking is that you do whatever you can to find out if there is a weapon in the hands of one of these groups and if so, where it is."

"What makes you think it would be anywhere in Indonesia at all?"

"We are not sure of anything at this point." Jack said.

Amir stared at the rug. He was silent for what seemed like a long while, but Jack decided to give him some time. Annie got up and went into the bathroom. Finally Amir spoke.

"Why are you involved with this, Jack, if you are not employed by your government?"

"I didn't choose to be here, Amir. I found the diagrams and the retinal scanner by accident. I was just trying to get hold of some stolen technical data for one of our clients. But now that I am involved, I guess you could say I

202

volunteered to help in any way I can. In any case, the important thing is that we find this weapon before it can be used."

Amir was silent again, staring down at his shoes.

"It would not be here, if such a thing exists."

"What do you mean?"

"Perhaps you are not aware of the history of this region. For many years a group that calls itself the Gerakan Aceh Merdeka has been attempting to gain autonomy for this region of Sumatra. The movement has been under attack by government forces for some time now. Although there has been somewhat of reconciliation, the military presence here is still very strong and the GAM has been often penetrated by the Indonesian intelligence services. This would not be the place to hide this weapon if it exists."

"So where do you think it might be?"

"That I cannot answer. Let me clarify, please, my knowledge of these organizations you suspect of conducting terrorist activities. I have been retained by my government as part of a planning committee. Our task is to help the economy of my country function more effectively. This is a very diverse nation, Jack. In the past, most of the regions have functioned autonomously and the result has been a large degree of political conflict and waste. The task is further complicated by the presence of groups who wish to establish an Islamic theocracy in Indonesia. Indonesia is 85% Muslim. Most people here, certainly most educated people, desire a democratic form of government, which has at its heart, Islamic Law. Unfortunately, there are many millions more of mostly poor, uneducated people who have been made to believe in a more radical form of Islam. I think it has always been so throughout history that when large masses of people are kept from building a better future for themselves, they fall prey to those who would destroy the status quo, and replace it with some variety of Utopia. It has happened many times before. Perhaps you are familiar with the writings of Alexis de Tocqueville after he visited your country many years ago. He voiced just this concern. That the judgment of the wise would be subordinated to the prejudices of the ignorant."

Amir paused for a moment, searching Jack's face for a reaction before he continued.

"The committee I work for believes the best way to keep Indonesia from becoming a radical Islamic state is a more equitable distribution of wealth and programs to educate and care for the poor. To give them a way up, so that they have an interest in sustaining a democratic form of government. My task is a difficult one as is always the case. Those with the wealth are not so interested in sharing it. You may believe, as many do, that these terrorist groups, as you call them, live in camps in the jungle. If that were the case, it would not be that difficult to find them. To the contrary, although there are some training camps, most members of these groups are dispersed throughout the population. Perhaps a cab driver or a janitor. Also, I am afraid, some wealthy and educated people who see this kind of turmoil as an opportunity for gain. In any case, I have no direct knowledge of anyone who is a member of one of these groups. I know, as they say, people who know people. That is why I do not believe I can help you."

Jack started to reply, but Annie interrupted.

"What about the money trail?"

"What do you mean?"

"Well, I think it is obvious the weapon was not given to the terrorists. Money must have changed hands. Probably a lot of it. Somewhere there must have been a bank involved."

"Perhaps, this is true, Annie, but it is not at all a certainty. In any case, it could take many months to investigate this possibility. If it is true that a weapon is already here in Indonesia, I doubt that there would be enough time. Such connections are normally investigated later on to assign responsibility. I am sure that is not your primary concern."

There was another lull in the conversation. Finally Jack spoke.

"I know this is difficult for you, Amir, and I don't want to expose you to any unnecessary danger. All we are asking is that you try to find out anything you can. Anything that could help us find this thing."

"I will help if I am able to do so. As you said, it is not in the best interest of my country that this sort of incident takes place. For now, at least, there is nothing more I can tell you."

"OK, Amir. I am going to give you a number you can call anytime, day or night. If you find out anything, no matter how trivial you may think it is, please call and let us know. I will make sure that no one is aware of your cooperation with us. We have no interest in seeing you harmed."

After Amir left, Annie started pacing the room. She was obviously agitated. Jack watched her for a moment, waiting to get her reaction.

"So what do you think of him?" He asked, finally.

"I don't know. He seems like he's telling the truth, but I would have to bet he knows more than he's letting on."

"Is the tail in place?" Jack asked.

"I'm sure they are on him. They are very good at what they do. I don't think Amir will spot them, although he may assume he is being followed in any case." She walked over and sat down in front of him on the couch. "What are we going to do, Jack? I feel like we need to be doing something."

"Unfortunately, a lot of this game is about waiting," Jack said. "You have to give things time to develop."

"But we don't have any time. This thing could be ticking away right now."

"That may well be."

"How can you be so calm about this? This is a disaster unfolding right before our eyes. It has to be stopped."

Jack studied her for a moment. He understood how she was feeling. He also knew that the kind of anxiety she was feeling could lead to panic. Panic never helped anything.

"It's a war, Annie. No one man, or woman, can fight a war. You are given a mission. It is one of thousands of missions. Sometimes they don't make any sense to you but you carry out your orders. You do your small part to the best of your ability and you hope for the best. I have learned over the years not to worry about the war. I only think about the mission."

"Well, it doesn't look like our mission has done any good."

"You don't know that. Amir may come up with something for us. We just have to give it time."

"Well, I can't just sit around here waiting. Jack. I'm going back to the consulate to see what's going on. Call me if you hear from Amir."

18

The next two days were like torture. Jack went to a near-by shopping center and picked up some decent clothes and a small suitcase. He didn't want to risk being out in public too much, so the rest of the time he spent wandering around the hotel and sleeping. His body was still pretty sore and the stress had taken a toll. Annie was staying at the consulate and they spoke on the phone several times a day. There was no news from anywhere. The trail had gone completely cold and everyone's nerves were on edge. Jack spoke to Charlie and had him wire some money. As expected, he was well out of the game. He was headed back to the States and the agency didn't seem to want any further involvement in the incident. No one was issuing checks. Amir had been followed to Jakarta but he was spending his days in the government complex and his nights in his apartment in the Menteng residential district. It had taken a day to get a bug in place but it had turned up nothing of interest.

By the morning of the third day, Jack was ready to pack it in. He had just finished breakfast and was about to call Annie to arrange transportation off the island when his cell phone rang. It was Amir.

"Is this Jack?"

"Amir? What's happening?"

"I cannot be sure, but I have found a man who may have some information to share with you. He wishes to talk to you. He is extremely frightened."

"What kind of information?"

"I cannot speak of it over the phone. I am in Jakarta. Can you meet me here, perhaps this evening or early tomorrow?"

"Sure. I mean I'll see what arrangements I can make. How can I get in touch with you?"

"I will give you my cell phone number. Please call me when you arrive at the airport. I will arrange transportation for you, and, Jack, you must come alone."

"I can't leave Annie here by herself, Amir. I have to bring her with me."

"If you insist, but I must warn you, there may be some danger in this for you, Jack. You may not wish to expose Annie to any potential harm."

"I understand. At least, I need to bring her to Jakarta."

"Jakarta can be a dangerous city. Annie should not move about alone."

"Can you arrange a hotel for us? I can leave Annie someplace safe while I meet your friend."

"He is not my friend, Jack. I do not know where his loyalties lie or what he hopes to gain from talking to you. I know almost nothing about this man except that he is acquainted with some highly placed individuals in the government. This is all I am able to say to you now. If you wish to talk to this man you must come quickly. I will arrange a room for you. It will be at the Hotel Ciputra near the airport. Take the shuttle bus and I will meet you at the hotel. Please call when you have arrived."

209

As soon as he hung up the phone he called Annie. She reacted as if she'd just won the lottery. He could hear the excitement in her voice as she fired questions at him, none of which he could answer. She put him on hold while she arranged the flights. They managed two seats together on Garuda International departing for Jakarta at three in the afternoon. Annie came by in a consulate car at noon. She had a passport and visa for Jack. They took a cab from the hotel. The airport was chaotic and there were armed soldiers everywhere. They were searched several times before being allowed to board and the plane was an hour late taking off. The flight was a little over two hours and Annie was still fired up, and talking a blue streak.

"I want you to take me with you when you meet this guy, Jack."

"No way. Amir told me to come alone and I can't risk it."

"When are you going to stop thinking you need to protect me? I can take care of myself. I think I've proven that."

"That's not the point and you know it. Whoever this guy is, there is a good chance he is taking a very big risk talking to me. We can't risk spooking him."

"Right, but what if it's a setup? What if they think you know too much and want to get rid of you?"

"That's just a risk I'll have to take."

"Well, if it isn't Jack the hero again. I seem to remember you didn't want any part of this thing a couple of days ago."

"Yeah, well I didn't realize how much fun it was going to be."

"At least let me put a bug on you."

"You mean a wire? Not a chance. If they search me and find it, I'm as good as dead."

"I don't mean a wire. It's just a small disk, about the size of a shirt button. I can hide it in your clothing somewhere."

"What's the range?"

"It's very short, but it's better than nothing. Come on, Jack. They'll never find it."

"What's the point? There won't be anyone near enough to do me any good. Listen, Annie, I want you to stay at the hotel. There are ten million people in that city and half of them wouldn't mind killing you."

"Hey, I worked there, remember? I know Jakarta better than you do."

"Yeah, well, then you know I'm right."

"Anyway we won't be alone. There should be a team in place by the time we arrive."

"What do you mean by a team?"

"I mean you will be followed to wherever Amir takes you and we will place 24 hour surveillance on whomever you meet up with."

"I hope your people know what they're doing. If we blow this, it could be our last chance."

"They are very good at what they do."

"I'm sure they are. That's not what worries me."

"What then?"

"I mean, as jittery as everyone is, I don't necessarily trust your people not to pick this guy up, whoever he is, and sweat him for whatever he knows."

"I can't guarantee that won't happen, eventually," Annie said. "In the short run, they are prepared to let you do this your way. After we find out what this guy has to offer, a decision will be made."

"How much?"

"How much what?"

"How much money do I have to play with here? I guarantee you this guy is not doing this for the good of humanity. He probably wants to live very comfortably, very far away from here."

"Well, it depends on what he has to offer, of course. If he actually knows where the weapon is, we would be prepared to make him a very rich man, believe me."

"Yeah, well he is going to want a big piece of the pie before he gives anything up. I hope you know a banker down here."

"That won't be a problem."

"OK, let's say he claims to know where it is and he wants ten million dollars, half up front."

"Tell him you need to speak to someone."

"OK, so then he hands me a cell phone and says 'be my guest'."

"Then call me and tell me what he has to offer."

"How soon could you get the money?"

"First thing in the morning. But he isn't getting a shilling until we have some kind of verification."

"You can get five million dollars first thing in the morning?"

"For this, I could get the Crown Jewels by noon."

They arrived at Soekarno-Hatta International Airport just before seven and were greeted by signs declaring 'Welcome to Indonesia, Death Penalty for Drug Smugglers'. The place was in chaos and they had to fight their way out to the street. As soon as they were outside, the smell hit them. Even though the airport was in a large, open area, the air was heavy with exhaust fumes. When the breeze was coming in from the city, there was the unmistakable smell of burning garbage and open sewers. They waited a half hour for the shuttle bus and when they got into traffic it was not much faster than walking. When the cars stopped, they were immediately swarmed upon by begging children. The traffic pushed through them like ships parting the waves and it was a miracle they weren't crushed under the wheels. No one gave them anything. When the hotel was in sight, Jack phoned Amir.

"Where are you, please?"

"We're in the bus, near the hotel."

"We must depart as soon as possible, Jack. Please meet me at the Marble Court Lobby lounge in one half hour."

They checked in and went immediately to Annie's room. She took a plastic case from her make-up bag and removed a small disk that had two thin wires protruding from it. She secured it under Jack's collar. He started to leave, but she blocked the door.

"Don't do anything stupid, Jack. I don't want to have to rescue you again."

"Why? You getting bored with it?"

"Seriously, be careful. You don't know who this bloke is. He could be Al Qaeda for all you know."

"If it's Osama bin Laden, I'll be sure to get his autograph for you."

She gave him a quick hug, and then backed away, looking more than a little embarrassed. Amir was waiting in the lobby. He was wearing a light windbreaker and had a crash helmet in each hand. He put one down on a table when Jack arrived and he extended his hand.

"It's good to see you again, Jack. I don't think you will be afraid to travel by motorcycle. I find it is the only way to manage the traffic here. If you like, you may cover your nose and mouth with a cloth."

It was a well-worn Suzuki T350, 2-cycle, and Jack was barely in the saddle before Amir gunned it and charged into traffic as if were in a motocross. Jack was a little surprised. He wouldn't have guessed Amir had a wild side but he proved to be a very skilful rider and, pretty soon, Jack just relaxed and enjoyed the experience. The whining of the small, air-cooled engine prevented them from talking and the traffic was so chaotic he had to put all of his effort into keeping his knees from being smashed by the crazed drivers. The lines in the street were evidently there for decoration only. Sometimes there were five cars abreast in what was supposed to be three lanes. A couple of times a car came at them head-on, driving on the wrong side of the road. Amir was all over the road and often off of it. He went up on sidewalks and jumped curbs. Once, to avoid a bus, Amir put the bike into a near slide and Jack's knee just grazed the pavement. If Annie's people were trying to follow him they would have to be crazier than Amir and he wasn't sure that was possible.

After about a half hour, the traffic began to thin out a little. They were headed east on highway 25 toward an industrial suburb called Bekasi. It had the distinction of having the largest open garbage pit in Indonesia. Three thousand people lived in the dump in makeshift shacks. A thousand of them were children, fighting each other for anything of value they could eat or sell. Jack never thought he would be grateful for the smell of exhaust fumes. The sky was starting to darken when they arrived at a cluster of factory buildings and Amir pulled off the highway and through an open gate. The parking lot was packed earth and looked as though it had recently been bombed. Amir maneuvered the bike around the water-filled holes and between the low, brick buildings until he came to a halt in front of a single story structure that looked like an office. Amir removed his helmet.

"The man you are to meet is inside. Regrettably, I will not be permitted to join in the conversation. I will wait for you out here, Jack. I will be prepared to depart quickly if this becomes necessary. I hope it does not. May Allah be with you."

The room was dimly lit and it took a few seconds for Jack's eyes to adjust. It looked like it had been looted. There was an old metal desk and a few filing cabinets, one of which was lying on its side with the doors sprung open. Papers and trash were strewn

215

across the floor. A man was sitting in a metal chair in the middle of the room, his face shrouded in shadow. He was smoking a cigarette and the smoke drifted toward the ceiling in a narrow plume before it disappeared into the darkness. What light there was came from grime-encrusted window and it was sufficient only to illuminate the floor. There were three other men, their forms just visible in the gloom, leaning against the far wall. He couldn't tell if they were armed. One of them came forward, carrying a metal chair. He placed it in front of Jack and indicated he should sit. No words were spoken. The atmosphere was tense, but he did not feel threatened. The one who had brought him the chair stood behind him. The man in the chair shifted his weight and dropped the cigarette on the floor, slowly snuffing it out with the bottom of his shoe. Jack could not make out his features. Finally he spoke.

"I am told your name is Jack."

His voice was high pitched and he sounded extremely nervous. He spoke with a distinct accent but his English was good.

"Tell this man behind me to get over where I can see him, sport."

"That is not a promising beginning to our conversation, but very well, I will do as you request."

He said something in what sounded like Javanese and the man walked over and joined the others.

"You are in no danger here, Jack. To the contrary these men are here for my protection. I am certain you can understand my concern."

216

"Who are you?"

"You may call me Hadi."

"Who do you work for?"

"That is not information I am prepared to share."

"OK Hadi, what do you have to tell me?"

"You wish to get to the crux of the matter. This I can understand as well. I have a story to tell you, Jack. It is a story passed along to me by a sea captain I am acquainted with. My work brings me into contact with many men of the sea. He is the captain of a Pinisi Schooner. Perhaps you are familiar with these beautiful wooden sailing ships from Sulawesi, each one with two Black Irian Jaya Ironwood tree trunks for its keel. They ply these islands carrying all manner of goods and people, as they have done for more than three hundred years. At the end of the story, we will discuss the value of some additional information, which I will keep for the time being. Are we agreed?"

"Go on."

"In July of this year, this captain was carrying a cargo of oil-cake out of Mindanao bound for Kagoshima in Japan. His radio was down and, had he known the ferocity of the storm he would soon be facing, he would not have risked the passage. The weather was turning worse by the hour and when he came through the Balabac Strait below Palawan, he was hit by the full force of Typhoon Koni. He had no choice but to take in sail and run before the wind, down the north coast of Borneo. This captain is an excellent seaman, probably the best in all of Indonesia. Otherwise his vessel would have

217

been lost. As it was, his ship suffered a broken mast and some other less serious damage. He could not maneuver well enough to get his ship into any of the smaller ports along the coast, but at last he was able to make the shipping channel entrance to the port of Bintulu on Sarawak."

The conversation was interrupted as Hadi lapsed into a coughing fit. Jack thought he was going to cough up his lungs. Finally, he spit on the floor and then took a handkerchief out of his pocket. He wiped his face and mouth. Jack waited for him to compose himself.

"Please, excuse me. My health is not good." He cleared his throat again and continued with the story.

"After he was safely anchored, this captain learned of another ship in distress. They listened to the drama unfold on the radio in the harbor masters office. It was a North Korean flagged vessel named the Pong Nam. She had also been blown off course and was a hundred miles south of the Spratly Islands, taking on water. Her generators were down and she could not use the pumps. The weather was too bad to send anyone out for a rescue attempt and it was feared she would be lost. Evidently, the crew was able to make repairs and the ship limped into Bintulu late on the following day. She was listing badly and everyone was amazed she had survived at all. A few days later, while my friend was supervising repairs on his vessel, he was visited by some men. They told him they had a cargo they required him to transport. These were difficult men and it was not a request. Not at all. In the early morning of his fourth day in port he was made to tie up next to the Korean vessel. They forced him to open his hold and throw some of his cargo overboard. A metal container, about the size of a large freezer was lowered into his hold. He was told to keep quiet and that if he told anyone he would be killed along with his crew, and his ship burned to the waterline. They left port a few hours later. Several of the men from the freighter stayed on board to guard the cargo."

"Did he tell you what the cargo was?"

"He didn't know. All he could tell me was that his crew was extremely frightened by it. The seamen in these islands are superstitious men and they blamed it for damaging the vessel that carried it. They were afraid a demon was going to come out of it. They called it the yaksa baga. It means the devil's womb."

"Where did he take it?"

Hadi didn't answer right away. Jack waited.

"The information I have just given would cost me my life, if certain individuals found that I had revealed it. These men here with me speak no English. Only you and I know what I have told. You must not reveal the source of this information. Are we agreed?"

"I'm not going to tell anyone who you are, Hadi. I just want to know where the hell this thing is."

"I am not a well man, Jack. I have a large family. I will be dead soon enough but the men I am speaking of would not hesitate to destroy my family in reprisal. If I am to reveal the destination of this cargo, I want enough money to move my family to the West. Perhaps to Europe. I was in London once. It is very expensive to live there."

"How much?"

"You know what this thing is, Jack. This yaksa baga. It is the thing the West has feared for so long."

"How much?"

"I would require one million British Pounds."

"Paid how?"

"I will provide you with an account number. As soon as the funds are transferred I will reveal to you what I know."

"If we transfer the funds, how do I know you will give me the correct information?"

"Indeed. This is always the dilemma in such dealings. I am not so naïve to think I could get away with cheating the British or the Americans, or whomever you represent. Eventually I would be found. I am not a well man, Jack. I do not have either the energy or the courage to attempt to deceive you. The information I have is accurate as of one week ago. I am sure you understand the urgency."

"How can I get in touch with you?"

"Contact Amir when you have an answer. He will get a message to a mutual friend. I don't think I need to remind you that time is of the essence. I will respond quickly once I have your government's agreement."

19

Jack gave Amir a brief account of what had been discussed when he was dropped off at the hotel. Amir went home and promised he would wait by the telephone for instructions. Annie made a call to the consulate when Jack finished his story and Trevor asked her to put Jack on the line.

"Nice piece of work, Jack. That is the ship we wanted to search several months ago. The one we found in Da Nang. This is the first real lead we've had in this thing. Did your contact indicate if Bintulu was the original destination of the Pong Nam before she encountered the typhoon?"

"He didn't say, but I doubt it. I don't think he knows."

"You may be aware that Bintulu is the home of the Petronas Liquified Natural Gas complex. It is the largest of its kind in the world and would make a spectacular target. It would be a very costly strike indeed."

"I don't think so, Trevor. You could probably light up that facility with a well-placed firecracker. If I had a nuclear weapon I wouldn't waste it there. I mean, aside from the port, you would just be blowing up a lot of jungle."

"Yes, you're right of course. On the other hand, we do not really know how reliable this information is. If it is a fabrication, the weapon could still be in the area. There is also the matter of the unaccounted for missile components. I don't suppose this man made

221

any mention of any other cargo being offloaded?"

"No, he didn't mention it."

"In any case, we will have people at the port in a matter of hours to get any information they can. What does your gut tell you about this man you met? Do you feel he is legitimate or perhaps an opportunist out to take advantage of the crisis?"

"I can't be sure, but he was very scared and I think he was telling the truth. Whether he will give us the right destination is up for grabs. Are you going to give him what he wants?"

"We will if we have to. I know time is critical but I would like you to make a counter offer of half a million pounds. Half to be paid up front. Half if the weapon is found. If he is as frightened as you seem to think, he may go for it. Be firm but if you cannot get him to waver, agree to his terms."

"I don't suppose you were able to get a tail on this guy."

"Regrettably, no. We did not anticipate Amir would be using a motorbike for transport. Our people were hopelessly blocked in traffic."

"I'll call Amir right away. I'll let you know what happens."

They got Amir's away message when they phoned, but he called back ten minutes later. Amir had seemed shaken to learn that the weapon most probably did exist and would no doubt be used. He promised again to help in any way he could. It was getting late, too late to call his friend. He told Jack he would initiate contact first thing in the morning.

Jack and Annie had taken separate rooms and Jack sensed some distance had developed between them. After their trek through the jungle and the craziness in Medan, he thought she was warming up to him a little. Now, he wasn't sure. He really wasn't sure how he felt about her anyway. She didn't seem to have much of a soft side. He liked being around her, but he wasn't sure if he wanted anything more. In any case, this wasn't the time to be dwelling on it. They had breakfast together in the morning. Annie had arranged to visit her friends at the Embassy, but she made Jack swear he would contact her as soon as he got word from Amir. Jack called him again at noon but he had not heard anything.

Annie got back to the hotel late in the afternoon. She had called Jack so many times he was starting to get aggravated with her. They met for dinner at six.

"What the hell is going on, Jack? Why hasn't he called?"

"He can't talk to the guy directly. I told you that. He is working through another contact. We just have to wait. There's nothing more we can do."

"I don't understand how everyone can be so calm about this. The clock is ticking. I mean, doesn't everyone realize what would happen if this thing isn't found?"

"Look, Annie, you do what you can. You wait when you have to. You think about what else might work. What you don't do is get yourself so worked up that you start making mistakes. Waiting can drive you crazy, but mistakes can get you killed."

"So, what aren't we doing? I mean, what are we not thinking about? There must be something."

"Well, at some point somebody needs to figure out what the target is. Even if we find out where the weapon was taken, there is no guarantee it will still be there."

"OK, so what do you think the target is?"

"I've been thinking about that since the beginning but I haven't really come up with anything. I guess we can narrow it down a little, at least. First of all, it will be a high value target. Something that will hurt the US or Western interests badly. I don't think they would use it on any of the major cities in South Asia. Too many Muslims would be killed. It won't be used anywhere in China for obvious reasons. On the other hand, it really doesn't seem like the target is in Europe or the States. I doubt that they would waste their time playing this kind of a shell game down here in the islands if it wasn't going to be used somewhere in the area. Those Pinisi Schooners are island hoppers. They are not used much to cross oceans. It would raise alarms if one of them tried to enter one of our ports."

"Yes, but their ship was in trouble. Maybe they just wanted to get it out of sight. They could have been afraid it would be found."

"That's probably right. The other thing is there may not be a target yet. They might be looking for a target of opportunity. I don't really think that is the case either."

"So what does that leave us with?"

"There's Australia and New Zealand. They've both been active against Al Qaeda and Jemaah Islamiyah."

"That must be it, then."

"I thought so, too, for a while, but now I really don't."

"Why?"

"Something has been bothering me about this thing from the start. Remember when you

224

first met me back on Sumatra? I told you the Chinese were involved.

The guy I took those papers from was a Major in the Chinese army. At the time we suspected the Chinese were fronting the money to buy the weapon but they were going to use Jemaah Islamiyah as a straw dog so they could keep their hands clean."

"Yes, but Trevor said you didn't have anything to fear from the Chinese. He said they were offering their help."

"Sure. But maybe they got caught with their hand in the cookie jar and now they don't want any part of this thing or else maybe this is some rogue group within the Chinese military with their own agenda. But I still think they had a target in mind when this deal was being hatched. Something that would help their position in the region and hurt the US. I don't think a strike against Australia would do much to help them and it wouldn't be worth the risk."

"What about a US military installation?"

"Yeah, I thought about that, too. The thing is, there just aren't many of them down here. At least, nothing big enough to be worth this kind of exposure. For the most part, the US shares facilities with sympathetic countries in the region. Many of them are Islamic countries and the rest don't want China to be pissed off at them. It wouldn't go over very well to have a US base on their soil."

"OK, so maybe now that the Chinese are out of the picture, the original target is not going to be hit. Maybe the terrorists have picked a new one. One that would further their own cause and to hell with the Chinese."

"That's the other possibility, and that's why it is so important that we find out where the weapon was taken. If you're right and they just wanted to get it out of sight, my guess is they moved it someplace where they could reach their intended target easily and without raising too more suspicion. Once we find out where it went, it will help us narrow down ..."

Jacks cell phone rang and he answered it quickly. He listened. Annie studied his face. She was practically crawling across the table to try to hear what was going on.

"OK, Amir. Let's get together in the morning and talk about our options." He hung up the phone.

"There's something wrong. Amir's friend has not been able to get in touch with our guy. He says the guy has dropped out of sight. Nobody seems to know where he is."

"Shit, shit. This can't be happening, Jack."

"Amir is going to meet us for breakfast tomorrow morning. There's still a possibility he will be contacted tonight. If that happens he'll call."

"Jesus. I can't stand this."

"I'm open for suggestions."

Annie sat back in the chair and stared blankly at the table. Jack worked on his coffee. After a few minutes she spoke.

"Listen, Jack. My people at the embassy asked me if I wanted to interview someone since I'm here anyway. I'm going to meet him tonight. Why don't you come with me? I won't be meeting him until late. We could get some drinks first."

"Who is he?"

"Remember I told you I was scheduled to meet someone with information about organ harvesting before I was kidnapped?"

"The same guy?"

226

"No, I assume that one is long gone, but this one may be even better. He claims to have had a kidney removed at some clinic in China where he was being held as a prisoner. If he is telling the truth, we can make a pretty strong case based on his testimony and the physical evidence."

"Do you think it would cause a problem? Me being there, I mean?"

"I doubt it. He may actually feel better about talking to a man. A lot of the male population down here thinks I should be off somewhere being pregnant."

"OK then, sure. It's not like I have anything else to do at the moment."

The meeting was set for 11pm at the Shangri-La hotel in the Sudaman district. Annie wanted it moved up but the embassy told her the contact was extremely nervous and feared for his safety. He apparently thought he would have a better chance when most of Jakarta's sober citizens had already retired for the evening. They decided to try one of the clubs, rather than wait around the hotel. They waited until nine and then took a cab downtown. It was the first time Jack had seen Annie dressed to have a good time. The dress was a red flowered print - short, low cut and tight about the thighs. She looked great in it but even in heels she looked like she could handle herself. It wasn't quite a swagger but enough to discourage anyone looking for an easy score. The makeup, just a little on the heavy side, highlighted her features, but failed to erase the look of determination that seemed to be permanently etched on her face. She looked a little like she had overdressed for a business meeting and her smile was thin and fleeting.

It seemed like rush hour lasted all evening and the traffic crawled as usual. They went to Blok M. It was the center of the bar scene in Jakarta and they picked D's Place. The upstairs bar was packed with skimpily dressed, Asian women grinding to the music, and a mixed group of men, many of them Western. It was a little too much neon and way too much noise. After a few minutes they settled on the downstairs bar. It was a relatively small room with a pool table pushed up so close to the wall that nobody seemed to be able to play from that side. Jack tried to order drinks, but Annie insisted on paying. She was on an expense account. Jack ordered a bourbon, neat, and Annie had a martini. They clinked glasses and Jack knocked down half of his glass in one gulp.

"Jeez, slow it down a bit, mate. The night is still young."

"That's just a warning shot across the bow, to let my system know what it's in for. Helps it mobilize the defenses."

"You know when I first met you, Jack, I thought you were probably a boozer but I haven't really seen you do much drinking. Unless you're hitting the mini-bar."

"No. There was a time when I could put it away but I reached the point where I knew if I kept it up I would wind up an alcoholic, and I decided I didn't want to go down that road. Not that I don't tie one on now and then."

Annie smiled. "You must have a lot of will power. Most people who get there can't seem to put on the brakes."

Jack just shrugged his shoulders. "Listen, Annie. Let's agree not to talk about this mess tonight. I think we both need to give it a rest."

"Fine, but it's going to take a few more of these before I can think about anything else. So you need to pick a subject. I'm not capable right now."

"OK, let's talk about your love life."

"No way. That's none of your business."

"OK, so you don't have one. Did you ever have one?"

"Of course, I bloody had one. More than one, if you must know. What, did you think I was a lesbian?"

"No, I don't really think that, but it did cross my mind."

"Well, uncross your mind. I'm straight."

"You're straight but you don't seem interested in getting involved."

"You mean I don't seem interested in getting involved with you."

"That, too. But I don't think it's just me. I think something is driving you and it doesn't leave room for anything else."

"Well, I've been a trifle busy just lately, trying to avert a world-wide catastrophe."

"In my experience, Annie, life is either one long catastrophe or a continuous chain of on-going minor disasters. If you wait for the all-clear signal, you might find out it's too late."

"It's never too late."

"Maybe not."

"What about you, Jack? You don't seem to be attached either."

He took another long drink. When he spoke, he was staring down into his glass. "She was killed. Murdered the night before I met you."

"Oh, Jesus, Jack. I'm sorry. I didn't know."

"There's no way you could have known."

"How did it happen?"

"I'll tell you about it some day. I really can't talk about it right now."

"You suffered that kind of loss and you were able to get us through the jungle and through that trouble in Medan? How on earth were you able to do that?"

"It's probably the only way I could have gotten through it. It forced me to go into the zone."

"What do you mean?"

"It's a survival reflex, I guess. Life becomes very simple. It starts with OK, I'm alive right now, what do I have to do next to stay that way? What are my choices? What is the best choice right now? If I make this particular choice, what are the likely consequences? It just keeps going on like that until either you get out of whatever shit you're in or you die. Once you understand you're on your own and nobody is going to help you, it becomes a kind of challenge. It really isn't even about whether you want to live or die. It's about not letting them beat you."

"Are you still in the zone?"

"Not really. But I'm pretty far away from being able to think about what happens when this is over."

"Was she your wife?"

"No, she wasn't really even my girlfriend. I wouldn't know how to explain it."

Annie finished her drink and ordered two more. After they were delivered she turned and studied his face.

"OK, Jack. Then I'll tell you about Geoffrey."

"Was he your husband?"

"No, but almost. Geoffrey was the perfect English gentleman. Rich family, old money,

230

grandfather in the House of Lords. Best schools. He was handsome and charming and intelligent and athletic and he adored me."

"So what happened?"

"I was swept away at first. After a while, I couldn't stand him. He was like a virtual image of a perfect man, but I couldn't find anything inside of him. When I tried to push it, he always had some politically correct, logical answer. He never lost his temper - over anything. I don't think he could actually feel anything. When I finally told him I was leaving, you know what he said? He said 'Oh but you're being terribly hasty, Annie, old girl. One shouldn't be rash about these things. Why don't you have a spot of tea and we'll talk about it after dinner?'. I lost it and punched him in the face."

Jack laughed. "You did? You punched him out?"

"I knocked him right on his perfect ass. You should have seen the look on his face. It was so far out of his realm of probable outcomes he went catatonic for a while."

"Angel punched me out once."

"Angel? Oh, was that her name? I wonder what you did to deserve that."

"I didn't do anything. It was just foreplay."

"Foreplay? You're joking?"

"No, she punched me in the face and then held a knife to my throat while we had sex."

"I don't believe you."

"I've got the scar to prove it." Jack pulled down his collar, revealing a faint red line from the center of his throat almost to his ear. "She told me if I didn't get it up she was going to cut it off."

"Jesus, Jack. She could have killed you."

"She could have. She decided not to. I probably wouldn't have let her, but I'm not really sure."

"Was that the way it was between you two?"

"No, it was never the same with her. In the beginning, I thought it was all acting but it wasn't. Angel had a thousand personalities. They were all real. The trick was to figure out who she was at any given moment. Sometimes she was docile as a lamb. Sometime she dressed up in costumes and became someone else entirely. Once she ran into the street naked, yelling rape at the top of her lungs. She was like a drug. I couldn't stay away from her."

"Were you living together?"

"No, it wasn't like that. When I was in Singapore I was with her all the time. The rest of the time she amused herself by getting rich men to spend their money on her."

"She was a prostitute?"

"Not really. She started out as a high-priced call girl but after a while she didn't really need the money any more. If she felt like having sex with one of her conquests, she did. Most of the time she just let them spend money on her. A lot of guys would pay just to have her on their arm."

He took another long drink and they were silent for a while. Finally, Annie turned to him.

"We should probably get going"

They took a cab over to the Shangri-La. The coffee shop was closed but Annie was feeling the alcohol and she needed some caffeine. They ordered two coffees at the bar. She wasn't expecting a long interview. Everyone pretty much knew the landscape already. Mostly, she wanted to be able to report to the commission that she had met an actual victim and had seen the scar, up close and personal. She brought a camera to document what she saw. It would add some weight to the large volume of anecdotal evidence they already had reported. If he could give then names and dates, so much the better. She would also offer help in moving the man out of the country, probably to Taiwan, where he would be out of the immediate reach of the PLA.

There was a live band and the music was a little off-key but not as loud as in the disco bars. They sat together, sipping their coffee and staring blankly out onto the dance floor. They were like two people waiting at an airport, spending an idle hour before departing for different destinations and to futures uncharted and as yet, unimagined. They had both run out of things to say. A slow number came up and Annie tapped him on his shoulder.

"Dance, sailor?"

"Sure, if you promise not to put your toes where my feet are stepping."

They went out on the floor and held each other, lightly at first, moving to the music. Gradually they moved closer until they were making full body contact. It was a conversation of a different sort. He held her firmly, but not so tightly that she couldn't speak to him with her body. She made him feel what was possible without committing to anything more. He was really getting into it when he felt her pull away. He thought he had gotten too close, until he followed her glance and noticed a small Chinese man had entered the bar.

"I think that's him, Jack. This shouldn't take long."

Annie walked over and introduced herself. They spoke for a moment and then moved to a table in the corner. She removed a small voice recorder from her purse and placed it on the table. The man looked at it doubtfully but evidently didn't object. The waitress came over but they waved her off. Jack took a seat at the bar where he could keep an eye on her. Annie slid her business card across the table, but the man did not reciprocate. There were not many professional women in Jack's line of work. The ones he had met, if they were attractive, wielded their sexuality like a weapon. Some overtly, most with a degree of subtlety he imagined took years to perfect. Or maybe it came to them naturally. It was like the bulge of a pistol under a guy's coat. Not really a part of the conversation, but something that couldn't be ignored. Annie didn't seem to be aware of her affect on men, or if she was, she managed to hide it pretty well. She was all business. He wondered how she had managed at being a hostess. She just didn't seem the type to put up with a lot of unwanted foreplay. The guy she was interviewing kept staring at her breasts, but she didn't let it become a distraction. If anything, she looked a little disinterested. Jack wondered if that was part of her negotiating skills or perhaps he just didn't have anything of interest to give her. After a while her attitude changed. She leaned forward. They evidently had become nervous about the recorder so she switched it off. She took a quick look over at Jack and her expression was something between excitement and alarm. Jack started to stand but he thought better of it. Something was going on and he didn't want to get in the way of it. If she wanted him, she would let him know. The conversation became more animated. Annie was leaning into him like a fighter, about to go in for the kill. The guy was raising his hands in surrender but she kept pressing. It went on for about ten minutes, until the man stood. He did not look pleased but when Annie reached out her hand, he held it briefly and then turned and walked out of the bar. She was excited when she walked over to him.

"So what's up?" Jack asked.

"I'm not sure really, but this could be something. Do you remember when Trevor was telling us about some shake-up in the Chinese intelligence apparatus? The second directorate or something?"

"Second Department. Yeah, why?"

"Well, this guy is trying to arrange political asylum for a couple of people coming out of China sometime in the next few days. A man and a woman, both Falun Gong members. He claims the woman is the wife of a high ranking military officer in Chinese intelligence. The woman claims that her husband has gone bonkers and is involved in some kind of unsanctioned action against the US. He apparently was best friends with that pilot, Wang Wei I think his name was. The one who was killed in a crash after colliding with that US surveillance aircraft a couple of years ago. Apparently this guy has lost patience with the Politburo and wants to push things along."

"Did you get his name?"

"No."

"Do you know what he's planning?"

"No, this guy I was just with was as nervous as a cat. I think he's been through the ringer himself. Either that or he's a bit of a dim bulb.

If he had more information he wasn't going to share it with me until I could guarantee asylum for these people. Oh, and by the way, for himself as well."

"What did you tell him?"

"I told him we would have to talk to these people before we offered anything."

"Do you know when they're getting here?"

"He claims he doesn't know. He says they keep the timing and the route secret in case somebody gets caught."

"So what do you plan to do?"

"I'm going to call it in. Trevor's going to want more than I can give him but I really think this guy was in the dark about most of it. We're going to have to wait until these people show up. More damn waiting, Jack, but I don't know what else to do."

"Yeah, well it might be something or it might not. We'll see how it goes."

During the cab ride back to the hotel, she was as animated as he had ever seen her.

"This has got to be it, Jack. This is what we've been waiting for."

"Slow down there, cowgirl. I admit it looks promising but we won't know until we talk to this woman."

"Do you think Trevor will start a search for her, after we tell him?"

"I imagine he will," Jack said. "But trying to find an unknown Chinese woman down here is like looking for a grain of sand on a beach. We don't even have a description of her, not that it would help much. I doubt he'll have any luck."

"I'm going to phone him first thing in the morning in any case."

"Yeah, he should know as soon as possible, even if it doesn't lead anywhere."

"This must be it, though, don't you think? You told me it could be some kind of rogue operation."

"I'm just grasping at straws, Annie. I don't know any more than you do."

"I can't stand this waiting, Jack. It's driving me bonkers."

When they got back to the hotel, Jack walked her to her door. She was having some trouble with the key and he took it from her and opened the door. She stepped inside and then turned and looked at him.

"What are we doing here, Jack?"

"Your guess is as good as mine."

"I mean, you and me? I can't figure it out."

"I don't know either."

"We're doing something, though. Aren't we?"

"Yeah, something."

She put her arms around his neck and held him in her arms. "Do you think we would have met if it hadn't been for this mess? Do you think we would have come across each other anyway?"

"No."

"Me either."

She pulled back and looked into his eyes. He reached down and kissed her on the lips and she responded.

"Would you stay with me for a little while, Jack? I don't think I want to be alone right now."

20

Jack was already in the restaurant having coffee when Annie walked in. Her skin was a little pale and she had the look of a woman who had spent too much time in front of a mirror before surrendering. She sat down without saying anything and buried her face in the menu. After a few moments, she stole a quick glance at Jack but turned away when he made eye contact. He could see she was unhappy. He also knew whatever he said would be the wrong thing, so he said nothing. The waitress came over with coffee and filled Annie's cup. Annie looked on attentively, as if it were a procedure of some great importance. She ordered and then reluctantly gave up the menu, leaving her defenseless. The silence was lasting too long. He could see her struggling for something to say and he decided to let her off the hook.

"How's the hangover?"

"How did you know? My head is killing me. I though I was going to be sick but so far so good. What about you?"

"Not too bad, except for the nail sticking in my left temple."

A brief smile that quickly faded. He decided to test the waters.

"Do you want to talk about it?"

"No."

"No as in not now, or no as in never?"

"No as in no. What did you order?"

"Two eggs over easy, why?"

"Just don't let me look at them."

Jack started to say something when he saw Amir walk in from the lobby. He looked upset

238

and Jack knew the news wasn't good. His thick lenses magnified the look of concern on his face and he looked like he might break out in tears.

"I'm afraid I don't have anything to tell you. The man you spoke to in Bekasi is missing. No one seems to know where he is. My friend spoke to his wife and she is very frightened. The police are now looking for him."

Annie looked stunned. "Do you think the terrorist's have him? I mean, what else could have happened?"

"I don't know, Annie."

"Maybe he got cold feet and decided to drop out of sight for a while. He was pretty nervous when I spoke with him," Jack said.

Annie was visibly angry. She slammed her hand down on the table, jarring the coffee cups. "I can't believe this is happening. We were finally getting somewhere."

Jack reached over and put his hand on her arm. "Maybe we can find the ship some other way. Doesn't someone keep track of ship arrivals and sailings, Amir?"

"Perhaps this is so, although if I remember what you told me, the captain was forced to depart. I doubt he was permitted to make anyone aware of his destination. Of course we can try. Did this man provide you with the name of the vessel?"

"Not that I can remember."

"Why don't you tell me again what was said? Perhaps we can think of something."

Jack started at the beginning and recounted the conversation in as much detail as he could remember. At the end Amir was silent for a while, going over the details in his head.

"Please tell me again what damage was sustained by the Pinisi boat."

"He only said one of the masts was snapped and there was other less severe damage."

"Yes. Perhaps that is something."

"What do you mean?"

"There are very few places in Indonesia that have the facilities and the skills to replace the mast of a large sailing vessel. The Pinisi Schooners are constructed in southern Sulawesi. For the most part on the beaches near Makassar. Perhaps we may surmise that once the boat completed its mission, it returned to this area to have its mast repaired or replaced. I do not believe there is anywhere else this work could be done. I also do not imagine there were too many boats with a mast snapped off in the typhoon."

Annie interrupted. "How could he go anywhere with a broken mast?"

"Most of these boats have diesel engines today. They are called kapal layar mesin, which means motor sailing ship. The sails are used to save fuel and when the engines are not functioning properly."

Annie's cell phone rang and she excused herself. Amir continued.

"Would you be prepared to travel to Sulawesi, to see if we can find this vessel, Jack? It may be our best chance at this point."

Jack didn't answer right away. He had that feeling again, of being dragged into a dark room where nothing good was going to happen. He could see the concern and determination on Amir's face and realized how dedicated he had become. Jack wondered what he was risking by helping them. He knew the answer was probably everything. Somehow he couldn't believe anything would come of their efforts and if the weapon were found at all, it would be by someone else, far away from wherever they ended up. Still, he was driven by the idea of finding the man who killed Angel and that was enough. There was not yet a world for him on the other side of her life. Something was whispering that there never would be, unless he got his hands on her murderer.

"Sure." Jack said finally. "I'll have to arrange tickets, but I think we could go there today if we can get a flight."

"Very well. I will need to make some arrangements. Please tell Annie I was sorry not to say goodbye. Perhaps she will accompany us."

"Maybe. We'll see."

Jack sat and drank his coffee. In a few minutes Annie returned. He couldn't tell if the news was good or bad.

"That was Trevor. They think they know what the target is. They believe it's the Ras Tanura oil terminal in the Persian Gulf."

"What makes them think so?"

"Apparently they have been questioning those men who were picked up in Medan at the house where you were being held. Trevor thinks it makes a lot of sense. It would virtually shut down the flow of oil to the west."

"Well, at least they'll know where to look if we can't find the weapon before it's moved, providing the information is accurate. Listen, Amir thinks the Pinisi Schooner would have needed to put in at Sulawesi to have its mast repaired. He doesn't think the work could be done anywhere else. He suggested I travel there with him and sniff around a little."

"Not without me, you're not. I'm not going to argue with you any more about this."

241

"OK, OK. But what about the Chinese woman? Don't you want to be here when she arrives?"

"Sure, but you said it yourself - we need to find out where the weapon is right now. I don't think she'll be able to tell us that. Besides, anybody at the embassy can debrief her. The important thing is the information."

"Alright, why don't you call Trevor back and tell him what we want to do?"

Annie's whole demeanor changed. Jack knew she wanted badly to be the one who found the weapon. For the most part it was a genuine concern for the catastrophe it would cause, but there was also a good bit of personal ambition involved. She was out to prove herself to someone and that could be dangerous. For her and for everyone around her.

"That's a great idea, Jack. I'll call him right away."

They arrived at Hasanuddin airport in Makassar late in the afternoon. From the air, they could see several large fires, and a plume of dense, gray smoke drifting to the southwest out across the Java Sea. The pilot bounced the plane down the runway but managed to keep it on the tarmac. It was another near riot at the airport. They were all exhausted by the time they made it to the street. Paotere seaport was a little north or the city and they decided to get rooms for the evening and get a fresh start in the morning. If the terrorists knew about Jack's meeting with Hadi, they were all in a lot of danger. He felt better to be out of Jakarta, but they were getting farther away from civilization and they were very exposed. In the morning, Amir insisted he go to the port alone and he was

242

right. Not only would a couple of Westerners probably not get answers, it was likely they would raise the attention of people they didn't want to meet. Amir told them that the local language was Buginese, named after the ethnic Bugi people. Back when the Portugese were trading spices in the islands they were often raided by local Bugi pirates. It was where the term boogieman came from. Amir did not speak the language well but he thought he could get by. Jack and Annie went out and walked about the city a little but they stayed close to the hotel. She had taken a private room and Jack didn't say anything about it. She was acting a little strangely with him. Not angry exactly but something less than friendly. He knew better than to try to figure it out, but it didn't do anything to help his mood.

The city had a lot of history and there were coastal fortifications that went back to the sixteenth century. The people were friendly and it was a surprisingly modern place but the smoke made it uncomfortable to breathe. Amir met them back at the hotel shortly after noon. He seemed excited.

"I have learned that a ship named the Angin Kidung had a mast replaced several weeks after the typhoon. I have been told that the captain of that ship is a man named Mochtar Hari."

Jack slapped him on the back and Amir seemed startled for a second. "Great work, Amir. Is the ship still at the port?"

"Regrettably, no. No one seems to know where it is at the moment. I have talked to one of the port administrators, however, and left him my cell phone number. He has promised to phone me if he learns the ships location. He will contact some of the other ports. He may know something soon or it could take a day or two."

Annie threw her hands up in the air. "This is so frustrating."

Amir nodded.

"Yes, it is difficult to wait. There is one more possibility, however. I have been told that some of the original crew of the Angin Kidung left the ship when it came into port for repairs. The crew had lost money on their voyage and they believed the ship was bad luck. A ship chandler gave me the name of the first mate. He is Chinese and goes by the name Shan Wu Jun. He hired on to a new ship called the Mongso Udan. It is currently in Parepare taking on a cargo of rice. If we hurry we may be able to catch it before it sails. Parepare is not far from here. About 150km to the north. It's about a four hour drive by bus."

"We should get going then," Annie said.

Amir thought for a moment. "Perhaps we should not all go."

"What do you mean?" Jack asked.

"We cannot be sure we will reach the port before the ship sails. Once we leave this city, my cell phone will be useless until we get near to Parepare and possibly there also. If the port official calls, he may not be able to reach me."

"Why don't you stay here, Jack? In case he calls," Annie said.

"Please, pardon me, Annie. I do not mean to insult you but it may raise suspicion if I am seen travelling with a Western woman. The customs here are quite strict in many regards. It would be better if you remained here. I will leave my phone with you. We will be back by tomorrow in any case."

Annie looked frustrated and she glared at Jack. Amir spoke again.

"If you are in agreement, Annie, I will call my contact at the port and tell him a friend will be answering his call."

Annie nodded her head. Jack put his hand on her shoulder but she pulled away.

"It will be better if you stay at the hotel, Annie," Jack said. "I know it's going to drive you crazy but we don't know who may be looking for us. Get a hold of Trevor and let him know what's going on."

The bus didn't depart until five but the Trans Sulawesi Highway was surprisingly good and there was not much traffic. The road took them past endless rice fields and Bugis villages with their thatched, wooden houses built on stilts. Jack just stared out the window, seeing nothing. He liked it better when he was being shot at. At least it kept his mind occupied. It was becoming more and more difficult to force the memories out of his head and to keep his anger under control. Amir watched him for a while and then he spoke.

"You know, Jack, it was not only for the reason I gave Annie for wishing her to stay behind."

"What do you mean?"

"I do not know Parepare well but I know the port can be dangerous. Especially at night. I would not wish to expose Annie to such risk. Also, if I am honest, I will feel a lot better having you close by. Still, if I am able to locate this man, it will be necessary for me to talk to him alone. I would imagine the crew of the Angin Kidung was threatened with their lives to keep them silent. It is fortunate for us that they were

245

not all killed once they unloaded the weapon. I believe we may need to provide him with some money to loosen his tongue. Are you prepared to do this?"

"Sure, but I only have about three hundred dollars with me."

"I think that will be sufficient. If we find him I will offer one hundred and allow him to bargain to two."

The bus terminal was a little south of the city and they had to take a becak to the port. The city was small but larger than Jack had expected and not at all primitive. Except for a few monuments, it was difficult to distinguish Parepare from any other city in Indonesia. The architecture was a little different but the streets all looked pretty much the same. It was late and the streets were not well lighted. They trusted to their driver to get them to the Cappa Ujung port. The streets near the port were quiet and Jack began to get the familiar feeling of being on hostile ground. They paid the driver and walked down the ramp to the quay. It was quiet except for the sound of water lapping against the hulls of ships and the creaking of the spring lines as the ships leaned forward against a rising tide. They could hear the faint sound of a bell in the distance, probably on a buoy serving as a channel marker out in the Makassar Strait. There were lamps on the pilings along the quay and out along the moorings. The little islands of light they provided did little but provide some atmosphere and indicate the waters edge. And there was the familiar smell of the sea and the scent of the land it bordered, carried by a failing wind now deprived of its energy by the setting of the sun. Jack was wary. The place had a bad feel about it and he didn't like being unarmed.

There were two schooners tied up at the port and their first guess was wrong. The second schooner was tied up at the end of the quay. It was sitting low by the waterline and looked like it was ready to get underway. The gangplank was still in place and they could see the faint outline of a man standing watch by the cabin house. They stopped in the shadow of a small utility shed. Amir looked nervous.

"I believe you should remain here, Jack. If you would please give me two hundred dollars as we agreed?"

Jack opened his wallet and handed Amir the money. "What are you going to do? Just walk on board and ask for this guy?"

"Unless you can think of something better. I cannot at this moment."

"Are you sure you don't want me to come with you?"

"I don't think that would be wise. However, if you here me screaming horribly, please come quickly."

"Try to stay where I can see you, Amir."

Amir smiled and Jack could see him summoning up his courage. Finally, he walked down the quay and stopped at the end of the gangplank. Jack couldn't hear his voice but he didn't understand the language anyway. After a brief conversation, Amir walked up the gangplank and disappeared into the deckhouse. Jack swore to himself. He felt helpless and he didn't have a good feeling about the outcome. A half hour passed and Jack was getting worried. He had just made up his mind to walk over to the ship when he heard a commotion. A man exited the deckhouse, running. It was Amir. Two men emerged behind him, screaming. Amir was running toward him in a panic. Jack ran out to meet him. Suddenly shots rang out and Amir stumbled. He fell to his knees and then collapsed onto the quay. Jack was still thirty yards away. He could see Amir was not moving. The men reached Amir and Jack saw one of them cock his weapon and fire two shots into Amir's fallen body. Jack yelled, and they turned their attention to him. A round hit close to his feet and he realized there was nothing more he could do without a weapon. He turned and ran down the Quay with the two men in pursuit. Several more shots were fired in his direction. He ran with all his strength. When he reached the port entrance he took a quick glance behind and saw no one. He stopped for a moment and considered going back but, in the end, he knew there was nothing he could do for Amir. The best thing he could do for everyone was to get back to Annie.

21

Jack ran through the port gate, checking again to see if they were following. No one was behind him. His mind was racing. If it was the port official that had sent Amir to Parepare, there was a good chance he was involved. Annie was in danger. She was alone in Makassar waiting for the phone call. He had to get back to her. He ran out into the street. There were no cabs or becaks at the port entrance. He wasn't about to take a pedal cab. He found a relatively busy road and started walking. There was still no pursuit and it made him wonder why. Unless they hadn't realized he and Amir were together. Nothing else made much sense. He forced himself to slow down and try to walk normally. A Westerner travelling alone and on foot in this part of the city at night was bound to get someone's attention but it wouldn't help to look like he was in a hurry. After about ten minutes, he managed to flag down a cab and got a ride to the bus station. There was a night bus to Makassar within the hour. He found a phone and called the hotel. She didn't pick up. Next he tried Amir's cell number, but he couldn't get through. When the bus started to load, Jack took a seat in the back near the emergency exit. He hunkered down and tried to avoid being noticed. Once the bus departed everyone dozed off anyway, and unless the bus was stopped, he figured he would be all right until they reached the city. He was trying to sort everything out but somehow it didn't add up. A lot of people who had tried to help him were dead. He wanted more than anything to get his hands on the bastards who did it, but it was like trying to wrestle with ghosts. There was something he wasn't seeing but he couldn't get his mind around it. Eventually, sleep took him.

The bus got in at three in the morning. He had to wait a while for a cab but the roads were nearly empty and he arrived at the hotel by three-thirty. When he got to the room, he knocked, but she didn't answer the door. After several tries he gave up and walked back down to the lobby to get another key. When he finally opened the door, he found the bed still made and the room empty. He felt himself starting to panic and he fought against it. He checked the bathroom and even the closet but Annie was not there. Her travel bag was still packed and sitting next to the dresser. He looked through it but her wallet and passport were gone. Then he noticed a note sitting on the desk.

Jack:

I hope you and Amir had some luck. The man from the port called and said he wouldn't have any information until tomorrow at the earliest. Trevor thinks we are wasting our time but he agreed to give us another day or two. He thinks the weapon has probably been moved again anyway. There has been a virtual blockade set up on all the sea routes approaching the Persian Gulf. Every ship of any size is being boarded and searched well before it gets anywhere near there. I know you are going to be angry with me but I couldn't stand sitting around here any more. The man who called gave me the name of a doctor who lives near the port and is a friend of captain Hari. I am going to pay him a visit and see if he might know anything. I'm sure I'll be back before you, but I thought I would leave a note just in case. Here is the doctor's number in case you want to contact him.

Yours,

Annie.

He checked the time. Calling someone at four in the morning was no way to get useful information but it couldn't wait. After a long delay, he managed to get an outside line and called the number Annie had left on the cover of a magazine. It rang a long time before he heard a foggy voice on the other end. It wasn't English, but pissed off sounds pretty much the same in every language.

"Is this Doctor Suharto?"

There was a long pause on the other end. When the man finally spoke he sounded calmer. "This is Doctor Suharto. Who is calling, please?"

"I'm sorry to call you so early in the morning, Doctor, but a friend of mine has gone missing and she left me a note telling me she would be visiting you. Her name is Annie Blake. Have you seen her?"

"Yes. She came to visit me last evening."

"What time was she there?"

"Near eight o'clock. She stayed for a brief time, but I was not able to help her. I'm sorry, that is all I know."

Jack heard a click on the other end of the line. Something had happened to her and he wasn't sure what to do. He looked through his wallet and found Trevor's number at the British Consulate in Medan. He got his away recording and left a message.

"Trevor, this is Jack. I went to Parepare with Amir last night to get some information. We found out the schooner that off-loaded the device from the Korean vessel was named the Angin Kidung.

251

Amir is dead. We were trying to talk to a crewmember who had been on the schooner in Bintulu when the weapon was transferred. I let Amir go on the ship alone and they shot him. I never should have let him go alone. When I got back to Mekassar, Annie wasn't at the hotel. She paid a visit to someone who knows the captain of the Angin Kidung around eight but she isn't at the hotel and I can't think of where else she would have gone. I don't want to go to the local police, Trevor. I don't have a picture of Annie anyway and they may want to detain me. I'm hoping she has been in contact with you. I don't have a phone with me, but I'll call back in a couple of hours or sooner if I find out anything. Can you have someone contact the police in Mekassar to report her missing and maybe fax over a picture and description? I don't know what else to do. I'll try to call you again in a couple of hours."

The answering machine beeped and Jack hung up the phone. He sat down on the bed and tried to sort everything out. There were not a lot of options. He didn't know the city or anyone who could help him. He knew he should notify someone about Amir, but he didn't even know what government agency he worked for. Amir was single and had not mentioned anyone as a personal friend or girlfriend. It would have to wait. He didn't know how to begin searching for Annie. It could have been a simple abduction for ransom, or worse it could have been a rape or murder. There was no way to know. He had to admit it was now more likely Jemaah Islamiyah had taken her. He didn't want to think they were that close, but it was starting to look that way.

Everything inside of him was telling him to walk away but he couldn't. He didn't know where to begin. He went into the bathroom to wash his face and when he reached for the towel hanging on the back of the door he saw it. The word Jayapura was scrawled on the back of the door in bright red lipstick. He stared at it for a moment trying to decide what it meant. He knew Jayapura was a city somewhere in Indonesia, but he wasn't even sure what island it was on. He didn't know if it meant that was where Annie was taken or if she found out where the weapon was just before they took her. He sat for a few minutes trying to decide the best course of action. In the end, he decided trying to find Annie in Makassar, alone without even Amir to translate for him, was going to be futile. The only real lead was Jayapura and that's where he decided to go.

On the way out, Jack stopped at the front desk to see if anyone had seen Annie leave the hotel, but it was a different shift and no one remembered her. He left Trevor's number with them in case anyone contacted the hotel about her and then asked if they had a map of Indonesia. He asked the manager if he would call Trevor's number in a couple of hours and let him know he was flying to Jayapura. They offered to make a hotel reservation for him but he told them it wouldn't be necessary. He found Jayapura on the map. It was located in Papua on the north coast of New Guinea, just on the Indonesian side of the border. There was a cab waiting at the curb. The driver was dozing at the wheel and he was startled when Jack jumped into the back seat.

"Take me to the airport. Do you understand? Airport."

The driver nodded and put the cab in gear. Jack stared vacantly out the window at the deserted streets. A light rain had begun to fall. He arrived at the airport around six AM. There was a Garuda flight to Sentani airport in Jayapura at nine. He purchased a ticket and then exchanged some currency into Kina just in case. He was told he would need to purchase an entry Visa when he arrived. He tried Trevor's number again but he couldn't get through. There was nothing left to do but wait. He picked up a copy of the Asian Wall Street Journal and had some breakfast at a coffee shop. The rest of the time he tried to stay out of sight. Nothing was going to happen at the airport, but he didn't want to take any chances. He looked out the large plate glass window at the runway. The rain was coming down hard now, the thick drops bouncing off the concrete like hail stones. The monsoon had finally arrived, like a messenger bearing bad news. The dark, rain-laden clouds cast a pall over everything. The voice in his head was telling him it wasn't going to end well but there was no other way. If he turned his back on Annie now, he knew he wouldn't be able to live with himself.

Jayapura is a small city of about two hundred thousand people that sits in a bowl at the foot of the Cyclops Mountains. It is not a big tourist destination, except for an occasional anthropologist studying Stone Age cultures in the interior of New Guinea. He purchased a Visa at the immigration checkpoint, telling them he was a tourist. They were mainly concerned that he was not a Western journalist. There had been separatist riots in the city in the recent past and some of the students were beaten in the streets. The police were not fond of Westerners with cameras or laptop computers. The officers at the security check point didn't speak English but Jack just kept throwing money at them until they shut up and let him pass. It seemed to him that the whole world had gone insane. He took one look at the city and the words 'end of the line' popped into his head. He had no idea where to start. There was a small shop by the ticket counters and he purchased a light, hooded rain jacket and a map of the city. After a few minutes studying the map he went out to the curb and hailed a cab. The only thing he could think to do was to look for a ship where they might be holding the weapon. He told the driver he wanted to go to Yos Sudarrso Bay. The rain was rolling across the city like a heavy, gray curtain blowing in the wind. He could barely see out the window. When they got down near the waterfront he spotted a Chinese restaurant with a good view of port. There were outrigger longboats pulled up along the beach and he could just make out some ships tied up at the wharf on the south side. He decided to get something to eat while he figured out what to do. It seemed like as good a place as any to start.

There were a few people ahead of him, waiting to be seated. Jayapura had been the headquarters for General MacArthur during World War II although it had been called Hollandia at that time. He stood in the foyer, lost in thought. After a few moments, he noticed a large mural on the wall, showing the history of the war and the island hopping campaign of the US forces. As he studied the map he wondered again why the weapon would be taken to this place. He just could not convince himself that the target was in the Persian Gulf. Something didn't seem right about it. If they had moved the weapon to Jayapura, it was moving east instead of west. But if not there, what other high profile target could it be? There were small US naval support facilities on some of the islands but nothing big enough to waste a nuclear weapon on.

Suddenly he remembered something he had read in the Wall Street Journal earlier, at the airport. He had left the paper on the plane. He pushed himself past the people waiting in line, eliciting some angry stares and some comments he didn't need to know Chinese to understand. There was a stack of Chinese language newspapers at the counter but nothing in English. He took one anyway and started to page though it. He found an article with the picture of a US Ship. He vaguely remembered what the Journal article had been about. It said the USS Blue Ridge command ship and the entire Seventh Fleet battle group with the carrier Kitty Hawk would be somewhere in the area before heading for the Persian Gulf. He couldn't remember where the ships would be laying over or when. He scanned the article to see if there was anything like a date. There was an old Chinese woman behind the counter. He showed her the article.

"Do you speak English?"

The woman shrugged her shoulders. She didn't understand what he was saying.

"English. Does anyone speak English?"

He was shouting and everyone in the restaurant turned to look at him. Finally a balding Chinese man in a stained white apron came out of the kitchen and hurried over to him. He wasn't too happy.

"No trouble here. You go now."

Jack showed him the article. "Can you translate this for me? What does it say?"

The man snatched the paper from him and glanced at the article. "Many ship go Guān Dǎo."

"Guān Dǎo? What is Guān Dǎo?"

The man took him by the arm and pulled him into the foyer. He walked over to the mural and pointed to Guam. "Guān Dǎo. You go now. No trouble here."

"When? When will the ships go there?"

The man looked at the article again, and then pointed to the door. "Three day. You go now."

Jack ran out into the street. His mind was racing. The idea that the target was the Persian Gulf oil terminal had never seemed right to him. The Chinese intelligence services were involved in the conspiracy from the beginning and it would make no sense for them to stop the flow of oil out of the Middle East. China depended on imported oil as much as the West. It would be a disaster for their economy. Taking out the fleet, on the other hand, would sway the balance of naval power in Asia for years. If they could accomplish that without being implicated, it would be an enormous victory. It was hard to believe they would take such a huge risk but there was no denying their involvement.

He needed to call Trevor. He found a hotel a few blocks up the street and he entered the lobby. There was a bank of pay phones in an alcove by the public restrooms. He walked over and began digging in his pocket for some change. Two men walked behind him, headed toward the rest room. Suddenly he felt something hard pressed into his side.

"We have the woman. Come with us now or we'll kill her."

22

He was walked out to a waiting car and pushed into the back seat. The car made a u-turn and, at the bottom of the hill, it turned into the commercial port entrance and drove down the quay. There were two ships tied up on opposite sides of the main pier and he could just make out the outline of a third ship riding at anchor out in the harbor. The car stopped at a floating dock at the end of the quay and he was pulled out of the back seat. They walked him over to a gangway and down onto the floating dock where a small tender was waiting. He was pushed on board and made to sit on the open rear deck. The lines were cast off and the tender headed out into the bay. He was drenched through and even though it was not particularly cold, his teeth were chattering. The water was choppy and it was all he could do to keep from sliding over the rail. As they got closer to the ship, he got a better look at it. It was a small tanker and there was something familiar about it. The tender cut its engines and drifted up to the pilot ladder dangling over the side, and that's when Jack saw it. A long horizontal crease running almost the entire length of the ship. The ship had been repainted, and no doubt re-flagged, but it was the Sulawesi Maru. The same ship he had sailed on out of Singapore. At last he understood why the ship had been taken and the captain killed.

They hadn't been after money or even the cargo. They wanted the ship itself. He knew the weapon would be on board and the thought crossed his mind that he and Annie were both going to regret finding it.

As he was pushed up the pilot ladder and onto the main deck, Jack felt like he was in a bad dream. It seemed as though everything that had happened since the night he had been thrown over the side had been a mistake, an unintended detour, and now fate had corrected the error and his journey would continue on to its inevitable conclusion. It was as if he and Annie were destined to die together on this ship, and he had been forced to go find her so they could meet their fate together. Like a man forced to dig his own grave. The anger began to rise within him. He was pushed through the ship and found himself standing in front of the same cabin he had occupied on the trip out of Singapore. He turned and looked at the deck. He could still see the dried blood where Sadik had fallen. They pushed the door open and shoved him inside. Annie was lying asleep on the bunk. She was dressed in tan slacks and a blue silk blouse but she looked dishevelled, like she had been sleeping for a long time. The door slammed behind him and he heard it lock. He went over to the bunk and shook her, gently. She stirred and rolled over to face him. Her eyes were glazed over and she didn't seem to recognize him.

"Annie, are you OK? Did they hurt you?"

"Jack? Where are we? How did you get here?

He voice was hoarse and she was having difficulty forming her words. He went over to the sink and filled a mug with water. Annie sat up, holding her head in her hands. He held the mug to her lips and helped her drink. She made a face at the taste of it.

"We're in Jayapura. Don't you remember? You wrote it on the back of the door at the hotel in Makassar."

"I didn't, Jack. I didn't even get back to the room. They grabbed me on the street in front of the hotel. I think they drugged me with something." She looked around the cabin. "Where are we?"

"We're on a ship. It's the same ship I was on coming out of Singapore, the one that was hijacked. It's been repainted. I'm sure the weapon is on board."

"Why would they bring us here, Jack? It doesn't make any sense."

"I don't know either."

"Jayapura? Isn't that in New Guinea?"

"Yeah, well, in Papua. The Indonesian side."

"That's a long way from the Persian Gulf."

"Yeah, but I think Trevor is wrong about the target, Annie. Remember what I said about there being no large US military installations in the region? Well, that's normally true, except it turns out the entire US seventh fleet is going to be stopping in Guam this weekend. It all begins to make sense. If the Chinese could eliminate the fleet, they would have no one to stop them in all of Asia. It would take us months or maybe years to rebuild our strength. They could easily invade Taiwan or let the North Koreans invade the south and we would

261

have to stand by and watch. They could never do it openly but if they succeed in making it look like a terrorist act they would be off the hook. I've got a bad feeling we've been led around by our noses for the past few days."

"But half the world must be trying to find this thing by now. Why would they go through the trouble to bring us here? If they thought we were getting too close they could have just killed us. Have you mentioned any of this to Trevor?"

"No. The last time I contacted him was to let him know you were missing. I had to leave a message. I left Trevor's number at the front desk and asked them to call him later and let him know I was going to Jayapura. I was trying to call him when they grabbed me. I hope he got the message, but even if he did, I didn't know that Guam could be the target. We are the only ones who know, and I don't see anyway to send out a warning at this point."

"Where is Amir?"

"They killed him."

"Oh, no! Oh, my God, what happened?"

"We went to the port together but he insisted on going to the schooner alone. I waited for him but they chased him off the boat and shot him before I could do anything to help."

Annie held her head in her hands. "What are we going to do, Jack?"

"I'm all out of ideas. I guess we just have to wait until we see what happens."

Annie got up and walked over to the basin. She wet her hands and splashed some water on her face. Jack was pacing the cabin, trying to come up with something they could do. Suddenly the ship shuddered and there was a low rumble coming from somewhere beneath their feet. The engines had been started and, in while, they could feel the ship rolling gently.

"Looks like we're going for a cruise."

They sat together on the bunk not knowing what to say. After a few moments the door opened and a man stepped into the cabin. They both stared at him in shock. Annie looked at Jack with a puzzled expression on her face. It was Amir. As Jack stared at him, the realization that he had been duped came over him and he struggled with the urge to break Amir's neck. A guard entered behind Amir and held a gun on them. Amir smiled and spoke.

"So you see I have been somewhat less than honest with you both. I am sorry to have lied to you but it is your own fault, Jack. There was no other way."

"What the hell are you talking about?"

"By your actions, Jack, you gave us no other choice than to bring you here. You will recall our conversation about the retinal scanner that you found in the briefcase with the documents?"

"What about it?"

"You must understand, Jack, that the people who have supplied us with this weapon were extremely worried it might fall into the wrong hands, or be used for a purpose other than the one they intended. As a precaution, they sent us the weapon without the security device, so they could insure it would only be used as they wished. For reasons you may guess, they did not

263

intend to be present at the time the device was armed. Once the weapon was in place and they were sure of the arrangements, they were to deliver the security scanner and witness for themselves the completion of the reference scan. You see, Jack, the scanner was designed so that the first scan it performed would be established as the reference. It contains a battery backup for this purpose. Thereafter, the only person who could commence the arming sequence for the weapon would be the person who was used to establish the reference. Because of your meddling, that person is you, Jack. You told me that the device scanned your eye when you investigated it. From that moment on, all of our efforts have been directed at getting you to this ship. We could not risk attempting to capture you until we had lured you away from your friends. We could not risk that you would be killed trying to evade us. I knew if we managed to capture Annie we could get you to follow. That was the reason for the little diversion on the dock in Parepare. We needed to separate you from Annie and have enough time to bring her here. Unfortunately for you both, it worked perfectly."

"So that was all crap? That story you fed me about not being a terrorist."

"I do not consider myself to be a terrorist, Jack, but I am a soldier. We cannot hope to fight the imperial powers of the West on their own terms, with their advanced weapons and huge military forces. Our only option is to use unconventional means."

"You mean by killing thousands of innocent civilians?"

"That is not our intention, Jack. We are not Al Qaeda. Until now the world has not much heard of our organization. That is about to change I assure you. As I explained to you before, our interests are to drive your forces out of this region. Beyond that we are content to let your immoral and bloated civilization decay on its own. The weapon we carry on the ship will be used against a military target. Fair game, as you might say, in the war we are conducting. As I told you before, I am not in agreement with many of the practices of the groups you refer to as terrorists. We merely share the same goals."

"So who are you, Amir? Are you calling the shots here?"

"No, you will meet the leader of our brotherhood shortly. In truth, you have seen him before although I am sure you took no notice of him. Fortunately for us, he was in the lounge at the hotel in Singapore when you and your accomplice stole the briefcase. He was performing surveillance on the man you robbed. That is how he was able to retrieve what was stolen from us. His name is Megawati and he is a great man. A visionary."

"He is a murderer."

"You are referring to the woman? I am sure she was aware of risk she was taking. She was not an innocent victim, and neither are you."

"I don't suppose you and your great leader Megawati are going to sail this ship to your target and die heroically for your cause."

"That would not be a prudent use of our resources, Jack. There are others aboard this vessel who have offered their sacrifice for this purpose. At the proper time, we will be departing. You, however, will be permitted to witness this great historical event first hand."

Jack sneered at him. "Yeah, you visionaries always manage to find somebody stupid enough to die for you."

"You think I am a coward perhaps? What you think is of no concern to me, but I will assure you that when it comes my time to sacrifice all for our beliefs, I will do so willingly and without fear."

Annie had been silent for the entire time. Finally she spoke. "You lived in the West, Amir. Jack told me you went to university in the US. You must have met people you cared about. You have to know they are not evil people."

"I learned many things in America, Annie. I learned that, in the West, a man such as I, is and always will be, something less than people such as you. No matter how intelligent, no matter how courageous, no matter how dedicated. It will always be true. The men with the power in the West. The wealthy white men. The ones who pull the strings of the puppets. They will steal and cheat and kill to make sure this never changes. So that it never has a chance to be otherwise. But that is not my grievance. Brown-skinned men have always been less. Everywhere in every country. Even often in their own. No, it's something else. Something that you yourselves do not see. Where is the point, Jack, when the right of a man to enjoy his fortune, bestowed upon him most often by inheritance, or favored circumstances or

266

by greed, or theft or dishonor or even if by his wits and by his labor, begins to prevent the less favored from having even the most modest of dreams for their own children? How much wealth does a man need? At what point do the many take up arms against the few? Is it perhaps when the wealthy build their mansions by the sea, and then come to believe they own the ocean? Is it when the white men, with their immoral financial schemes, have stolen so much from the people that the people's dreams are broken and their children are sick and have no future? Or is it when a government is no longer run by honest and right-thinking men, but by dogs who bay after the briefcases filled with cash as if chasing a bitch in heat? It is not just your country. It is everywhere in the developed world and even here. The sultans build their palaces, the priests build their cathedrals, the generals build their armies and the people grovel in the dust. It is not a system that can be adjusted, Annie. There are no small corrections for such a web of injustice. There is only what I carry with me in this vessel."

Jack interrupted. "You're talking about human nature, Amir. Do you really think things would be different if men like you were in charge? Revolutions stir things up for a while but, even when they succeed, they just create a vacuum. In time, the world looks just the same. Only the faces of the greedy change."

"Not this time, Jack. This time, the world will be run by men who owe their allegiance only to Allah. Where men who steal from the people are not rewarded with wealth, but instead have their thieving hands removed by the sword. But enough of talking. I have duties to attend to. I have grown quite fond of both of you, truly. It troubles me that we have been forced into these circumstances, but there is noting to be done about it. We will come for you when our preparations are completed."

Amir turned and the guard opened the door and stepped out. Amir started to follow but Jack stopped him. "Amir, can I talk to you for a second. Outside?"

Annie started to object but Jack looked at her and she went quiet.

"I don't think there is any reason to continue our conversation, Jack."

"Just for a moment, please."

"Very well, but be brief. Time is not in abundant supply."

Jack followed them out into the hallway. When the cabin door was closed Jack turned to Amir.

"Take Annie with you when you leave the ship, Amir. There is no reason to make her stay here."

"As much as I like Annie, I'm afraid that will not be possible."

"Look, she is just an innocent victim here. She didn't have any part in disrupting your plans."

"Perhaps, but we know she is an agent of the British government. That is reason enough."

"She's not a spy. She works for some commercial branch of the government. Besides she would be a lot more valuable to you alive than dead?"

"How so?"

"I am sure the British government would pay plenty for her safe return, and I'm guessing you could use the money. Besides, she isn't any danger to you."

"On the contrary, Jack, she knows me and will soon meet Mr. Megawati."

"Well, it's not like this thing is going to be some big secret, Amir. What do you think is going to happen when this thing explodes? The whole world will find out who was responsible. Look what happened to Osama Bin Laden. I'd bet your friend Megawati wouldn't mind being mentioned in that company. Talk to him. See if I'm not right."

"Very well, Jack. I will do as you request. I would not be too hopeful of the outcome."

23

Trevor was alone in his office, sitting at his desk. He was as worried as he had ever been in his long career. Scores of ships had been stopped and boarded in the sea-lanes leading to the Persian Gulf, to no avail. He had always recognized the possibility that they had been given disinformation regarding the target but none of their other efforts had born fruit, so they continued the search. He hadn't heard anything from Jack or Annie and that worried him, even though he never believed they would come up with anything useful.

The frustration of sitting and waiting was nothing new to him but there had never been more at stake. His phone rang and he picked it up absently. He didn't speak.

"Hello, hello, is this Trevor Martin?"

"This is Trevor."

"This is Nigel Williams at the embassy in Jakarta. I'm happy to have found you in."

"What can I do for you, Nigel?"

"Well, about an hour ago, a little Chinese woman came knocking at our front door. The woman told us a rather incredible story. To tell you the truth we probably would have sent her packing but we, of course, have been told someone might be contacting us about defecting. We have also been briefed on the current crisis and I though it would be a good idea if you heard what she had to say. The documents she brought with her seem to corroborate her story."

"Which is?"

"It's most extraordinary, really. She claims to be the wife of an officer in the Peoples Liberation Army. She indicated that she was running away because her husband has gone insane. She got out of the country with another man who was some kind of political prisoner. She claims her husband and a group of officers in his command had gone mad and were plotting an attack against the West. She says a nuclear weapon is involved. She claims they were afraid to talk to anyone in their government because they didn't know who to trust."

"How did she end up in Jakarta?"

"That part is a rather long tale. Apparently their escape was arranged by a group of individuals from a religious group called Falun Gong. The man they were travelling with was to meet someone from our embassy to disclose information about the persecution of group members in China. To make a long story short, she claims her husband and a few others are planning an attack against the US naval facilities on Guam."

"Good God man! Have you informed anyone else about this?"

"Not yet. I wanted to run it by you first."

"Yes, well done. Is the woman still there?"

"Yes we are holding her. Actually she seems extremely frightened. She asked us if we could protect her. She indicated she would like to seek asylum in the UK."

"All right, keep her there and make sure she is given a thorough debriefing, but be gentle with her. She mustn't feel she is being interrogated or that she is being charged with anything. What ever you do, don't frighten her

271

any more than she is already. Make her as comfortable as you can. I'll arrange transportation. I should be there in no more than three hours."

Trevor put down the receiver and then immediately picked it up again and dialled another number. "This is Trevor Martin. I need to be put through to the Prime Minister."

"I'm very sorry, Mr. Martin. The Minister is sleeping. He has asked not to be disturbed. Are you aware of what time it is?"

"Yes, I bloody well know what time it is and I am telling you this is a matter of national security and if you don't go and get him for me immediately I will have you shot. I also suggest you raise the Chinese Embassy and advise them the ambassador will be receiving an urgent call within the hour."

24

When Jack returned to the cabin, Annie was glaring at him.

"What the hell was that all about?"

"I'm trying to get you off this ship."

"How do you expect to do that?"

"I tried to get Amir to appeal to this asshole Megawati's ego. My guess is he wants to be some kind of terrorist super-star. Otherwise he wouldn't try something this crazy. I think he'll like the idea of impressing you. If they do take you with them, you'll be held hostage, but I don't think Amir will let them hurt you. They'll try to get your government to ransom you."

"Do you think it worked?"

"I don't know, Annie. I gave it my best shot. Amir likes you. I think he'll argue in favor of it. We'll just have to wait and see."

"I'm really scared, Jack. I don't think I've ever admitted that to anyone in my life."

"I know. But scared isn't a bad thing. It helps keep you focused. Just don't panic. Panic gets you dead. You just need to convince yourself that this is going to turn out okay and then just deal with it as it happens. I know you're going to be alright."

"How do you know?"

"I just know. I'm never sure how things are going to turn out for me, but I usually get a feel for the people I'm in the tank with. Like Sadik, the captain of this ship when we were hijacked. I knew he wasn't going to make it."

"How could you know a thing like that?"

"I can't describe it really. It's almost as if I know somehow that I'm with somebody at the end. Like I'm watching the final act of a play that I've seen before."

"That's pretty creepy."

"Yeah, I know."

"Well if you ever feel that way about me, don't tell me."

"You're going to live to be an old maid, Annie. Don't worry about it."

"What the hell do you mean an old maid?"

"That's what happens to girls who punch out their fiancées."

Annie was silent for a while. Finally she looked at Jack and she held his eyes. "What about you, Jack?"

"I don't know. One thing I'm sure of is this guy Megawati killed Angel, or at least had somebody do it for him. I've got a lot of motivation to stay alive so I can get my hands on him."

"I don't think that's a good reason to want to stay alive."

"Show me a better one."

"How about me?"

Jack looked at her and he could see she was serious. He wasn't sure how to answer. "We would never work," he said finally.

"Why not?"

"You don't know me, Annie."

"I think I know you pretty well, after all the hell we've been through the last couple of weeks."

"Yeah, well that's not me either, not really. It's been wall-to-wall mayhem since I met you. I'm not as much fun when people aren't trying to kill me."

"I know more about you than you think."

"Like what."

"Like I know I can trust you. I know you would look out for me. And it's not just me. I saw the way you looked after the girls back in the jungle. You would have risked your life for any one of them. Even Amir, before we found out he was playing us. You were concerned about him. I could see it."

"I've done a lot of things, Annie. Things I wouldn't tell anyone about."

"We've all done things we aren't proud of. You can't carry it around with you all the time. It just drags you down. You have to let go of it."

"Some things won't let you."

"Maybe you need to have somebody to help you unload it."

Jack didn't answer. He just sat on the bunk looking at his shoes. Annie put her arm around his back and just held on to him. When he finally spoke it was like he was in a trance. The words came out flat and strained.

"Do you remember what I told you about Brad? About blowing up that guy's house?"

"Sure. How could I forget it?"

"Well, what I didn't tell you was that one of his daughters was home that day. The newspaper said she was sick in bed. I never noticed there was only one kid in the car. I should have paid more attention. That little girl died in the house that day. She was burned to death, and I did it. I killed that little kid just as surely as if I had put a gun to her head and pulled the trigger."

Annie gasped. She started to pull away but then she paused and buried her face against his arm.

"Nothing I ever do for the rest of my life is going to change that. Nothing will ever wipe it from my memory."

After a while, Annie spoke. "You made a mistake, Jack. It was a terrible mistake and someone died, but you didn't intend for it to happen. If you had blown up the house knowing she was inside, that would be a different thing. But that's not what happened."

"She's still dead. And I did it."

"You've got to find a way to forgive yourself for it, Jack. That's the only way you'll ever get free of it."

"I can't do that."

"Then I'll do it for you. I forgive you, Jack. I forgive you for everything you've ever done."

Jack looked at her. She was crying. "I don't think it's up to you to forgive me."

"Of course it is. I love you, Jack. I need you. I need you to survive so you can be with me. Don't you dare give up on yourself. That's the one thing I won't forgive you for."

He put his arm around her shoulder, and then they embraced. In a while they lay back on the bunk and held each other.

"There's something I want to tell you, too, Jack. It's difficult for me but maybe it will help you to know. I've really never talked about this with anyone except my mother. I mean, a lot of people know about what happened but they don't know what it did to me inside. Maybe it will help you to know."

Jack held her gaze. He knew she needed some assurance from him. He didn't have the words for it but he didn't look away and that was enough.

"I was nineteen. There was this boy I'd met at chapel. Roger. We were so much in love. You know how it is when you're that young. We used to take the train into London on the weekend. A friend of mine told me there were a lot of great

276

pubs in Brixton and I made Roger take me there. I never had any problem getting served. It was kind of a dangerous place but I guess I didn't think anything bad could ever happen to me. We went to a few pubs and had some drinks. The crowd was a little rough, but no one bothered us. We both had a little too much to drink. It was a beautiful night. I told Roger I wanted to take a walk in Brockwell Park. He didn't want to. He said it was dangerous to be in the park late at night, especially in that part of town. I got really mad at him and we fought. I called him a coward. I made him go."

Annie's voice started to quaver and she stopped for a moment. There were tears in her eyes.

"There were three of them. They beat Roger unconscious. They held me down and made me watch. They killed him right in front of me and then they all laughed about it. When they were done with him they took their time with me. It went on and on, like they were having a party. I just wanted to die. I don't know why they didn't kill me. I wanted them to kill me. When they walked away I wanted to scream at them to come back and finish it. They just left me lying there on the ground, naked, bleeding, so cold. I don't know how long I lay there. I didn't want to get up. I don't think I even moved any part of my body. I had come to the end of my world and there was nowhere else to go. In a funny way I was at peace with it. I just kept staring at Roger, knowing it was my fault he was dead. I wanted to be with him. Some people found me - they were out walking their dogs - or I probably would have died there. I can't even remember what they looked like."

Jack held on to her. He didn't know what to say.

"It took a long time for me to even look at a man again, Jack. Somehow I blamed Roger even though I knew it was my own fault. I guess I couldn't bring myself to take responsibility for it. When I met Geoffrey I somehow felt secure for the first time in years. I thought it was him but it wasn't. I guess it was that aura of invincibility the rich have about them. Like nothing could ever touch them. When I realized it wasn't Geoffrey who was making me feel safe, I started to resent him, too. He was a terrible ass after all, but it wasn't really his fault it didn't work with us. He was just being who he was. I suppose I should have told him what was going on inside of me, but he wasn't someone I could tell that kind of thing to. I don't know why really. I guess I was afraid he would make some inane, patronizing comment and I would end up hating him for it. It wasn't fair. I know it wasn't."

She looked at Jack but he still didn't say anything. He just held her a little tighter.

"After that, I gave up trying to find someone. I couldn't understand why it had happened to me. I kept looking for some reason I might have deserved it. Even trivial things I had done. Nothing made any sense. And now, twice in a fortnight, I've been abducted, threatened, beat up, drugged and soon maybe killed. Do you believe in reincarnation, Jack?"

"I don't think about things like that."

"I can't think of any other reason these things should be happening to me. I just think I must have done something horrible in a past life and now I'm paying for it."

"I don't know, Annie. Most of the time I think it's just random. Ninety nine percent of your fate happens before you even know who you are. If you're born in Bangladesh or Somalia or someplace like that, your life is pretty much going to be a nightmare. A lot of what has happened to me has been my own damned fault, but I've seen plenty of innocent people get screwed over, just from being at the wrong place at the wrong time. There are some lousy bastards out there who live to be a hundred. There are kids who die because of who their father is. Like I told you back in the jungle, I don't want to know 'why me?' I don't need to wonder why I might somehow deserve it."

"The thing is, Jack, we have been through hell together since we first met and yet I still feel safe with you. I feel safe with you even though we're nothing like safe. I can't explain it. Maybe it's just that if I'm going to die, it's OK as long as I am going to die with you. Do you understand? I don't want them to take me off the ship. I don't want to die alone in some bloody jungle. I'd rather be blown to pieces with you than live without at least knowing you made it, too. That, at least, you are alive somewhere, doing what you do. It's all I have left to hold on to."

"If I can't get you off this ship, Annie, we're both going to die. If they take you with them, you'll live and I might still have a chance."

"How?"

"I don't know how. I just know there's always a way. At least, there always has been up until now. We'll see what happens. Anyway that card has been played. Either they are going to take you with them or not. Nothing I do or say now is going to change that."

279

She wrapped her arms around him. "Whatever happens, don't you dare give up on yourself. Don't give up on me."

25

The Nimitz-MacArthur Command Center PACOM, at Camp H.M. Smith, Hawaii was fully manned and the atmosphere was tense. Satellite images, some indicating the disposition of the 7th Fleet and some showing the image of a single, small tanker, were projected on large overhead screens. Admiral Thomas Jennings, Commander, Compacflt had flow in from Yokosuka Japan earlier in the morning and was in conference with Admiral James Clark.

"What is the current location of the suspect vessel, Jim?"

"She's now 270 miles southwest of Guam and making about 17 knots."

"And all attempts to hail her have gone unacknowledged?"

"That's right. There is very little doubt that this is a rogue vessel. Whether she is carrying a weapon, or otherwise has hostile intent, is still unknown."

"When will the interdiction commence?"

"It's already underway. The DEVGRU is assembled at Andersen field and will be feet-wet within the hour."

"Who is the Task Unit Commander?"

"This is Bill MacGregor's Unit. In the meantime, I have ordered the fleet to sea and they are preparing to weigh anchor as we speak." He indicated a point on the large tabletop map display with a pointer. "The Shiloh and the Curtis Wilbur will screen the fleet from positions, here and here, as a precaution. They will have firing solutions on the suspect vessel and will be prepared to launch at your command. The Fitzgerald will be delayed in port for an estimated 3 hours for repairs on her rudder."

"And where will the interdiction take place?"

"Approximately here. About two hundred miles southwest of Guam."

"Any indication there could be other vessels involved?"

"There's nothing else out there that hasn't been accounted for."

"What about submarines?"

"We have a round the clock P-3 umbrella. So far, their sonobuoys haven't picked up anything. We have the Houston patrolling below the thermocline, in this area, just north of the trench."

"What do we know about the suspect vessel?"

"She is apparently sailing under a Sri Lankan flag of convenience but is not listed in the International Ship Registry. The name on her stern is the Maluku Kelasi. There is no ship of that name in any of the commercial logs."

"How the hell did we find her?"

"We got a tip from the Brits regarding a possible terrorist attack on the fleet during its layover in Guam. The information suggested the attack would be carried out by ship. Our Intel people have been trying to track down rumors of what they believe is a small-yield nuclear device that found its way into the hands of one of the terrorist groups down here. I'm sure you've been briefed on it. We don't know much more than that at this point. We checked out every major vessel within 300 miles of Guam and turned up the Kelasi sailing out of Jayapura."

"How did we get caught with our pants down on this one, Tom?"

"Well, I can't comment on how this weapon might have gotten loose. No one is saying. If it is what they think it is, I'm sure we will be briefed on it eventually. Every vessel that comes within a hundred miles of the fleet is accounted for and boarded if necessary. I don't believe they could have caused us any harm."

"How large a weapon is it supposed to be?"

"Nobody knows for sure. The Brits think it may be something on the order of the Hiroshima bomb."

"That'll make a hell of a hole in the ocean."

"Well, that's all it's going to do."

"What are Captain MacGregor's orders?"

"They will proceed to a position five miles from the target vessel and then hold for final authorization. Once authorized, the team is to board and secure the vessel. It will be thoroughly searched and if a weapon of any kind is found they will stand by for further instructions."

"Any chance this thing could light off while our men are on board?"

"We don't know. If we are dealing with terrorists, there is a possibility they could pull the trigger if they are boarded. Intel seems to think the weapon, if it exists, is probably on a time delay. We don't expect to find a whole lot of crew on board."

"If that's the case, can it be deactivated?"

"We won't know that until our people have a chance to look at it."

"Those are some damned fine men we are sending out there, Tom. If there is any chance this thing could go, I'd rather send that ship to the bottom."

"Well, that's our other option. Their current course takes them directly over the Mariana Trench, in fact, almost directly over the Challenger Deep. It's the deepest point in the Pacific, more than thirty six thousand feet."

"What would an explosion at that depth do? Does anyone know?"

"We've had some discussions about it. There were several detonations at Bikini Atoll in the Marshal Islands, right after the war."

"I thought they were air bursts?"

"The first try, codenamed Abel, was an airburst but it didn't hit the required ignition point. The Baker test was detonated ninety feet below the surface. The Saratoga and the Japanese Battleship Nagato were sunk in that test. There was also an H-bomb test there in 1954. The thing is, the waters there are shallow so there is probably no relevance to our current situation. There was also a test known as project Wigwam in the mid fifties. A thirty-kiloton nuclear weapon was exploded at a depth of 2000ft. There was almost zero detectable thermal radiation and fallout was minimal. There's a possibility, though, that this ship would never make it to the bottom. If the core of the device is subjected to enough pressure, there's the possibility it could light off by itself. We don't know. And no one is sure what the pressure wave from an explosion at these depths would do. Water doesn't compress as you are well aware. If the thing detonates at depth it will no doubt be felt all over the region."

"Very well. I want to get on the horn with the Joint Chiefs. It will be their call. Let me know if there is any change and advise me when our interdiction team is on station."

26

Jack and Annie awoke when the cabin door opened. The ship was no longer moving. Amir came in with another man they had not seen before. He was short, and heavy-set with an oily looking, dark, pockmarked complexion. He looked to be in his late thirties or early forties. From the smug look on his face, Jack knew immediately who he was. He vaguely remembered seeing his face at the lobby bar at the Grand Central. He wasn't the kind of man Jack would take much notice of, and that was probably his greatest asset. The most dangerous men were often the ones you would never suspect of being capable of anything more deadly than a dirty look. Jack knew he could kill him quickly, before anyone could intervene, but he didn't want Annie to be harmed. He also wanted Megawati to know why, before he killed him.

"I am Megawati. You know why you are here and I require that you come with me now. I suggest you cooperate fully, Mr. Lawrence. I am quite prepared to pluck out your eye if you force me to do so. I will tell you that Amir has suggested a better use for the woman than to die with you on this vessel. There is some logic to his proposal and I have agreed to bring her with us when we depart. That is, providing you give us no further trouble."

He indicated to his men and Jack and Annie had their hands cuffed behind their backs. They were lead out into the passageway and then down several decks to a long fore-aft corridor. Annie kept looking at him, looking for reassurance he supposed, but he had none to give. In spite of what he had told her, he really didn't see any way out for himself. It wasn't that he had no hope. He just had a feeling that he had finally come to the end, and some part of him felt relief. Maybe, he thought, that was what he needed all along. Something to give it some meaning. If he succeeded in saving Annie's life, that would be something. That would be enough.

As they moved aft through the compartments, the temperature steadily increased until they entered the engine room. The noise was deafening. There was a man, stripped to his waist and sweating profusely, working on a large, partially disassembled valve. They passed through another door and entered what looked like a maintenance compartment. The overhead was open through several decks to a large hatch through the main deck. The hatch was closed. There was a lathe and milling machine along with an assortment of tools and spare engine parts strapped to pallets and on several steel worktables. The center of the compartment had no deck plates and was surrounded by a steel railing. A labyrinth of pipes and cables ran under the deck toward the engine room. The weapon sat against the far bulkhead of the compartment. It had been bolted to supports, welded to the deck plating and the cover was sitting open. Jack laughed ruefully when he saw it. It looked like nothing more than an oversized beer cooler. Amir stood to the side with Annie. Megawati had his men pull Jack over to the device. He flipped a toggle switch and an LED display switched on, showing a row of twelve zeroes. Megawati turned to Jack.

"Now, Mr. Lawrence, you will proceed."

Jack looked him in the eye. "Before I do this, Megawati, I want you to know that I am going to kill you."

Megawati laughed. "Perhaps your ghost will attack me at some future time. For now, you will do as I say."

Jack knew there was no use in resisting. If he were to have any chance at all, it would lie in cooperating until he could get Amir and Megawati off the ship. He knew there was a possibility they would kill him the moment the retina scan was complete, but he didn't think so. He guessed Megawati would enjoy the idea of his enemy being strapped to a nuclear weapon, watching the numbers tick away his life. If he resisted, they could easily knock him unconscious, tape his eyelids open and complete the scan anyway. He placed his eye to the lens and Megawati pushed the switch. Once more he saw the green point of light, which held steady for a second and then completed a counter-clockwise scan of his eye. He pulled his head away and looked at Megawati. The smug look had returned to his face and he indicated to his men to take Jack away. They held him while Megawati entered numbers into the display. When he entered the last digit, a whirring sound emitted from deep within the device. Megawati looked at the display and smiled. He looked over at Amir and they both lifted their fists into the air and shouted 'Allahu Akbar'. The guards repeated the chant. Finally Megawati turned to Jack.

"You have killed many of my people, Mr. Lawrence, and caused us a great deal of trouble. You are a courageous adversary and I do not hate you for it. On the contrary, I salute you and will now bestow upon you the greatest honor a warrior may experience. You will die, knowing that you have held back nothing. That you have given your all to the fight. Even though you have failed, you will know that of all the great forces of the West, only you came near to stopping us. Indeed, it is very important to me that you should be here to see the end. I will sleep better at night knowing that you will never again interfere with my plans."

Jack started to say something but the blow came down upon the back of his skull and blackness enveloped him. The last sound he heard was Annie, screaming.

Annie was taken by the arm and led back through the ship, struggling to turn to see if Jack were still alive. Fearing the worst. They took her up the gangway and along a passageway to a door that was open in the side of the hull. She could barely see through her tears. There was a platform beyond the door and when she stepped out, the rain and wind tore against her. It was dark but she could see the lights of a large yacht that had been tied up beside the ship. A steel stairway led down to a second ladder that seemed to dangle in the air next to the smaller vessel. Her hands were still cuffed at her back and she was afraid of falling into the sea, but two men took her by the arms and moved her across the gap to the deck of the yacht. She was immediately taken through a door and down a corridor. It was a boat built for the wealthy. The bulkheads and deck were of mahogany and teak with brightly polished brass fittings and railings. They stopped in front of a door and she was taken inside and then forced to sit on the bunk. A man she hadn't seen before entered the cabin. He was holding a syringe. She starting screaming and backed away but they held her tightly and she felt the needle enter her arm. She suddenly felt too tired to stand and then she slid back onto the bunk.

27

For a brief moment he thought he was dead. The darkness was absolute, like being immersed in a pool of black water. It was the throbbing in his head that made him think otherwise. That, and the steady beat of the engine. As the sensation gradually returned to his body he became aware of the cold steel deck, and the rhythmic movement of the ship. He tried to raise his right hand but quickly discovered it was cuffed to a pipe. He started to feel the panic rising but he fought against it. His left hand was free and he felt the back of his head. There was a sizeable lump where he had been struck and his hair was matted with dried blood. It seemed that the bleeding had stopped but he couldn't be sure. As he started to sit up he became dizzy and the pain intensified. He felt nauseous and had to fight the urge to vomit. He had no sense of time or place, but he guessed they had cuffed him where he had fallen. The weapon was somewhere out in the darkness. Close by. Ticking its way to oblivion. It was like some unimaginable beast, lurking in the darkness, waiting to obliterate his world. How much time? That was the first thing he needed to know. Maybe the only thing.

His head had started to clear and he reached down to his right shoe, feeling along the seam where the heel was attached to the sole. He probed the seam with his fingernail and finally managed to withdraw a slim sliver of metal. He concentrated on holding it tightly between his thumb and index finger as he located the key slot. He wedged the end of the sliver against the small post in the center of the handcuff lock and began probing for the release. He worked at it for a few seconds and finally felt the lock give. He carefully replaced the piece of metal in his shoe. Before he stood, he extended his arm above his head to make sure there was nothing above him. Finally he rose unsteadily to his feet, gripping the steel railing for support. His head began to throb and his legs felt weak. He tried to remember the layout of the room but he had no point of reference. He began to inch his way forward with his hands extended, as he felt for anything solid. After a few steps his foot bumped into something. He reached down and felt a wooden pallet. It had some metal objects banded to it. The pallets he had seen were on the deck against the starboard bulkhead, so he now had an idea where he was. He made a right turn and slowly moved forward. After he had gone a few feet he began to hear a faint whirring sound and he knew it was the weapon. After a couple of more steps he felt it. The cover was in place and he reached around the perimeter looking for a latch. As his hand moved around the long side of the device, he felt the metal getting warmer until he felt the beginning of a slug of steel between the cover and the base of the device. Someone had welded the cover in place. He didn't know if he had ten hours or ten minutes, and he would never know. He sat back down on the deck, unsure of what to do. In the end, he thought about Annie. He could hear he voice, telling him not to give up, no matter what. There was no way to stop the weapon, but at least he could try to stop the ship. He had to find a way out of the compartment.

He worked his way slowly back to where the door was located, holding his hands out in front of his face to avoid smashing into anything. He tried the handle, but it was locked from the outside. He felt around the perimeter of the door for a light switch but wasn't able to find one. He needed light if he were going to have any chance at all.

He thought for a few minutes and an idea came to him. Slowly, he worked his way back toward the weapon. When he reached it, he got down on his hands and knees and felt around the deck. After a few minutes he found it, sitting on a wooden pallet on the far side of the weapon. They hadn't bothered to move it. It was a small, metal box that was still warm to the touch. He worked his hands along the box and found two heavy cables. They each terminated in a large alligator clamp, one of which still held a welding electrode. He took the other clamp and attached it to a deck cleat and then felt around the unit until he found the switch. Holding the electrode in the air he threw the switch and the unit immediately began to hum. He stepped onto the pallet and then shielding his eyes, he touched the electrode to the deck. There was a blinding flash of light, but his eyes didn't have time to adjust. He kept tapping the electrode against the deck as he looked around the room, being careful not to look directly at the arc. After a few seconds, he began to recognize objects. It was like seeing a room with a strobe light, with the ghost of the previous image transposed on top of the next. The sparks were burning his hand and melting through his shirt. He didn't see a light switch anywhere. He looked up. There was a catwalk above him and in the bulkhead that separated the compartment from the engine room there was a small access hatch. It looked like it could be opened from the inside. After a few more taps, he located a ladder against the far bulkhead, behind some machinery. He turned off the welding unit and waited a few seconds for his eyes to readjust to the darkness. Then he made his way carefully over to the ladder.

It was a tight squeeze but he managed to mount the ladder and start to climb. He was still a little dizzy and that, combined with the movement of the ship and the darkness, made the climb difficult. After a few steps he felt like his head was spinning and he held on with all of his strength. He concentrated on keeping three-point contact and worked his way up to the catwalk. He crawled carefully along the steel walkway until he reached the hatch. It was small, but large enough for a man to pass through, if he crouched over. He pushed on the latching handle and felt it give. Once the latch was free he pulled gently on the hatch until it opened just a crack and he was able to see into the engine room. The metal hinges squealed but the sound was drowned out by the throbbing of the engine. He pushed the hatch open cautiously, and crept through onto a platform on the other side. He could see one of the crewmen. He was sitting at a table against the opposite bulkhead, reading a magazine. Jack looked around the compartment. He didn't see anyone else. The catwalk extended along the hull and then along the opposite bulkhead where it terminated at another ladder that went down to the deck. It passed directly over the table where the crewman was sitting. He didn't look like a man who knew he was about to be incinerated. Jack guessed he had no idea what was about to happen to him. It was pretty loud in the room but if the crewman looked up, there would be no place for him to hide. The floor of the catwalk was just steel grating. You could see right through it from below. It was risky but there was nothing to do but go for it. He crept along on his hands and knees, his eyes fixed on the crewman. The steel grating cut into his knees. When he had moved about halfway along the catwalk the crewman suddenly stood and stretched. He raised his arms above his head and tilted his head back. Jack froze. The light was dim but the guy seemed to be looking right at him. His heart was pounding, but finally the man turned and walked over to the engine and examined a panel of gauges. With the crewman's back turned Jack stood into a crouch and made his way quickly over to a position above the desk. He pushed himself back into the shadows and waited. The crewman was taking his time, walking around the perimeter, turning valve handles and listening to the sounds of the engine. Finally, he seemed satisfied and he walked back over to the desk. As he started to sit, Jack stood, grabbed hold of the railing and jumped over the side, landing on the crewman's back and knocking him to the floor. The crewman was stunned and Jack sprang to his feet and finished him with a kick to the jaw. He searched the man for a weapon and then quickly searched the engine room. There was nothing he could use to defend himself, aside from some large wrenches. It was time to make a decision.

In the end, it came down to where he wanted to make his stand. He had a little experience with engines and he knew he could damage it enough so they would never get it restarted in time. As soon as the engine stopped, someone would be calling down from the bridge for an explanation. It wouldn't be long before they sent someone to investigate. He didn't know how many there were and there didn't seem to be any other way out, aside from the one door they would be attacking. He didn't want to be trapped. He went over to the door to the maintenance compartment and found a light switch on the bulkhead. He unlocked the door and stepped back into the maintenance compartment. He looked up at the large hatch through the main deck but it didn't look like it could be opened from the inside. There was no other way out. He went back to the door and wedged a section of pipe against the lever so that it couldn't be opened from the engine room side. Then he went back over to the ladder and climbed back up to the catwalk and through to the engine room. If he were forced to, he would make his stand on the catwalk on the other side of the small door. It would give him the high ground and plenty of cover. With the main compartment door jammed, it was the only way they could get through. He could hold them off indefinitely if he wasn't able to get by them. Small comfort, but the best of his limited options.

He reached the deck and started to examine the valves and piping around the engine. There were brass tags on the valves but they were not written in English. He found a three inch pipe leading to a sea cock that penetrated the hull and lead to what looked like the raw water cooling system. He turned the large hand wheel until the valve was fully closed. Next he climbed up to the top of the engine and found what appeared to be the lubrication piping. He closed every valve he could reach. Next he opened the drain valves on the water and oil accumulator tanks to bleed out the remaining fluid. Without cooling and lubrication, the engine would eventually seize up. He just didn't know how long it would take. When he got back onto the deck, he looked at the temperature gauge. The needle had already begun climbing slowly toward the red area. It was going to happen sooner than he thought. In a while, the engine seemed to be laboring and in a few minutes an alarm began to sound and a red light was flashing on the gauge panel. Suddenly he heard someone calling on the intercom. He had only minutes to prepare himself. He grabbed a wrench and took up a position next to the open engine room door.

His luck held. They had only sent one man. As he stepped through the door, Jack hit him on the back of his head, knocking him to the deck. The man had a sidearm and Jack removed it from the holster. He checked the chamber on the weapon and then ran back over to the gauge panel. The temperature indicator was in the red and smoke was beginning to come off the engine. It was starting to vibrate badly. He didn't want to leave until he was sure the engine was stopped but there wasn't much time. He waited. The noise from the engine continued to rise and, after a few more minutes, it was shaking so violently he thought it would tear itself off its mounts. Suddenly there was a loud bang and the engine stopped. A plume of smoke rose and spread across the overhead. He rushed back over to the door and started down the passageway. When he had gone a few yards two men appeared at the other end, both armed with assault rifles. Jack drew down on them and fired two shots killing the lead man. The second man ducked for cover and Jack dashed back to the engine room. He leapt through the door just as the rounds started rattling off of the surrounding steel. He fired back but missed.

He didn't want to close the door because it was his only way out. He glanced through the doorway and saw several men advancing on him. He slammed the door closed and was about to wedge it shut when flames leapt up behind him. Some of the lubricating oil had run onto the deck and had caught fire. The compartment was filling with thick smoke. Jack climbed the ladder and dashed across the catwalk to the access door. He crawled through and took up a firing position from the other side. He couldn't see the engine room door from his position but he heard it being thrown open followed by the sound of gunfire. It was difficult to see through the smoke and it was starting to burn his lungs. After a few seconds he heard the sound of a fire extinguisher and his visibility was reduced to zero by the white, chalky discharge that quickly filled the compartment. He heard what sounded like an exhaust fan and the smoke began to clear.

One of the men crept around the side of the engine and began firing at him. Another one had climbed up on some piping and he opened fire from that position. Jack returned fire, but they were alternating and ducking quickly out of sight. He could hear men moving on the other side of the compartment and in a while he heard a popping sound followed by the orange glow of a cutting torch. He looked below his position and within a few seconds, he could see sparks coming through the bulkhead around the main compartment door. He slammed the small access door closed and dogged it down. There was nothing to jamb it with so he crawled over to the ladder and climbed down to the deck. He took up a position behind the milling machine where he could fire on both doors. He wondered again how much time was left. The sparks from the cutting torch were spraying into the room and in a few moments, he heard a piece of metal hit the deck. Then the muzzle of an assault weapon poked through the hole and suddenly there were rounds zinging off the steel around him. He looked up and saw the dogs slide open on the access hatch and as the sparks started again at the main door, the access hatch flew open and he began taking fire from above. Jack tried to conserve his ammunition but after a brief, intense exchange he was out. Out of ammunition and out of options. At least he had stopped the ship and he didn't think they would be able to repair the engine any time soon. It was cold comfort. He looked over at the weapon, almost wishing it would go off. At least then he would know if he had done any good, before he died.

28

The radio chatter was coming in over the loudspeakers as the interdiction force moved into position. The duty officer turned to Admiral Cook.

"The team reports they are in position and are awaiting authorization."

"Any change in the course of speed of the vessel?"

"No change in course, sir, but the vessel seems to be losing speed. Now down to ten knots."

"Very well. You may..."

"Hold on a second, sir. The P3 is reporting propeller sounds. They are reading what they believe to be a submarine off the port side of the suspect vessel at a distance of thirty six hundred yards, and depth of sixty feet."

"Where the hell did that come from? Is it one of ours?"

"Negative sir. The Orion says it appears to be a Kilo Class, diesel electric boat."

"A Russian sub, Tom?"

"Possibly, but the Russians also sold a few of those boats to the Chinese. They're damned quiet and difficult to detect."

"Is there any way we can raise her, find out what the hell her intentions are?"

"We are attempting to contact the boat."

"How long can our interdiction team stay over the target?"

"No more than about twenty minutes. After that they would have to refuel to make it back to Andersen."

"Do we have refuelling capability in the area?"

"We can have a KC10 on station in thirty minutes."

"Very well. Let's get the tanker into the air. Tell MacGregor to hold his current position and await further orders."

"Aye-aye sir."

"Sir, the Orion is reporting torpedoes in the water. Tracking the suspect vessel."

"What the hell. Are they sure?"

"Confirmed Admiral. One minute, twenty seconds to impact."

"Do we have visual?"

"Negative sir. We won't have a satellite in range for another fifteen minutes."

The room went quiet.

"Captain, I want our team out of there, just as quick as those birds can fly. Have a rescue team remain on station to search for survivors."

"Aye, aye, sir."

"Twenty seconds sir, ten..."

They advanced on him cautiously. He was out of ammunition and out of ideas. At least the ship would never make it to Guam, he was convinced of that. He looked over at the weapon and it seemed to him it was throbbing, like the malevolent heart of a monster, bent on destroying the world. He wanted it to go off, there and then, in the middle of an empty ocean where it could harm no one. He didn't want them standing over his body thinking they had beat him. He thought about Annie, held captive in some jungle, waiting for him to come rescue her and about Angel who was dead because of him. A deep rage overcame him. He made up his mind at that moment not to go quietly. There was a short piece of pipe on the deck. He stooped down to pick it up but his hand never found it. There was a tremendous explosion followed quickly by a second and the entire ship seemed to break in the middle and lift out of the water. The machinery shielded Jack momentarily from the main force of the blast and the flying debris, but quickly the compartment filled with water and Jack found himself in the middle of a whirlpool swirling up toward the main deck. The lights went out and it was pitch black again. He struggled to hold his breath as he was smashed around the compartment and slammed into the bulkheads. He could feel the pressure increasing on his body and he cupped his hands over his ears and screamed. As the rising water compressed the trapped air in the compartment, the main hatch blew out, and Jack was lifted up and expelled into the air above the ship in a geyser of swirling water and steam. Within minutes there was nothing left but debris floating on a sea of burning diesel fuel. The last thing he remembered was pulling himself onto a floating pallet and then the darkness came over him.

29

Jack awoke in a hospital room. There was one other patient in the room, but he was unconscious and almost completely covered in bandages. Jack tried to sit up but his efforts were rewarded with an agonizing stab of pain from his rib cage. His left arm was in a sling and there was a constant, high-pitched ringing in his ears. His hands were both bandaged and there was an IV drip in his arm. The last thing he could remember was being trapped on the ship and running out of ammunition. By some miracle he had survived and a part of him was genuinely amazed. He thought about Annie. The door opened and a nurse entered the room. She wasn't smiling and when she saw he was awake, she spoke to someone out in the corridor. Jack got a glimpse of an armed soldier next to the door. They were guarding his room and that probably wasn't a good thing. The nurse walked over to him and took hold of his wrist, looking at her watch.

"Where am I?"

"This is the naval hospital on Guam."

"How did I get here?"

She didn't answer. Instead, she jammed a thermometer under his tongue and began putting a blood pressure cuff around his right arm. She pumped up the sleeve and then watched the gauge. There was a clipboard hanging at the end of the bed and she jotted some notes on it. She took a look at the IV drip and then pulled back the bandage on his arm and examined the area around the needle stick.

"The doctor will be in to see you shortly."

With that she turned and left the room. It looked like they thought he was a terrorist. Probably not a bad assumption, in light of what had happened. He wondered how difficult it was going to be to convince them otherwise. The last thing he wanted was a trip to Guantanamo Bay. His ribs were killing him and every time he tried to move it felt like a knife was jammed under his rib cage. After about twenty minutes a doctor entered the room. He was a Navy doctor with a tan military uniform under his white coat.

"How are you feeling?"

"Like shit. How long have I been here?"

"You were brought in early yesterday morning. Can you tell me where you are experiencing pain, if any?"

"It would be easier to tell you where it doesn't hurt."

The doctor picked up the chart and leafed through it. "I don't doubt it. Well, let's see. You have sustained a concussion. You've managed to fracture four of your ribs and you also have a simple fracture of the left radius. You have moderate to severe bruising on your legs and back and a contusion on the back of your head. Are you feeling any vertigo or nausea?"

"Not at the moment."

The doctor removed a penlight from his pocket and examined Jack's pupil response. Then he looked in each ear. "There are second degree burns on both of your hands and your left ear drum has a fairly severe rupture. There is the possibility it will heal itself in time. You probably will retain some hearing in that ear, through bone conduction in any case. The right eardrum also shows some scaring, but not quite as bad. I imagine you have some ringing in your ears."

"More like a siren going off."

"That should ease up in a few days, although it will probably be with you for a while. It's too soon to know. We'll have to see how it goes. Other than that you seem to be in pretty good shape. We performed a CT scan and didn't find any internal damage. All in all, I would say you are a very lucky man. Do you remember what happened to you?"

"I remember being on the ship. There was an explosion."

The doctor unwrapped the bandages and examined Jack's hands. They looked like raw meat. "Could be a lot worse. You'll probably have some scaring, hopefully not bad. Anything else bothering you? Any visual distortions, feeling like you are going to pass out? Do you feel any numbness in your feet or legs?"

"No, nothing like that."

The doctor made some notes on the chart and then returned his pen to his pocket. He looked at Jack. "In fact, your ship was torpedoed out of the water. Not by the US Navy, in case you are wondering. Our team found three survivors. One died on the way in. The other one is over there. It's about even money he isn't going to make it. Somebody must be looking out for you, big time."

"Well, thanks. For pulling me out of the drink, I mean."

"Don't thank me. I just patch up what they send me. I have to advise you that you are currently in the custody of the US Government.

There are some people waiting to ask you a few questions. Do you feel up to it?"

"Do I have a choice?"

"Sure. I don't have to let them talk to you if you aren't medically able. Sooner or later, you are going to have to answer their questions. It's up to you."

"It's OK. I may as well get it over with."

"Good enough. I'll be back to check on you in a few of hours. We've given you something for the pain. If it isn't doing the trick, ring for the nurse."

With that he turned and left the room. No one else came in for a while and Jack had just started to doze off when the door opened again. Two men entered. One was in uniform; the other was in civilian clothes. They pulled some chairs up to his bed. The officer took a small recorder out of his pocket and turned it on. He set it on the side of the bed. The civilian spoke first.

"I'm agent Danzinger with the FBI. This is Lieutenant Commander Eckert with US Naval Intelligence. Can you give us your name please?"

"I'm Jack Lawrence."

"And you are a citizen of what country?"

"I'm a US citizen."

"We want to ask you a few questions, Mr. Lawrence. I have to tell you that at this moment you are in the custody of the United States government and are suspected of being involved in terrorist activities in the region, including, but not limited to a possible plot against US Naval forces. You have the right to remain silent. Anything you say can and will be used against you in a court of law. You have the right to an attorney. If you cannot afford legal council

305

the court will appoint representation for you. Do you understand your rights?"

"Yes. Look this isn't necessary. I intend to tell you everything I know. I'm not a terrorist."

"Very well. What can you tell us about the ship?"

Jack started with his trip to Singapore. He told them everything that had transpired in as much detail as he could remember. They seemed to be mesmerized as they listened to his story and they only interrupted a few times to ask for further clarification. When he had finished, they looked at each other and shook their heads. Finally agent Danzinger spoke.

"That's a hell of a story, Mr. Lawrence. Is there anyone we can contact for corroboration?"

"Sure. If you call the British Consulate in Medan and ask for Trevor Martin, I'm sure he can back up everything I've told you."

"Rest assured we will do that. In the meantime, you are confined to this room. Please don't make any attempt to leave. Is there anyone you would like us to contact?"

"Just call Trevor."

"We'll be back to talk to you later. Do you have any other questions?"

"Yeah. Did it go off?"

"I'm afraid we can't comment on your case, at this time."

They stood without saying anything more and left the room. After a while, Jack fell asleep. They brought some food in for him later in the afternoon and he did his best with it. He didn't have much of an appetite. After dinner a different nurse came in. She helped him get to the bathroom and, when he came back, she asked him if he wanted anything to help him sleep. Whatever they gave him worked pretty fast. He had a vague recollection of someone coming in during the night but when he finally awoke it was morning. His ribs didn't feel any better and, when he coughed, it still felt like someone was jabbing a knife into his side. They brought breakfast in on a tray and he was working on his coffee when a whole crowd of people came through the door. One of them was an Admiral. Lieutenant Commander Eckert was with him. He walked over to the bedside.

"How are you feeling, Jack?"

It was 'Jack' now, not Mr. Lawrence. He guessed that was a good thing. "About the same."

"I'm pleased to tell you that we have spoken to Mr. Martin and others in the British government and you have been cleared of any wrong-doing in this matter. As soon as you are able, you are free to go. We may have a few more questions for you before you are discharged, if you don't object. Not now, of course."

"Anything you want to know."

"This is Admiral Clark. He wanted to meet you."

The Admiral stepped forward. "Well, Mr. Lawrence, I would personally like to shake your hand, but I won't, at least until the bandages come off. I've been briefed on your efforts to head off this unfortunate incident and I would like to personally offer the sincerest gratitude of the United States Navy. If I could give you a medal, I would. If there is anything we can do for you during your stay here do not hesitate to ask. For starters you will be moved to a private room in this facility and, let me assure you, you will be given the best care we have available. Once you have recovered, there are some people back in Washington who are going to want to buy you dinner, at the very least. Thanks again and you have our best wishes for a full recovery."

The Admiral turned to leave, but Jack stopped him. "Can I ask you what happened with the weapon, Admiral?"

Admiral Clark hesitated and then looked at Commander Eckert. He whispered something in his ear. Then he turned to the other people in the room and asked if they would mind waiting in the hall. When they had gone, and the door was closed, the Admiral turned back to Jack.

"Officially, Jack, this incident never happened. It would not be in the best interest of the United States for it to become known that anyone came this close to creating such an unimaginable disaster. For your information, it is very unlikely that the ship would have reached the fleet, even if we hadn't been given advanced warning. That in no way minimizes your bravery and your contribution to preventing this from happening. Officially, there was no weapon. There was no attack, planned or otherwise. Since you are no longer a member of the uniformed services, I cannot swear you to secrecy, but I am asking you, on you honor, never to mention this incident to anyone, ever. There will probably be other agencies of our government that will wish to talk to you about these matters. All accounts of this incident will be classified top secret, so were you inclined to mention this to anyone, it could never be verified. I don't believe you will choose to do that, Jack. I think you understand what is at stake. I also believe a man of your personal integrity can be counted on to do the right thing. Am I wrong?"

"No sir, you're not."

"That's what I thought. To answer your question, an underwater seismic event was registered at approximately sixteen hundred hours yesterday. It was detected by recording stations all around the Pacific Rim. Officially it was a magnitude 5.4 earthquake. The epicenter was close by the Challenger Deep. We have no confirmation that the event was the result of an explosion. As far as we can tell, there was no release of radiation into the atmosphere. Of course we are continuing to monitor the situation. There has been no word of any tsunami activity in the region. Does that answer your question?"

"Yes sir, it does."

The Admiral reached out and placed his hand on Jack's shoulder, then he turned and left the room.

About a half hour after the Admiral's departure, Jack was moved to a private room. He had become a VIP and, for the next few days, there was a steady stream of people, medical and otherwise, cycling through the room. He was questioned several more times and asked for additional details on some of the events leading up to the sinking. He was also asked to look at some photographs but he couldn't identify any of the faces they showed him. He gave them a description of Amir and Megawati. He didn't really like all of the attention but it helped keep his mind off of Annie. Trevor called him several times but there was no word from Annie and no one even knew where to start looking for her. There had been no ransom demand and, although neither of them would say it, they both feared she might end up paying the price for the failed attack. Jack wondered if he had done the right thing by getting her off the ship but, deep down, he knew she would not have survived the sinking. He was in disbelief that he had survived himself. In the end, he took it as a sign that he had been saved for one purpose only - to find Annie and get her someplace safe. It took precedence over anything else, including finding Megawati and making him pay. There would be a time for that, but it would have to wait. They kept him in the hospital for three more days. His ribs didn't feel much better but they had removed the bandages from his hands. They still looked pretty bad and the ringing in his ears had not subsided. More than anything else, his head hurt from trying to come up with a way to find Annie.

On Christmas Eve morning he boarded an Air Force C141 and was flown to Jakarta. The British embassy put him up at a hotel and he was invited to their Christmas day dinner. He accepted, for lack of anything else to do, but he was really feeling the absence of Annie and he was anxious to get on with finding her. After dinner he spent some time with Trevor, discussing what had been done to date to try to locate her. Amir's apartment in Jakarta had been under surveillance since Jack's conversation with Trevor from his hospital bed. The apartment was not leased to Amir and no one had shown up at the place. It was beginning to look like a blind alley but they would continue the surveillance indefinitely. They agreed to meet on the following day to share ideas and discuss what part Jack would play in the search. There had been ongoing intelligence efforts, for years, to locate terrorist's camps on the many islands of Indonesia, but the task was daunting. Jack, however, had one lead they hadn't explored. It was a long shot, and if it was going to work at all, he knew he would have to keep it to himself.

30

The next morning, Jack awoke to the sound of commotion in the street below the hotel. He looked out the window and saw people running. Something was wrong. He flicked on the television. An earthquake in the Indian Ocean, off the west coast of Sumatra, had triggered an enormous tsunami. They were showing the devastation at Banda Ache and similar reports were coming in from all over the region. As Jack watched the tragedy unfold, his heart sank. The thought that Annie could be trapped somewhere that was in the process of being wiped from the face of the earth was too much to take. He stayed by the television for most of the day, unable to turn away. He wondered if the weapon might have somehow triggered the disaster. It took him all morning to get through to Trevor and, when he did, the news was not good. All of the embassy's local assets had been thrown into the tsunami rescue efforts. It appeared Annie was going to have to wait. He understood why, but he was not about to sit still until the disaster was over. He had spoken to Pramana, the embassy's interpreter, at the dinner on the previous evening and Pramana had been very concerned about Annie's safety. He had given Jack his number and asked him to call if he could help in any way. The telephone system was overloaded and it took Jack an hour to get an open line. Pramana was not in, but Jack left his number and he received a return call later in the evening. He told the interpreter what he had in mind and Pramana agreed to help. The government of Indonesia was in crisis and it was difficult to find anyone with the time to conduct normal business. It took Pramana nearly a week to get back to him with the information. Trevor had given Jack the keys to a safe house they used in Jakarta and an embassy car, but there was nowhere to go. He felt like a caged lion, but the recovery time was good for him and by the end of the next week he was beginning to feel a little more like himself again, at least physically.

The information he had given Pramana was the license tag number from Amir's motorcycle. There was no guarantee Amir owned the bike, but if he did, it would give Jack a place to start. The address was in West Java, just past the outskirts of Jakarta in a town called Bintaro. Pramana agreed to visit the address, pretending to be searching for an old friend. He found that Amir's mother still lived at the house. It was the break Jack was hoping for. He drove out to the address on the following morning. There was a park across the street and he spent his time walking beneath the palm trees and sitting in his car watching. He felt a little conspicuous but with the crisis going on, no one seemed to take much notice of him. He left only to get some food and use the bathroom but he continually moved his car to different locations to avoid attracting attention. Jack knew there was no guarantee Amir would even show up at the house but he hoped Amir would eventually want to check in on his mother. It just seemed like something he would do. He would not perceive it as much of a risk. As far as Amir knew, the only person who knew he hadn't been killed on the dock at Parepare, and could connect him to the attack, was Annie. She was in no position to tell anyone. It was mind-numbing work, but Jack didn't have anything else to do anyway. On the evening of the fourth day his patience was rewarded. The lighting along the street was dim but when Amir drove up, Jack recognized him right away. Amir returned to his car two hours later and as he drove away Jack sat up in the back seat and held a gun to Amir's temple. Amir was trembling uncontrollably and he almost ran the car off the road. Jack gave him the address. Amir was begging for his life but Jack remained silent. He didn't intend to kill Amir, but he wanted him to think he was about to die.

Jack made Amir drive around to the back of the safe house and then he pulled him out of the car. Jack's ribs were still bothering him, but Amir didn't struggle. He was whimpering like a puppy. Jack almost felt sorry for him. Inside, Jack forced him into the sitting room and pushed him down onto the couch. He pulled up a chair facing him. Amir had started to weep.

"Not so much the brave warrior now, are you sport?"

"Please, Jack. I know I have harmed you but it was not personal. I only did what was required to complete my task."

"That isn't going to cut it, Amir. You left me to die out there on that ship. How do you think I feel about you now?"

"Please, Jack. You know, at least, I tried to save Annie. I showed compassion for her sake."

"What do you mean tried? If any harm has come to her, I will kill you right here, right now and I will take my time with it."

"No, Jack. She is fine. She has not been harmed. I swear it."

"I believe you, Amir. That's the only reason I haven't killed you already. Let me tell you how this is going to be. I have two questions to ask

314

you. If you give me the right answers, I am going to let you go. I'll give you a running start. That's more than you gave me. Maybe with everything going on down here right now you'll be able to get away. That's the only offer you're going to get. If you lie to me, or if I find Annie has been harmed, I will kill you, here in this house. Slowly. Just to be sure you aren't lying; you are going to be my guest for a few days. There is a little private room waiting for you in the basement. It's sound proof. Once I finish what I have to do, if you have been honest and Annie is safe, I will release you. Do you understand?"

"Yes, completely. What is it you wish to know?"

"Where is Annie being held?"

"She is at one of the training camps on the Island of Ceram, near the village of Bula."

Jack grabbed Amir by the collar and pulled him to his feet. He pulled him over to a map of Indonesia that was hanging on the wall. He took the map down and put it on the coffee table. "Show me."

Amir pointed. "The island is here. The camp is on the northeast coast, perhaps five thousand meters inland from this cove. There is a river that flows down from the central mountains. The camp is near the river."

"What is the ground like?"

"Excuse me?"

"The ground, the terrain. What is it like?"

"It is very thick jungle. Very difficult to move through, except by the known trails. The trails are watched."

"What about the river."

"It is very fast moving at this point and not really accessible by boat. There are many rapids

315

and waterfalls. It rains very much here. During the entire year. The island has not been well explored because it is so difficult."

"Is there a clearing? Any place to land a helicopter?

"The center of the camp is open. It is not a large area but I suppose a landing could be attempted. I think it would be difficult. Also, if I remember correctly, there is another area to the north of the camp. It is a slightly larger space."

"How many men?"

"Not more than twenty at this camp but there are some other camps in the area."

"How many men in all?"

"I am not sure. Perhaps fifty or sixty men at any time."

Jack handed Amir a pencil. "Mark the camp where Annie is being held and then mark the locations of the other camps."

Amir made some marks on the map. "This is to the best of my recollection, Jack. I have only been to the area twice. I am not very sure about the locations of the other camps."

"Are you sure this is where Annie is being held?"

I am quite certain."

"Is there any chance she will be moved in the near future?"

"I don't believe so. They believe it is time to be still."

"OK, Amir. You better pray she's there when we drop in. Now the second question. Where is Megawati?"

"At the moment, I do not know."

Jack grabbed Amir by the throat. "Wrong answer. Now think again."

"Please, Jack. You must understand. He is constantly moving. He is very nervous at the moment, since the attack has failed. He does not stay at the same house for more than a day. Often he is on a large boat. A yacht that belongs to a friend. "

"How do you get in touch with him?"

"I have a number. He does not answer. I leave a message. He calls me back at a later time. It has always been this way."

"Alright, I want you to call him. I want you to set up a meeting."

"He will not meet with me."

"Well you better give him a reason. Otherwise I'm going to kill you. You've told me where Annie is. I'll get to Megawati eventually. I don't need you alive if you can't help me."

Amir was rocking back and forth on the couch. He was sweating profusely, and Jack thought he was going to pass out. After a few moments, he spoke.

"Perhaps there is a way."

"What way?"

"Perhaps if I tell him I have money for him. He is badly in need of cash at the moment.

"Tell him whatever you want. But whatever it is, it had better work."

"Do you wish me to call him now?"

"No. I have some other business to attend to first. Besides, I want to have someone with us when you call. Someone who speaks the language. For now I'm going to show you to your accommodations."

"You know Megawati will kill me if I betray him."

"I wouldn't worry about that, sport. Right now you better worry about me. Besides, Megawati is not going to be in any position to harm you or anyone else when I've finished with him."

317

"I must tell you I am very concerned for Annie in the long run, Jack. She can identify Megawati and I don't know what he might do."

"If she dies, Amir, you die."

Jack took Amir by the arm and walked him over to a door in the hallway. He opened it and turned on the light. He pushed Amir ahead of him down the steps. It looked like an ordinary basement but Jack pushed Amir over to some shelving along the back wall. He reached down and pulled a lever. The shelving moved forward slightly and Jack pulled it the remainder of the way. Behind the false wall was a heavy steel door. Jack unlatched it and turned on the light. He pushed Amir inside. It was a panelled, carpeted room with a couch and a table and chairs. There were some books and magazines and a small refrigerator. A bathroom was off to one side. There were no windows.

"I'm going to leave you here for the time being, Amir. It's a lot more comfortable than the place you left me."

"For how long, please?"

"For as long as it takes."

"Please, Jack. I am very frightened of being enclosed. I will not do well in this room."

"It's the only option you have. Either this, or I kill you right now. Give me your car keys."

Amir handed Jack his keys. Jack walked out of the room, closed the door and threw the latch. He pushed the shelving back into place and then went back to the sitting room. He removed the map from its frame and then turned off the lights and left the house. After checking to see that the residence was secure, he drove Amir's car back to his parent's house, leaving it a few blocks away. He walked through the park and got into his own car.

318

Trevor was elated when Jack told him he had found out where Annie was being held. The problem would be getting the proper assets together to launch a rescue mission. He didn't think they could even get their hands on the helicopters they would need for several weeks. Trevor told Jack he would do what he could, but they would have to be patient. Patience was not Jack's strong suit, but it was difficult to know his best course of action. He wanted very badly to get his hands on Megawati but he couldn't be sure what would happen to Annie if Megawati were killed. In the end, he decided he would wait until after the rescue was attempted. If it failed, he reasoned Annie would have the best chance of surviving if Megawati was alive and allowed to follow through with a ransom attempt. Otherwise his people would surely kill her.

31

The raid on the terrorist camp on Ceram was late by a matter of hours. Trevor had called in some favors and managed to get the helicopters and equipment required to mount a rescue mission. It took them three days to obtain satellite surveillance and to develop a plan, and the better part of a week to get the assets in position for a strike. They swooped in at first light, only to find a deserted camp with the cooking fires still warm. Satellite surveillance had shown activity at the camp on the previous day but it had been abandoned sometime during the night. It appeared they had been tipped off. When Jack got back to the safe house two days later, he was pretty rough with Amir. Jack knew it would have been impossible for Amir to communicate with anyone but he didn't care. He was prepared to lean on Amir until he came up with something. They were running out of time. If Annie was still alive, it was only because Megawati thought she still had some value. If push came to shove, he would try to trade her for his life. He was on the run and probably near panic after the failed rescue attempt. He hadn't impressed Jack as a man who could take the heat and, the longer it went on, the more Annie would start to feel like excess baggage. More than anything, Jack worried she could become collateral damage, which was why he wanted to find them first. If the Brits found her and launched an operation, they would do everything they could to make sure she was protected. If it was the local police it was likely to turn into a blood bath and they would sort out the bodies when it was over. The entire region was still in chaos but the Indonesian authorities had at least circulated Annie's picture. The emergency made it easier for Megawati to move around but he would not have the time for careful planning. Sooner or later, Jack knew he would make a mistake. He had to find them before they were able to get out of Indonesia and a lot of time had already been wasted. Amir had attempted to reach Megawati on several occasions, but he didn't call back.

In the end it was a bit of unexpected good fortune that provided the lead he needed. A group of Australian scuba divers on an excursion to East Timor had seen a European woman, apparently unconscious, being lowered into a skiff from a motor yacht. The yacht was anchored in the Areia Branca Cove off of the city of Dili on the north coast of the Island. They reported the incident to the Australian embassy, not wanting to get involved with the local police. Word reached Trevor in Jakarta the following morning. He called Jack and asked him to come by.

"This could be just another blind alley, Jack. You know that. We will, of course, have our people at the consulate do some investigating."

"Do you have people down there who know what they're doing?"

"We have security personnel on staff at all of our consulates. They would coordinate with the local police."

"I'm not sure we should be getting the police involved."

"Why on earth not?"

321

"Somebody tipped these assholes off to our mission at Ceram. How do you know you can trust these people not to tip them off again? According to Amir, they have sympathizers in most of the local governments on these islands."

"I take your point. What do you suggest?"

"Get me down there. I'll have a look around and see what I can find out."

"I don't know that I'm comfortable having you freelance on this, Jack. If Annie is being held there, it will take a well-planned and adequately manned rescue effort to extract her safely. I don't want you charging in like some cowboy and shooting up the place. You would very likely get her killed if you were to try to do this on your own. Assuming she is actually on the Island to begin with."

"I don't think we have much time, Trevor. I have a bad feeling that if we don't find her soon, we never will."

Trevor stood and paced the room. Jack could see the strain on his face. He had taken a lot of heat for using valuable and badly needed resources to mount a futile rescue mission on Ceram. He was on a short leash and he knew it. There would be no chance of mounting another rescue without rock solid intelligence and that would take time. Time they very probably did not have.

"Alright, Jack. I'll have my people arrange transportation for you. But for God's sake, be discrete."

"I'm going to need some equipment. A weapon and some other things I won't be able to take aboard a commercial flight."

"That does not exactly sound like discrete to me."

"Look, Trevor, you know what these people are like. I can't just go down there unarmed."

Trevor stared at him for a moment and then shrugged his shoulders. "Very well. Tell Richard what you need. We'll have it sent to the consulate in Dili by diplomatic pouch. You should have it shortly after you arrive. Please be aware you have no legal status to carry a weapon in Indonesia. If you are detained by the local police, we would have limited options in trying to help you. If you find yourself on the run, and can get to the consulate, we will provide diplomatic immunity. Just don't get yourself arrested and, for the love of God, don't do anything to put Annie's life at risk, or your own for that matter."

Jack arrived at Comoro airport the following morning. He found the consulate and met the security officer who had been advised of the situation by Trevor. He was sympathetic but could not offer much in the way of support. He asked Jack to keep him advised. Jack rented a car and took a room at the Central Maritime Hotel, which was a converted cruise ship. He really didn't know what he would do next, but his instincts told him he was close. They also told him this would be his last chance to save her. Dili had been nearly levelled in the separatist fighting in the late nineties and it wasn't easy to keep a low profile. Fortunately, it was the height of the tourist season and even with the tsunami, there were still enough European and Australian divers and back packers to keep him from looking too conspicuous. He didn't think any of Megawati's men would recognize him but, still, he remained cautious. He kept to the cafes and coffee houses

323

and spent a lot of time at the Caz Bar near the cove. There was a yacht anchored off the Fatucama headland where the huge statue of Jesus kept watch over the waterfront. It reminded him of Rio de Janeiro. He didn't know if it was the same yacht the divers had reported but he watched it anyway. There were villas along the beach roads dating back to when the Portuguese claimed the island. They had survived the general destruction and Jack guessed if Annie were in the city, that's where she would be. He purchased a pair of high-power field glasses, rented a sea-kayak and spent two full days watching from the bay. Nothing turned up. He had the consulate confirm with the Australians that the yacht anchored in the cove was the same one the divers had reported. It had been boarded but nothing suspicious was found.

On the third day after his arrival he received a call from Trevor. A ransom demand had been mailed to the British consulate in Bali. A phone number was provided with instructions to call on noon of the following day. It was a cell phone but probably a pre-paid throw away with no GPS locator. They would be able to trace the call to the closest cell tower, but that wouldn't be enough. No one really believed Annie was being held on Bali, but they would play it by the book. Megawati would assume the Brits would demand proof of life, which meant Annie was probably still alive. He figured he had about twenty-four hours until they killed her. It would be dangerous going in on his own, but there was no time to wait for help. If he couldn't save her, it would be too late. There was only one card left to play.

Jack parked his rental car in a hotel lot near the beach road. The embassy had provided him with a Browning HP, 9mm, fitted with a suppressor. He left the pistol and satellite phone in the trunk and then walked back to his hotel. He had dinner in his room and got the remainder of his equipment ready. Then he set his alarm for 3 am and tried to get some sleep. Jack knew he was going to need some luck to make it work. He wasn't sure how much he had left. The moon was nearly full, but it hid behind a low layer of cloud and cast dim shadows over the cove. It was deserted, except for a few drunks passed out on the beach. He had learned to cultivate stillness. It was not just being silent and knowing how to move. It was a state of being, so acute, that every sound and every shadow became part of a single living image. An image in such fine balance, that he would feel a change, before his senses told him where to look. He moved quietly across the beach to where the kayaks were chained to a piling. He paused for a moment and let the wake of his movements settle. The padlock was old and rusted and he had it open within a seconds. He stowed his gear and then headed out into the cove with strong steady strokes. The yacht was anchored about a half mile out and Jack put his back into it. The water was choppy and a light rain had started to fall. Bad enough, he hoped, to keep anyone on the yacht off of the weather decks. It was a good bet they had already swallowed enough booze to put them out for the night. He was counting on it. When he neared the yacht, he slowed down and let the kayak drift. He flipped on his night-vision goggles and did a full circuit of the vessel. There were a few lights on but no sign of movement. He slowly pulled the kayak up to the dive platform on the stern of the yacht and secured it. Then he climbed quietly up and over the railing. He squatted in the shadows for a moment and listened. After a few moments, he moved forward. The boat rocked gently in the light chop and the deck was wet and slippery. He carried a simple incendiary device. A plastic bottle filled with gasoline and a battery powered igniter controlled by a digital timer. He didn't want to use a bomb; it would wake up half the city. The fire would most likely destroy the yacht but, if not, it would be badly disabled for a long time. Either way, Megawati would not be able to make his escape on it. If he did his work well, it would look like an engine fire and if his luck held, it would also tell him where Megawati was hiding. Once the boat went up, Megawati, or at least his people would probably head for the waterfront to see what was going on. If he didn't see what house they came from, he would at least be able to follow them back to it. It was a little bit thin. But there wasn't time for anything better.

He crept forward and found the engine hatch. The hinges groaned when he opened it and he froze for a second, letting the silence return. He dropped down into the compartment and placed the device next to the diesel engine. He opened a fuel oil drain valve and let it run, and then set the timer for forty-five minutes. He removed the fire extinguishers from their mounts and detached the wires to the fire alarm system. Finally, he went back up through the hatch taking the fire extinguishers with him. The whole operation took less than five minutes. He dropped the extinguishers quietly over the side and climbed over the stern. There was plenty of time now and he conserved his energy as he paddled steadily toward the beach. The headlights of a car moved slowly along the beach road but other than that, the city was quiet. He pulled the kayak up onto the beach and checked his watch. Fifteen minutes until ignition. He walked along the road to the hotel lot where his rental was parked and then drove to a position where he could see the yacht out in the cove and also several of the villas along the beach. Jack knew if it all went bad and Annie was killed, the blame would fall on his shoulders. He also knew in his gut that there wasn't time to wait. Once the ransom demand had been made, it was only a matter of days, perhaps hours until they killed her. There was no way they would return her safely. She had seen too much. He sat in the dark, watching the yacht through his field glasses. His mind flashed back to the day he had driven that FedEx truck up to the mob house and changed his life forever. He couldn't let this go bad. He had to get Annie out safely, even if it cost him his life.

When it happened there was no sound at all, just a muted flash of light. In a couple of minutes, he could see flames and, in a short time, the entire stern of the yacht was burning. Suddenly he heard the sound of the yachts horn, like a scream in the night. Jack watched the row of villas. A few lights came on but no one emerged. A fire siren went off in the city. Finally, Jack spotted a car coming toward him on the beach road at a high rate of speed. Jack got the license number of the car as it passed. It slid to a stop by the beach and four men exited, running toward the shoreline. They quickly untied a Zodiac and headed out toward the yacht. Jack started the engine and made his way up the road, watching the villas for signs of activity. Another car raced by and Jack thought he saw Megawati in the back seat, staring anxiously out the window toward the cove. Jack rounded a bend in the road and then he saw it. The garage door was open and the lights were on all over the house. He didn't know how many were inside, but he was sure this was the place, and he knew there would never be a better chance. If all went well, he would have her out before Megawati and the rest of his men returned.

He drove past the villa and pulled over a few hundred yards up the road. He grabbed his backpack from the trunk and then ran back toward the house. The yacht was fully engulfed and it was lighting up the entire cove. He guessed anyone still in the house would be watching the fire, so he kept to the road. Once at the house, he worked his way around to the side where the electrical service entered. He opened the backpack and removed a small package of C4 wrapped in plastic. He quickly molded the explosive into a cord, wrapped it around the main conduit, and inserted a detonator. He went back to the front door and quietly tried the knob. They had left it unlocked. Jack flipped down his night-vision goggles and then hit the remote trigger. There was a sharp thump and a flash, and then the lights went out all over the house. He moved quickly. He did a quick circuit of the first floor finding two armed men in a dining room, staring out at the burning yacht. He got them both with the Browning before they knew he was there. He raced to the stairs and crept up to the second floor. He started on his left and began opening

328

doors. Three men emerged from a large room in the back of the house with a flashlight. Jack opened up on them. Two went down and he caught the third in the back as he leapt down the stairs. He waited for a moment, listening for movement but the house had gone dead. He knew that didn't mean there were no more of them. If they were there, they had gone to ground. He continued clockwise, opening each door in turn. On the far right, he found a locked door and he knew he had found her. He checked his back and looked over the railing to make sure no one was coming up the stairs, then he kicked the door in. He crouched and swept the room but there was no one there. No one but Annie. She was lying on a large bed and one of her wrists was handcuffed to the iron bed rail. She was conscious and she put her hand up to protect herself. Jack rushed over to her and removed his goggles. She started to scream, but he held his hand over her mouth until she recognized him and then she sat up and tried to hug him.

"Be still, Annie. I have to get these cuffs off."

32

By the time Megawati reached the harbor, the yacht was already fully engulfed. He could do nothing but stand on the beach and watch it slowly disappear beneath the waves. All that remained was a cloud of dense smoke, drifting out toward the open sea. It was not until the smoke had dissipated, that it finally occurred to him the fire could have been a diversion. He ran back to the car in a panic, and ordered his men to return to the house quickly. They arrived at the front door, just as Jack and Annie were coming down the stairs. He looked at Jack in disbelief, unable to comprehend that he was still alive and had once again foiled his plans. A deep rage came over him, but as he watched Jack draw his weapon and open fire, his rage was quickly replaced by an overwhelming fear. At that moment, Jack appeared to him as some kind of avenging angel; deadly and unstoppable. Megawati turned and ran, leaving his men behind to cover his escape.

It took a long time for the disjointed fragments, the sounds and the images of that last night in Timor, to finally resolve themselves in Jack's memory. Megawati's silhouette in the doorway and the muzzle flashes of the weapons. Feeling Annie's body shudder as a round slammed into her. The feeling that she had no weight at all as he lifted her over his shoulder, and that he did not feel the bullet that passed through his own shoulder. The acrid fumes of spent gunpowder burning his eyes and the screams of dying men as they fell in front of him. The sickening feel of her blood running across his flesh. In the end, the thing he remembered most was that exact moment when he stood in the doorway of that house, watching Megawati running toward the beach, slipping from his grasp. He knew at that moment his time of choosing had come. A door into a different life stood open, and all that was required of him was to deny, with every ounce of his being, those things that had driven him all of his life. His instincts and his hatred and his need for revenge. In the end that's how he knew he was in love with her. Because it really was no choice at all.

His wound had healed quickly, but Annie was going to need some time. When he carried her into the emergency room, the doctors didn't give her much of a chance, but she was a fighter and Jack stayed by her side, holding her hand, talking to her. She regained consciousness after a week but she wasn't able to talk to him, except with her eyes. When she was out of danger, they moved her to a better equipped hospital in Jakarta. It was going to take some time, but the doctors were optimistic she would recover fully. They couldn't tell him how long it would be, but he didn't care. The embassy had provided her with a private room and they moved a cot in so he could stay with her. He slept a few hours at a time, always driven awake by the violent images that had become the stuff of his dreams. The only peace he found was sitting with her and reciting his life to her, like a long confession, as she drifted in and out of consciousness. Trevor had been furious with him at first, but he knew Jack really didn't have a choice. In the end, he conceded Annie would probably have been killed if Jack hadn't acted when he did. The incident was meticulously documented and then buried in a Top Secret file that would never see the light of day.

Jack let Amir go as he promised but he didn't think he would last long. He was not the kind of man who could live life on the run. By the time he was released from the safe house he had become a broken man. His fear was the only prison he would ever need to keep him away from the dark side for the rest of his life. Megawati was another story. He had vanished into the shadow-world of international terrorism but his name was placed on the terrorist watch list and he was about to find life a lot less comfortable. Jack vowed not to waste another second thinking about him.

In the weeks that followed, Jack felt as if his life were peeling back, like layers of paint on an old house that had been inhabited over the years by different men. Somehow those lives had never been completed, only painted over for a while until the cracks started to appear, and fragments of his past emerged. For a long time he had been all of those men, and none of them. Allowing his life to lead him on, unable to change its trajectory. In the end he had become a man drowning in his own existence. And then fate pulled him out of the sea and dragged him up onto that beach on Sumatra and into the arms of the woman he would love for the rest of his life.

ABOUT THE AUTHOR

Wallace Brown's first novel, **The Shepherd Sleeps**, was published by Writers-Exchange in 2008. It is available in paperback or as an e-book at www.writers-exchange.com/wallace-brown.html. It is set in New Orleans at the height of the Vietnam War and the counter-culture revolution of the 1960s. As with his second novel, **Jayapura**, a sense of place and historical setting, permeates the narrative, providing the reader with the sensation of walking the streets of the French Quarter, or of navigating the dense jungles and teeming cities of South East Asia.

Wallace lives in suburban Philadelphia, Pennsylvania and is a graduate of Villanova University. He is an avid reader of both literary and genre fiction, particularly espionage thrillers. His favorite authors are Alan Furst, John LeCarre, Joseph Conrad and Somerset Maugham. To contact Wallace, log onto his website at www.wallacefbrown.com. You will find a link there to his e-mail address.